TASMANIAN GOTHIC

MIKHAEYLA KOPIEVSKY

BY MIKHAEYLA KOPIEVSKY

DIVIDED ELEMENTS

Revelation (A Divided Elements Origin Story)
Resistance (Book 1)
Rebellion (Book 2)
Revolution (Book 3)

TASMANIAN GOTHIC

MIKHAEYLA KOPIEVSKY

1 3 5 7 9 10 8 6 4 2

KYRIJA
North Arm Cove, NSW, Australia
www.kyrija.com.au

A CIP catalogue record for this book is available from the National Library of Australia

ebook ISBN 978-0-9954218-6-8
paperback ISBN13 978-0-9954218-9-9
paperback ISBN10 0-9954218-9-9

Cover Illustration by Ethan Scott

For Elijah

ONE

The small apartment was a hothouse and Solari was firmly cocooned within it. Sweat ran a silent river down her forehead, itching along the scar that split her face like a trench. Distracted, she dragged her sleeve across it, swearing as droplets of residual worm mucus mixed with the salty perspiration in a rush of bright, hot pain. Her fingers twitched, desperate to rip off the heavy respirator mask, but she ignored the temptation. Only idiots opened their mouths to breathe underwater when their lungs screamed for oxygen.

Grimacing, she topped up the small vial gripped in her gloved hand, keeping in check the tremors that always affected her at this part of the cook. At the last minute, she turned her head and averted her eyes, emptying the blue liquid into a large glass beaker dominating the kitchen bench. The rush of fizzing sounded like her brain melting.

Heat continued to build in her too-small studio, the stained plaster walls seeming to press in from all sides and suffocate her. Black plastic covered the only two windows and every vent was either patched closed or clogged with the gum of previous cooks. In the corner of her apartment, a pedestal fan regarded her without sympathy, its silent blades illuminated by a battery-powered torch hung from the ceiling. Worth a month's takings, the chunk of metal was useless without electricity, and there had been no electricity in the city for days.

Only after the fizzing stopped and the harsh, astringent smell faded did Solari turn back to the counter. The beaker, its glass scratched and discoloured, cradled five large crystals of tetrahydron. Enough to make fifty kilograms of snowrock. Enough to make local crime lord, Yevgeny Worcsulakz, happy.

Fifty million dollars would make me happy as well.

There had been a time when she had considered going rogue and creating her own stash of snowrock—not enough to attract attention, just enough to set herself up after her contract ended; enough to protect her from stumbling back into Worcsulakz's clutches. A 'get a better life' fund, not just a 'get out of trouble' fund. But making the highly potent, hallucinogenic drug was the easy part. Moving it in Tasmania's Southern Reaches? That was a death wish.

Her fingers ripped off the mask and she gulped in lungfuls of stale air. She glanced past the fan to the small vent in the far wall; hidden inside was her nest egg, a multi-coloured assortment of notes she had scraped together over eight years of cooking tetrahydron. It wasn't much—just over five hundred dollars—but, it would be enough to get her out of the next messed-up situation when it arrived on her doorstep. Always a matter of when, never a matter of if.

Some nights, the sound of its impending arrival was louder than others, echoing with the crack of gunfire in the war-ravaged streets of Hobart. Tonight, it was deafening, merging with the screams of the wounded and the ululations of the ascendant; a hideous symphony that reverberated violently off her apartment walls.

Sighing, Solari pulled off her gloves and threw them into the sink. As contaminated as they were, she should have discarded them; but she had better things to do with her money. Water shuddered from the tap, tainted yellow and smelling funky. Somewhere in Hobart's industrial sector, the city's water treatment plants were sitting idle like her fan.

It was possible the brownout was merely symptomatic of Southern Tasmania's dysfunction, something born of neglected infrastructure or labour strikes. More likely, it was rival crime lord Pierre DuPlessis sending alpha teams into the heart of Worcsulakz's territory to create chaos; the city's major substation just another casualty of the decades-long war between two monsters who would burn the decrepit world around them in order to gain more power.

The sound of gunfire grew nearer, transformed from distant popping to explosions of sound that rattled the windows. Solari glanced around the apartment, spying her hooded flak-jacket lying on the stained, tattered carpet near the door. Flecks of mutant grass seed dotted the bulky fabric, smuggled remnants of her last foray into the Fringes. It had been days since she had travelled across the city into the wild organic mess of mutated life that stretched for thousands of hectares to the west coast of the island. She would need to return soon to gather more ingredients for her tetrahydron, but walking through a hot conflict zone was the kind of disincentive that kept her at home and scraping the barrel of her existing inventory.

On tired legs, she walked slowly towards the jacket, sweat itching between her shoulder blades in protest against any consideration of putting it on. The gunfire was louder now, only streets away, but even it couldn't mask the heavy banging that erupted into her studio.

"Slaari!" Anders' voice, thick with alcohol and insolence, slurred its way through the apartment door in-between rounds of banging. Her ex had always been an unpredictable drunk. "Sollllaaari." Sing-song. Provocative. The calm before the storm. "Come on, baby doll. Open up. Open up, baby doll. Anders needs a fix."

She stared at the door, heart thundering in her chest, silently willing Anders to give up and go away. Sometimes he did — sometimes he got bored, or came to the conclusion she wasn't at home or didn't have any snowrock to steal; sometimes he turned paranoid at the thought of someone else turning up, or found an easier way to feed his addiction.

The banging erupted again. Each crash of his fist against the flimsy wooden door set Solari's heart racing faster. Subconsciously, she rubbed at the raised white line of scar tissue on her wrist — a permanent reminder of Anders and his temper.

"Solari!" He was angry now. The melody gone from his voice. "Open up, you bitch. Open this fucking door." The banging was insistent, shattering. The door shuddered on its hinges. "I know you're in there. I can smell your fucking sweaty stench from here."

She bent down slowly and picked up her flak jacket. It wouldn't be beyond Anders to fire a round into the apartment just to release some rage. The heat was already a thick blanket around her, but she shrugged into the long black sleeves regardless. Pulling up the zipper to her chin, she cringed at the rustling of fabric and clicking of interlocking teeth.

Loud thuds shook the door. Anders had replaced his fists with his shoulder, or his foot. It was the circuit-breaker she needed; no longer caring if he could hear her, she ran to her phone. Fingers poised above the screen, she paused, grimacing before she punched in the only number that could help her.

Two rings in and an unfamiliar male voice answered. "Details."

"Solari Peterov. ID 161115. Precursor Manufacturing." Her voice was shaking.

Another thud. The door would not hold forever.

"Someone's trying to break into my home lab. I have five tetrahydron crystals ready for collection."

"Priority dispatch is on its way. Secure the rocks and await advice."

The line went dead. Solari grabbed the beaker and ran for the bathroom. The small room was crowded with vats of chemicals—her poor attempt to keep the precursors cool during the power brownout. She pushed the large plastic tubs aside to make some room. The smell was caustic; every breath burned her nostrils and left her gasping for air.

She looked back frantically at the mask lying on the kitchen countertop. Another thud and the door groaned loudly—a begging for mercy, a forewarning of imminent submission.

There was no time left. Solari took a deep breath and locked herself in the bathroom.

The inevitable coughing and spluttering split her skull, the chemical fumes making her light-headed and nauseous. Solari gripped her phone, tempted to patch another call to Worcsulakz's protection racket even though it would do no good.

A final thud and then a loud crash. Anders was yelling, his vitriol no longer muffled by the thicker external walls. "You're going to pay for this, you fucking bitch!"

The sound of glass shattering and wood splintering punctuated his grunting. He was tearing her place apart, looking for the crystals that shimmered in a glass beaker on the broken tiles of her bathroom.

She gagged, bile rising up her throat. Chemical residues alighted on her skin, causing her to itch, and her breathing fell shallow and ragged. Her eyes could no longer focus, her vision fracturing the space into triplicates that shivered and stuttered. Anders' voice shifted to a high-pitched whining, the buzz of a thousand drones.

A cool touch unexpectedly caressed her cheek. Through a fog of incoherent thoughts came the realisation she had slumped to the floor.

Like a bad recording loop, the sound of the banging returned.

"Solari." Anders' voice was muffled. A thousand *broken* drones, with shattered wings and spluttering power devices.

There was a time when she had enjoyed the sound of her name from his lips. Back when he was a courier, before he went from merely transporting shards to sampling them.

The cracked floor tiles turned sticky, her meagre breakfast of soybeans and rice ejected from her compromised body, its sickly-sweet smell a quiet accent against the harsher vapours.

She stared at her wrist. Through an explosion of colours and black spots she could make out the scar that Anders' knife had carved just over a year ago—when he had been aiming for her throat. The damaged skin moved feebly, her pulse erratic and slow, a whispered stutter.

Her vision blurred, the scar losing definition and disappearing from focus. Gratefully, the smell of chemicals and her vomit also faded. Her brain—which only moments before had felt as though it was embedded with a thousand spikes—now felt like a soft, mushy blob.

And silence. Finally there was silence. No more thudding, no more screaming, no more Anders…

Until it shattered. The silence and the bathroom door, together.

***

Solari woke up wet and stinking of vomit.

Pieces of plastic debris from the broken bathroom door lay scattered around her. The glass beaker and its blue crystals were gone.

The effort of sitting up exploded grenades of pain in her head.

"Take it easy, Solari." She knew the deep voice that addressed her, pictured the bulky frame attached to it. "You've been whacked with a decent chemical cocktail."

Jerath. Her usual courier.

"Anders?" She croaked, pushing past the pain to prop herself against the bathtub.

"The piece of shit with the gun?"

Despite the pounding in her head, details began to coalesce; Jerath stood in the empty doorframe picking his nails, a large leather satchel slung casually over his shoulder, the scuffed glass of her beaker poking out the top.

"I gave him a bit of a touch up," Jerath continued, smiling as though recounting a funny story. "Sent him on his way with a warning."

He looked down at her, his face turned serious. "Not sure he's the type to listen to reason, though. How does he know you?"

The question came laced with a more subtle menace; a hidden threat.

Solari and Jerath got on well enough. Jerath was less pushy than the other couriers, less smug. And Solari didn't give him the grief that other manufacturers did — no lip, no begging for extensions, no tasting the merchandise. They did their transactions, swapped a bit of banter, and moved on to the next job. Simple. Just the way they liked it.

She stared at his hands, the way his thick fingers flicked quickly about each other. He would have no hesitation strangling the last breath out of her if it was necessary. If Worcsulakz ordered it. Or merely suggested it with the cock of an eyebrow.

'How does he know you?' Jerath wasn't making small talk. He wanted to know why a drug freak was belting down her door. How he knew about Solari, knew that she manufactured. It reinforced her earlier conclusion—going rogue would be a death wish.

"He's an ex. Used to be a courier, before he started skimming."

Jerath nodded and looked around the apartment. "He did a number on your place. What were you doing cooking here, anyway?"

Another question. Maybe calling in protection was a bad idea. With only a year left on her contract, she just needed to stay quiet and play it safe. Staying under the radar was the only way to survive the gangland war and it seemed to her that she had stuck her head out a little too far. Far enough to have it hacked off.

"I know it's against protocol, but with the power out, I can't access the coolroom in the lab."

Jerath offered no indication of whether he was satisfied. Solari held her breath, her stomach still queasy from the chemical sauna and jacked up on adrenalin.

In the end, he shrugged. "The brownouts are pissing off Worcsulakz as well. He's hearing rumours DuPlessis' thugs are running raids on the power grid."

It seemed Worcsulakz's arch-rival was getting bolder.

"You got the crystals?" she asked, changing the subject, drawing his attention back to what she could offer, what she was best at—why some breaches in protocol should be forgiven.

"Yeah, I'll deliver them tonight." He stared at her, his body still. "You know, we can arrange a more *permanent* solution to this ex problem of yours."

Images of Anders' head spiked on a borough marker flitted pleasantly through her shattered mind. But negotiating another deal with Worcsulakz would only tighten the noose he had fitted around her neck.

"Thanks, Jerath, but I'll manage."

"Your call." He pushed off the bathroom's door frame and exited through the hole in the far wall where her front door used to be.

Wincing, Solari pushed herself up on unsteady legs. Jerath had understated the level of damage Anders' rampage had exacted. Her life lay broken and scattered on the floor—a microcosm of the outside world, a diorama of gangland decimation.

Broken glass crunched underfoot, blood blooming against a shattered picture frame to paint a red filter over the photograph below. She bent slowly, ignoring the rush of vertigo, and picked it up. Dragging gentle fingers over the broken glass left red smears behind, but afforded her a better view of the picture. Her favourite.

A young Solari—maybe ten years old?—stood leaning against a taller boy. His shock of black hair fell thick around his face, hiding his eyes and giving him a roguish look. Denavim, her brother. He looked so young, so vibrant in that photo. Robust. Invincible. Untouched by the cancer that would take his life less than five years later.

She pulled the photo from its confinement and let the frame slip from her fingers. Cradling the picture in one hand, she pulled her flak jacket tighter in the other, and found a place where the destruction was not as severe: a patch of carpet, littered only with discarded books and broken vinyls.

Slowly she crouched down, the burning in her legs flaring brighter than the pain in her head. With a trembling hand, she swept away the relics of her past—treasures she had collected, remnants of a life before violence; beautiful, inconsequential things she had spent too much money on. Things that would never die and leave her like her family had.

Collapsing on to the carpet's worn threads, she pulled her knees up and hugged them tight against her chest. And screamed until her hoarse throat gave out.

TWO

The flak jacket scratched against Solari's fingertips as she pulled the hood up. For two days she had stayed curled on the floor of her apartment, shuffling from the spot only to take a piss or nibble on weevil-infested oats. If not for Jerath's promised return to pick up the tetrahydron batch, she would have stayed there instead of venturing to the Fringes.

She moved quietly along Hobart's streets, taking the long way to avoid the more dangerous boroughs and sticking to the morning shadows cast by crumbling buildings. The streets were empty, save a few junkies who lay dazed and mindless in the gutters. They stirred as she walked past, her boots crunching on loose debris. Some muttered sleep-filled curses, others merely grunted and rolled over on their sides.

In her earliest memories and the stories of her father, this part of Hobart had once been a vibrant cityscape. Now, abandoned shopfronts sat idle—their walls pockmarked with bullet holes, their shattered windows sprayed with promises and threats, their doors tagged with the blue trident of Worcsulakz and, occasionally, the orange anchor of DuPlessis.

More than once she had played with the idea of moving to a quieter part of the city, away from the conflict streets and the centre of the war. There were cheap rentals in Richmond, where she had grown up: tall, red-brick apartment blocks built at the turn of the century, with toilets that flushed and modern air conditioning units.

But, the memories were thick in Richmond. And besides, it

was too far from the Fringes.

A low, rumbling groan snapped her out of her thoughts and drew her attention to the body lying haphazardly in the doorway of what used to be a church. The stench of stale urine and decay assaulted her nostrils. The figure coughed, a hacking of phlegm and blood; their face, partially hidden by a hood, was covered in dirty, green scales.

Solari recoiled and looked away, quickening her steps to put distance between her and the church. As she walked, she clicked her tongue, working it around her mouth to dispel the bad taste left behind by the sight of the mutant.

It was over a year since she had last seen one. Mutated humans were uncommon in the western boroughs of Hobart—reviled by both sides of the conflict, they were easy pickings for sadistic fighters with torture on their minds and time on their hands. Most sought sanctuary in one of the enclaves outside the city, others wound up dead.

After a while she slowed, the stench gone and memory faded. Ahead, the wild beginnings of the Fringes rose on the urban horizon, drawing Solari's thoughts back to her mission. In other places, it was the city's agricultural holdings that backed onto the wilderness—a parasite on the lush, dangerous swathe of organic life. But, here, so close to the city, there was no gentle transition to the wild mass of scrub, trees, and vines; one minute there was the gravel of an abandoned industrial lot, the next there was the Fringes.

The cooler temperature brushed against her cheek as Solari stepped into the shadows of its wilderness. Epiphytes dragged hidden thorns along the exposed skin of her neck and leaf litter slushed underfoot. The noise of the Fringes was quiet at its edges, as if the wilderness was holding its breath. The silence should have been a comfort from the constant gunfire of Hobart, but Solari knew that the dangers of the Fringes were every bit as lethal.

With each step into the dark heart, the itch between her shoulder blades grew more insistent. Fear and desire twined together uneasily. There were unseen nightmares in the Fringes. Monsters. But there were also treasures; exotic chemical compounds hidden away in mutated organisms. With each step into the Fringes, she tempted one and coveted the other.

The path she tracked was familiar; crushed undergrowth and bent grasses revealed the route of her previous visits. She scanned the tree trunks for the purple moss and lichen that gave tetrahydron its potency, slashing and pulling at pieces that were useful, carefully avoiding the stinging nettles and acid-spitting dionaeas that grew nearby.

At regular intervals, she pulled her scarf tighter around her face and readjusted her gloves; while the mutant DNA she sought would gift her the precursors she needed, it could also just as easily infect her if she became rash or careless. It wasn't that the mutations were contagious—there was no chance of her sprouting horns, or growing extra limbs, or waking up with vines instead of fingers—it was the infection, the violent rejection of any mutant DNA by otherwise healthy bodies, that Solari feared. Stories of people dying horrific deaths from rampant infection after the smallest mutant scratch or bite were enough to justify the extra caution.

Moving deeper into the Fringes, she methodically hacked with her machete and filled the pockets of her jacket. It was hard work and, even with the cooler temperatures, a sweat quickly broke out along her skin. The hours dragged on and her pockets filled close to bulging. Only a few more samples, and she would have enough precursor to last for weeks.

As she crouched and hacked away at the fine, lilac tendrils of a prominent epiphyte, the sound of a breeze came whispering through the wilderness. Solari allowed herself to pause and lifted her face up, ready for the wind's cool touch.

It never came.

She stood and looked around in confusion. The sound of the breeze continued, but there was no shivering of leaves, no swaying of vines. With stealth and silence, she moved away from the tree, pocketing the epiphyte but keeping her grip on the machete.

Her belly fluttered, her mind yelling at her to walk the other way, back towards the city, towards home. But, a smaller voice, her rebellious spirit, urged her to inch towards the mystery sound. To satisfy her growing curiosity.

The rustling was louder, now—a midge too close to her ears, a lover's note crumpling in her fists. And then she saw it.

The moth was as long as Solari was tall. Its short fuzz of fur was a shock of vibrant colours—bright pinks, yellows, and purples. Impossible colours. But the wings—Solari could not draw her gaze from them. They fanned out from the shuddering body like a cheap entertainer's cape, fluttering to reveal a second wing segment that twitched and shimmered below the first. A kaleidoscope of swirls and whorls changing colour before her eyes.

She stepped closer. The moth erupted into a violent thrashing, the death throes of a beast attacked by a hidden assailant; viruses, parasites, microscopic bacteria, overburdened organs—there were a hundred ways to die in the Fringes. A hundred sources of torture and torment.

The thrashing stuttered; wings weakly beating against the ground, sweeping aside twigs, crushing desiccated leaves. Solari hesitated. The sound would be a beacon for the other monsters who had mutated in the unfiltered ozone that once streamed from the skyhole directly above Tasmania. Some, like the moth, were benign—nothing more than morbid curiosities. Others were deadly.

She should leave. Just turn around and beat her path to the city and her apartment. But it was rare to be gifted the opportunity to harvest from mutant insects. The moth was already dying; it would be a mercy kill to dispatch it from its torment.

With every second of deliberation, the risk of another predator appearing increased. Solari knew that she needed to act, and there were only two options: flee or kill.

Her heart hammering against its ribcage, Solari took a few tentative steps towards the beast. The flashing of colours and patterns was hypnotic, unnerving. Nausea swelled in her belly, and her pulse, compact and bright, fired in her temples.

The machete was a heavy weight in her hand, its steel flashing in the refracted sunlight drifting through the tree canopy. Small, beady eyes regarded her unblinking. Solari could see her silhouette reflected in them.

The wings flashed more urgently, expanding to brush against her jeans, leaving a silky residue of fluorescent colour. Antennae lay limp against the leaf litter. Solari brushed them aside with the toe of her boot, her breath now fast and shallow.

Crouching down, her knees trembled and pushed her off-balance. She pitched forward and threw her arms out to brace against the impact, her hands falling into the soft cluster of fur that ringed the moth's neck like a stole. Cursing, she wiped frantically at her jeans, her fingers itching with the ghosted feel of the mutant's body, despite the gloves that protected them. In a rush, she thrust her knife down into the space between the two eyes, averting her gaze at the last minute as a spray of black goop exploded like a geyser.

The fluttering of wings stuttered and stilled.

Her hands trembling with adrenalin, Solari scooped up the black head muck with some of the containers set aside for lichen collection. She worked quickly, her ears straining for the sound of predators.

Screwing the lid on the last jar, she stood up to regard the moth. The wings, while still spectacular, were quickly losing their transient colours and patterns. Reaching down, she pulled at one, testing its weight and integrity. It was light and soft. Almost stretchy.

There was a market for mutant curiosities closer to the border wall, rumours that guards would pay good money to then sell them to bored Northerners. And even if no-one bought the wings intact, she could always break them down and harvest the DNA for some new precursor. It was all money that would help her break clean of Worcsulakz when her debt was paid.

Breathing hard, she knelt again beside the moth. With quick, clean strokes she set about carving the wings from the body. Roots, like tentacles, twitched in her hands. Gagging, she kept working. The stench of the moth's blood filled the air and heat rose in waves from its corrupted body. Bile tickled Solari's throat and she gagged again.

Her hands moved expertly, the machete following the lines of tissue and sinew to remove each double segment of wing until the moth was denuded of all its majesty. She sat back on her haunches and tried to regain composure. Sweat coated her skin and her breath came fast and rough.

She had stayed too long. The smell, the heat, the sound — it was everything a mutated predator had been built to detect.

Casting her gaze around the nearby scrub, she worked quickly to secure her treasure. With trembling hands, she pressed the wings together and rolled them up tight, the roots still twitching with morbid energy. Solari hefted the bundle over her shoulder, the roots dangling down her back, and hurried through the wilderness to find her usual path.

With each step, the wing roots tickled the space between her shoulder blades. Solari cursed and shivered, picking up her pace. Breaking through the final web of epiphytes and underscrub, she exited the Fringes with a bellow and threw her bundle of wings to the ground. They landed with a dull thud, crushing the pale shoots of young grass.

Solari bent double and heaved up a meagre stream of vomit. Breathing heavily, she stayed head down, waiting for the nausea and adrenalin to leach from her body.

Slowly, normality returned. She straightened and looked over at the discarded bundle. The wing patterns were reacting to the new onslaught of sunlight, shivering in aftershocks of colour. It was a welcome distraction from the roots, which still twitched and twirled about themselves like an orgy of snakes.

Solari reached under her hood and pulled at the scarf wound tight around her hair. Dark strands spilled forward and she brushed them away impatiently. With deft fingers, she wrapped the wing roots tightly until their twitching was nothing more than a faint tremor. Grunting, she pulled the bundle up again, carrying it under her arm and resting its bulk against her satchel.

Step after shaky step, she pushed her legs to ignore the cramping that sent sharp spikes to her thighs. It was late and her apartment was still over an hour away. Surviving the terrors of the Fringes would be for nothing if she became victim to the horrors of the city.

THREE

The sound of gunfire grew louder as Solari approached her apartment building. Her detour in the Fringes had cost her precious time and her flagging energy had made for a slow return. She had arrived back too late; the fighting had recommenced in earnest and her safe passage was cut off. Sweating under the bulk of her jacket and her shoulder tingling with the dragging weight of the moth wings, Solari made a snap decision. Turning away from home, she headed north, picking her way along empty back streets to her laboratory.

Curtains fluttered aside in the windows of nearby apartment buildings as she approached the lab. Solari was an anomaly in these parts and the residents were wary of her presence. She visited infrequently, using the space only to break down source materials into their basic chemical components. But, still, the residents noticed the strange hours she kept, heard the strange noises that occasionally broke through the lab's walls.

Solari ignored their furtive glances. They could look all they wanted; there was no danger in looking, only speaking, and she knew they would hold their tongues. Those that survived in the war's epicentre knew that staying alive meant staying quiet: cockroaches only came out at night, and when they did, they stuck to the shadows and were satisfied with forgotten crumbs. Or they got squashed.

Still, she bowed her head and avoided eye contact. There was no point in tempting their tongues.

Inside the lab, the hum of the coolroom hinted at returned power, but flicking on the light switch did nothing to dispel the shadows. *So, just the generator then.* Solari sighed and propped open the lab door to invite the muted evening light in to illuminate the room.

Stepping forward, her foot tangled in an unseen obstacle, tipping her off-balance and sending her falling. Her hip slammed into a set of shelves, white-hot pain springing from the spot and radiating down her legs. The impact toppled glass beakers and jars to the floor, and threw the bundle of wings from her arms. She fell heavily to the floor, her leg screaming as glass shards sliced through worn denim and dug into her skin.

For a few seconds, she lay there, her breath ragged and heavy. And then, with trembling arms, she pushed herself up from the floor and groaned as the pain in her leg flashed bright and hot.

Exhaling through clenched teeth, Solari limped around the large steel benchtops and hauled the bundled wings into the lab's coolroom. The heavy door slid open with some resistance, the blast of cold air a relief to her sweat-drenched skin.

Inside, the space was crammed with jars and containers full of organic material sourced from the Fringes. On the far wall, a column of shelves stood stacked with distilled compounds—dangerous chemicals glittering in the red downlights. Her entire livelihood— her future—contained in that cold, hard space.

Solari fingered the soft, almost downy, material of the wings. Freezing them would slow down decomposition, but she worried the frost would damage them. Leaning the bundle against one of the racks, she grabbed the nearby fire blanket and gently wrapped it around the full length of the wings—it would be enough to protect them until she figured out what she would do with them.

She had already decided that getting to the border wall and finding a buyer for the wings was an unnecessary risk; it would be easier to break them down into chemical compounds and find local buyers. And while her mind was full of possibilities for new precursors, she didn't have the time or the energy right now to hack into the wings, dehydrate them, and grind them to dust. Shutting the coolroom behind her, she banished thoughts of future work, pushed aside the pain in her leg, and got to work on developing the azurei liquid required for the tetrahydron. The tetrahydron that Jerath would be coming for the next day.

Thoughts of Jerath reminded her of his offer of a more permanent solution to her Anders problem. She had used Worcsulakz to get her out of trouble before—the crime lord had been all too eager to rescue her from DuPlessis and secure a cooperative biochemist for his drug trade. But dealing with Worcsulakz was never cheap nor easy.

Solari rubbed the piece of scar tissue that traversed her eyelid. She had been blind in that eye for days following her escape from DuPlessis. Radical surgery by Worcsulakz's private surgeon had saved it, but even then, it wasn't enough to eradicate evidence of the torture—the ugly scar a perfect accompaniment to the white iris.

She could have had both fixed—Worcsulakz offered the cosmetic surgery as an additional bargaining piece for a more restrictive manufacturing deal, so certain she would take it. But, Solari had learnt her lesson about getting too entangled with crime lords. And besides, her new flaws marked her as damaged goods—a distinct advantage in her efforts to isolate herself and fend off overtures of intimacy and connection.

Over the years, her caution in maintaining a safe distance from the crime lord had not lessened. She had seen him tighten the noose on others; it never ended pretty. She would just have to deal with Anders herself.

Solari laughed—the harsh bark ricocheting around the sterile lab. It was an impossible challenge. Easier to tell herself to grow wings and fly over the border wall to the Northern Zone.

In any case, Anders—like the wings—was a problem for another time. Shutting her mind to any more distractions, she turned back to the work at hand and concentrated on distilling the precursors.

Hours slipped by, marked only by the sound of chopping and tearing and blitzing. Vial after vial filled with a deep blue liquid, until a row of twenty were lined up on the bench.

Solari's bag fell heavy as she deposited the jars into the inner pockets. The pain at her leg had reduced to an insistent throbbing and she readied to leave. Casting a final glance around the lab, her gaze stalled on the coolroom and her previous doubts about frost-damaged wings were resurrected.

Sighing, she pulled the bundle from the chill. The lab was more ordered than her apartment and she soon found a spray bottle of preserving liquid that was still mostly full. Unwrapping the wings on a stainless steel bench, she sprayed the roots liberally with the serum, shuddering at their every twitch and flicker. With each dowsing, they darted and danced with more urgency, brushing against her skin and attempting to coil around her arm in search of a nutrient source.

She worked faster, hands trembling as she tried to ignore the insistent twitching of the roots. Pain exploded again in her leg. The roots had pushed aside the torn denim and burrowed into the open cuts. Roaring, Solari pulled at them, gagging as they disengaged with a thick slurp and violent thrashing. Adrenalin screaming through her veins, she slammed the roots on the cold bench and smothered them with the blanket until the twitching quietened.

Her hands still shaking, she roughly rolled the wings up in the blanket and secured them tightly with a nearby roll of gaffer tape. Against her better judgement, she looked down at her leg, pulling aside the denim to inspect the cuts. In the muted light, it was impossible to tell how much damage the roots had caused, or what genetic material, if any, they had left behind. Wincing, she let her hands drop and focused her attention on retrieving a bottle of antiseptic and some antibiotics.

She grit her teeth at the sharp sting of the antiseptic—the neighbours had heard enough strange noises from her lab already, and she couldn't afford any unwanted scrutiny. Shaking out some pills from a small plastic bottle, she swallowed two and then another two for good measure, only hoping they were still in date and had enough active ingredients to ward off infection. At least until she could get back to her apartment and inspect the wound more carefully.

Pocketing the antibiotics, she threw a hateful glance at the bundle of wings still on the bench, and limped towards the door. They could stay there until she returned in a few days' time, when she would exact her revenge and begin the full dissection.

***

The darkened sky brought with it a cool breeze as Solari journeyed back to her apartment. She moved as quickly and silently as her leg would allow, hoping the hour was late enough for the fighting to be concentrated in the central boroughs alone.

Rounding the last corner to her apartment block, Solari's heart leapt to her throat, though not from fear of being caught in crossfire. Anders stood leaning against the building, flanked by three unsavoury-looking characters. The female was instantly recognisable, her brash makeup and too-short miniskirt the same as when Solari last saw her, attached to Anders like a rancid smell.

Instinct told her to protect the azurei and without hesitation she slung the satchel off her shoulder and hid it behind the pile of concrete rubble at her feet. Slowly, she backed away, keeping her eyes on Anders, careful to not draw his attention. Every part of her screamed with the need to turn and run; the strain of ignoring the primal urge pushed pins and needles along her spine.

Paranoia whispered to her, tempted her eyes to cast their glance towards the hidden satchel, to ensure it was still out of view. Breathing heavily, she instead kept her focus on Anders; years of training herself to ignore raw emotions and desires would not be so easily undone.

She was close now; the corner she turned just moments ago was only a few short steps away. Her foot crunched on unseen debris, twisting awkwardly under her weight, and she gasped as the pain in her leg reasserted itself. Her eyes swept from the female to Anders, fear of discovery flashing bitter across her tongue. But they remained oblivious, too high or self-absorbed to catch her stumble.

Relaxing, she took another step backward. So close to the corner, her brain switched from high alert to planning her escape. She would head back to the lab; there was a sleeping bag there for times when she had to pull long hours. She would come back the next day for the satchel—it would have to be early if she was to complete the cook and get the tetrahydron to Jerath when he came calling. And she would have to do something about Anders—his constant appearances were starting to cause trouble.

A crack echoed against nearby buildings, followed quickly by an avalanche of broken bricks and shattered glass. She stared in horror at it, her gaze quickly shifting to the figures outside her apartment block.

The female shouted and grabbed at Anders' arm. A wicked smile alighted on his face. "Hey, baby doll," he crooned. The female punched his arm. Anders' paid her no mind, Solari caught firmly in his gaze.

He advanced, slowly, like a predator. The others followed, laughing and jostling amongst themselves. He called out to her again, laughed as she took another faltering step backward. She looked around for an escape route, a safe haven, a weapon. Bending down, she grabbed a large piece of jagged concrete and waved it in front of her.

Anders laughed again—a low, menacing rumble. "Don't be like that, baby doll. We just want some shards. Just enough to take the edge off, y'know?" The sing-song, seductive voice reverberated around her.

They were getting closer, unperturbed by her manic waving of the concrete. She tested her leg, the extra weight amplifying the throbbing and turning it white-hot. There was nothing for it; she would have to run.

Pain exploded up her leg as she pushed off and raced around the corner. A loud cry sounded behind her and she knew that the group had given pursuit. Hobbling, she scanned the streetscape urgently. Her gaze flitted from empty storefront to collapsed wall, seeking refuge somewhere. Anywhere.

Ahead, a shattered window glinted under distant streetlights, the gap large enough for her to step through without making additional noise for Anders to follow. She limped as fast as the pain allowed, whipping her head around to look for her pursuers. There was still time.

Reaching the window, she kicked in the last of the jagged

shards and stepped through. Her boot caught and she stumbled, falling to the concrete floor inside. Glass fragments tore up her arms and hands, and her palms became sticky with blood she couldn't see. Suppressing a cry, she rolled over and scrambled to the far corner, where it was darker. The store had long been looted, with nothing but scraps left behind. Nothing to shelter her, nothing to protect her.

She cursed under her breath, wishing desperately for the phone lying nestled beside the azurei in her satchel. Pressing her back as tightly as she could against the plaster wall, she picked out the glass embedded in her hands and tried to control her breathing. Her fingers trembled as she grasped uselessly at the tiny slivers that refused to come out.

The shouts of Anders and his crew echoed louder. Solari hugged her knees to her chest, forgetting about the miniature glass daggers in her palms. Her heartbeat thundered in her chest, making her lightheaded.

Please let them pass. Please. Please let them pass.

The crunching of gravel and wild, incoherent yelling echoed in the empty space. Her pursuers appeared on the other side of the street, swaying and stumbling, switching between uninhibited joviality and aggression. The female giggled as she kicked at little pebbles of broken concrete with her gaudy high heel.

"Solariii," Anders called.

She shivered, caught between wanting to clamp her eyes shut and not being able to look away.

Anders was looking around and, for a moment, it seemed as if their gazes met. Solari's heart stuttered. And then the moment passed. Anders looked the other way, his head sweeping left to right as he and his friends advanced down the road.

Solari forced herself to keep watch as they moved out of sight, their laughter and shouts becoming softer and softer until she couldn't hear anything but her heart beating and the usual soundtrack of gunfire in the distance.

As the light outside faded, she slumped to the floor and curled in on herself. Her breath tickled the back of her hand and the smell of blood filled her nostrils. Eventually, the tension and fear dissipated and her eyes drifted shut.

*****

The crunching of glass echoed in her sleep state, but she didn't wake; the flak jacket was warm against the chill of the concrete floor and she snuggled in tighter. But, the low, throaty chuckle that followed triggered a surge of fear that wrenched open her eyes and shot her up to sitting.

While she had slept, darkness had invaded. The sun had long since set and the only light available was that from a distant streetlight. And, there, standing over her, backlit and dominant, was Anders.

"Hello Solari." His voice was calm and clear; the intoxication had worn off—replaced by a cold sadism.

A machete glinted in the soft light and her fear spiked into a clear, bright panic. Solari scrambled backwards, casting around for the piece of concrete she had carried in from the street, wishing she had grabbed one of the shattered glass panels as she'd scrambled inside.

Anders laughed again.

"Your friend gave me a new present." He pulled at his flak jacket, revealing a long, jagged scar tearing along his forearm. "Figure I should return the favour."

He crouched down. Solari kicked out, aiming for his crotch. Anders was quicker; his hand dropped to grab her foot, wrenching it until she cried out, and then wrenching it further.

"Tsk, tsk. Is that any way to treat your lover, baby doll?" He leaned in close, his face inches from hers, the traces of whiskey still on his breath. She hurled a gob of spit at him. It splattered uselessly against his chin. He didn't bother wiping it away, just backhanded her with a force that speared lightning bolts through her skull.

Anders sat on her legs, his full weight bearing down. Her fists struck out, wild and desperate, but even when they connected, Anders barely reacted. There was a feral energy in him now.

He grabbed one of her wrists and dug his fingernails in deep. "Now be a good girl and don't scream."

It all happened quick—him slamming her bound wrist to the

floor, pinning it to the concrete even as her free hand still punched and clawed—until it all went slow.

The machete twirled in long, lazy circles before Anders drove it down. Stars exploded behind her eyes and a high-pitched shriek pierced through the wall of buzz that built in her ears. The shriek grew louder, more urgent.

Her shriek. Her voice screaming even as her throat burned with the effort. While Anders grinned down at her, hacking off her finger.

FOUR

Solari drifted in and out of consciousness. The sound of Anders rifling around her buzzed in her ears, a low droning coming in and out of earshot. He was saying something, yelling something. Her eyelids flickered, everything appearing in static, a frame by frame telling of a nightmare. And then the darkness came to shut it out.

The darkness was still there when she came to, the streetlights laid low by another brownout. Time flowed against her, the tiniest of movements a battle. Her left hand reached for her right, a slick, sticky wetness coating her fingers as they made contact with her offending hand. The ring finger and pinkie were gone, roughly-hewn stumps in their place.

Her chest exploded as the sob was wrenched from it. The silence shattered, and she waited, stricken, for Anders' laugh. It never came; the room remained silent. She was alone.

Frantically, her hand skittered across the floor, searching for her missing fingers. Her palm, still burning with the lacerations from her earlier fall, sung with fresh pain as it ran over dirt and debris. She cast her search wider, a small voice inside her brain growing louder and more insistent; *the sick bastard has taken them for trophies.*

Tears streamed down her cheeks. Cradling her broken, deformed hand, she maneuvered to a standing position. Her flak jacket was wet and she stank of urine. The tears fell heavier as she realised Anders had pissed on her as his parting gift.

Slowly, her blurry eyes grew accustomed to the dark; enough to make out the broken window. She stumbled towards it, crouching to make her hesitant exit to the street. Thoughts of her satchel tempted her back towards the street corner, but fear of Anders lying in wait pushed her in the opposite direction. As if hijacked, her feet beat out a path unknown to her brain, and it was only when the sprawl of shanties appeared on the horizon did she realise where she was going and who she was seeking.

Scores of bonfires painted the night sky orange, illuminating the haphazard rows of stacked and rusted shipping containers amongst the concrete blocks and corrugated iron. Unlike the empty streets that surrounded Hobart's central boroughs, the gypsy quarter thrummed with life. Laughter and voices raised in song and anger drifted on the salt-tinged breeze. Somewhere beyond the towers of makeshift shelters, the Pacific Ocean swelled and tumbled.

Solari's shoulders relaxed. There was a small comfort to be found in that hotbed of human activity, in its sights and smells and sounds. Turning away from the activity, she located the large stack of shipping containers painted bright yellow and crisscrossed with dozens of ladders. Her hand throbbed, her leg ached, and her mind felt as though it had erased itself miles ago. Still, she plodded down the steep embankment to the timber lean-tos and scrap-metal humpies.

Children darted around her, squealing as they played out their game of chase. Years had passed since she had last ventured into the gypsy quarter, a lifetime since she had seen signs of life and hope and joy.

A little one, with his mess of blonde hair and dirt-stained cheeks, paused to regard her. Despite herself, Solari managed a weak smile. The boy exploded into peals of laughter and ran to catch up with the others. She followed him at a distance, watching as he bounded over rubbish, darting between cookfires and around junk piles. Ahead, the yellow container stack loomed large. The children's squeals grew louder as they got closer, peaking as they leapt at the rickety ladders, their small hands grasping and pulling at the rungs.

Solari watched them enviously, her absent fingers twinging, fire racing to her wrist. Tentatively, she reached for a rung. The chilled metal bit against her tortured hands. She paused, letting the ice battle the fire, and then she pulled away her right hand and reached for the next rung.

Pain erupted as the stumps pulled and tore at the damaged tissue, and with each new rung the pain built to a crescendo. Her legs trembled and her hands struggled to maintain what little grip they had. A small, traitorous voice inside her brain whispered to her, tempted her to let go—to halt the ratcheting pressure, the grating of raw skin on metal, the tearing and pulling of sinew.

She grit her teeth and kept her eyes on the tiny limbs of the children who scampered above her. Never at her hand. Never down. Climbing until the ladder intersected the second level balcony, her head breaching the gap in the floor like a newborn babe.

Gaggles of children streamed along the narrow walkway, greedy fingers clutching at the lollies Elysia squirreled away for them. Once upon a time, Solari had been one of those greedy-fingered children with her cheeks full of boiled sweets. The gypsy healer could never say no to a cheeky smile or hungry belly.

Solari stumbled onto the balcony, her hands tingling with pain and relief. The children brushed past her at speed, lost in their games and with no respect for the rickety balcony or the drop below. They tumbled one after the other, easily navigating the rabbit hole Solari had only just emerged from. The youngest one, the familiar one with his blonde hair, flashed her a victorious grin as he passed, his fingers popping another ball of hard sugar into his cherub mouth.

Something in that grin, that irrepressible spirit and hint of rebelliousness, reminded her of Denavim.

No.

It wasn't the time for memories, for lingering in the past. The past was sticky—stay too long and she might never return.

Elysia's container was at the far end of the balcony. Reaching the rough-cut door, Solari expected to be confronted with a crowded space, but the container was quiet. Elysia, her grey hair bent in earnest over a slender figure, turned at the sound of Solari's entrance. Her pale eyes widened in surprise and then confusion, finally dropping to the hand that leaked dark, coagulated globs of blood on to the floor.

"Solari!" Her voice was still as Solari remembered — a soft, gravelly rustle. It was the last thing she heard before the world turned black.

*****

Solari woke to a high-pitched squealing in her head — a kettle reaching boiling point, a pig being slaughtered. The pressure built in her skull, even as the sound faded. It settled into a constant thudding and then switched, sharpening and finding new definition, the pain breaking like a fever.

Beads of sweat exploded over her skin, immediately cooling on exposed patches, building uncomfortably under her flak jacket. She pulled at the jacket, her hands grabbing at a light, soft fabric instead of the heavy and coarse kevlar. Her eyes, still sticky with sleep, prised open and blinked against the daylight filtering into the room.

Pain, like an assassin's blade, slid almost imperceptibly into the base of her skull. A tingle, a hint that something was wrong. And then she saw the red-stained bandage that bound her hand, and the pain exploded into blinding, hot fragments.

Her body ricocheted upwards, a scream pulled from her core to explode against the metal walls of Elysia's shipping container. She waited for the sound to fell the gypsy quarter around her, only to realise that no sound escaped her lips; that the scream was trapped inside her mind.

"Calm now, Lareya." *Lareya*, Elysia's pet name for Solari. A name from a lifetime ago.

A sharp prick at her hand pierced the veil of her confusion and blackness faded in.

*****

There was no pain when Solari next woke, just a wall of fuzzy, half-formed, half-forgotten thoughts.

"I was wondering when you were going to wake up." The voice was familiar. Solari tried to focus her gaze, pulling it away from the view that stretched beyond the rough-cut window, a vague mess of orange embers and silver clouds. "Drink this."

The voice materialised into a stern face. Elysia. She looked older than Solari remembered—grey hair falling in ribbons, wrinkles abrading her olive skin from too much laughing at impish children and too much frowning at the weak and injured. Her hands, too, were older—thin and papery skin rustling as she handed Solari a small, porcelain cup. The pattern was faded and the edges chipped; Solari remembered it from her childhood and knew that the brew inside would taste terrible yet do wonders.

She sat up and took the cup in her left hand. The bandages made it awkward, but she was grateful there was no residual pain from the cuts on her palms. At the first sip, her tongue shrunk back at the bitterness and bile rose in her throat, threatening to expel the concoction before she could swallow it. Grunting, she drained the liquid, gulping heavily to keep it down.

Elysia's frown was still there, furrowing her forehead and deepening the creases around her eyes. She lowered herself onto the lounge next to Solari. The feel of warmth, where the older woman's shoulder touched her own, shattered the last of Solari's resistance and pushed aside the tattered remnants of her bravado. Tears budded in her eyes. It had been so long since she had felt the comfort of another human.

When she had been a child, there was no scraped knee or tummy bug that Elysia couldn't fix. Her father would bring her to the container tower and let the medicine woman work her magic, never quite trusting the doctors that were left behind in the Southern Reaches. But, it wasn't the medicine that was Elysia's magic—it was her touch, the gentle smile, the quiet words. That was why Solari had returned.

Elysia placed a small, frail hand on Solari's knee and squeezed, but Solari couldn't look up at her. Shame, spiky and insistent, bubbled below the surface of her mind. Shame at how long it had taken her to return to this place of comfort and peace, to visit an old friend. Shame at arriving late and unannounced as a victim, at knowing it took brutalisation at the hands of her drug-addled ex to bring her back.

Tears slipped down her cheeks. Out of habit, she raised her right hand to wipe them away, immediately feeling the unevenness of her hand, the missing fingers, the ugly stumps. The tears fell harder and she fell into the crook of Elysia's arm, resting her head against the bony chest and sobbing until there was no energy left to dredge the breath from her lungs.

The older woman remained quiet through it all, speaking only when Solari descended into shivers after the tears and sobs faded. "Hush now, child. You are safe here."

Slowly, Solari's body relaxed, the gentle voice and bitter tonic softening tight muscles and a fractious mind. She sat up and finally turned to Elysia, confronted by familiar blue eyes—the one thing that had not aged.

"Unburden yourself, Lareya. Tell me what happened."

The words came haltingly at first, Solari tripping over the timeline and stuttering as she recalled the more violent events. Elysia didn't react, just sat there listening. And, as Solari moved deeper into the retelling, something shifted—shame making way for anger and determination.

"I need that satchel, Elysia."

The old woman beckoned to a small child that had arrived unnoticed by Solari and who was now camped under the dining table, listening to the grisly tale in rapture. At Elysia's insistence, he scampered forward. Solari recognised him as one of the older boys she had followed through the rows of humpies. His hand reached out and snatched the lolly that Elysia proffered.

"Be quick, Matteo. Do not stop along the way, do not talk to anyone. A brown satchel at the corner of Hajile Lane and Eilyk Street."

The boy nodded, his mouth full of the hardened sugar, and raced out of the container.

"Now," Elysia said, turning her attention back to Solari. "I have a request of you."

***

Elysia locked the door to her container and led Solari to the small storage room at the back wall. As children, Solari and Denavim had hidden in there, cramped tight against the boxes, hiding from their father while he pretended to look for them in the small space of the container. Pretended to ignore the squeals and giggles as he called out to them, "Solari-ara! Denavim-vimvim! Where are you? Your papa is looking for you!"

The container seemed bigger then, an endless world of possibilities—an exotic island perched high in the even more exotic sea of the gypsy quarter. She smiled faintly at the memory, but her chest tightened; thoughts of her father and brother were always tainted with sadness.

Elysia reached for the storage room door, the wood panel coming away from its frame with a light click. Solari expected to see the same landscape of boxes, jars, books, and bandages from her childhood. But the space was empty—its shelves dismantled, its inventory removed.

The entire room was cleared, except for the half-naked boy sitting huddled with his arms gripped around his knees. Closely-cropped hair framed an adolescent face, guarded eyes peering up suspiciously at her. But, Solari's gaze quickly shifted from his face to the green scales that ran along the length of his spine and up his neck, her stomach turning at the way they glittered in the soft light of the container.

The mutant boy shifted under her gaze, looking questioningly at Elysia.

"He missed the scheduled run to the Second Enclave," she said, watching the boy but speaking to Solari. "I need you to take the truck and make the deposit."

Solari groaned, earning a sharp look from Elysia. The older woman shook her head, turned a comforting smile back to the boy, and shut the storage room door.

"Open the container door," Elysia said, tiredness and tightness creeping into her voice. "I can't have people getting suspicious."

Solari did as she said, grateful no children since Matteo had snuck in. Even with the wild tales that young tongues spun, talk of a mutant hiding would be enough to pique adult curiosity. And outrage.

"Elysia, what are you thinking?"

"Now, now, Lareya. I helped you didn't I?" The older woman sat down at the dining table and Solari reluctantly joined her. Despite the fondness she felt and the debts she owed to the healer, her gut twisted at the proximity to the mutant boy.

"But, I've known you for years," Solari countered. "And I am not a mutant."

Elysia shook her head again, frowning in disapproval. "Don't be like that, Solari. Don't be like them."

"Like who?"

"Like all of the misguided, self-righteous, ignorant bigots that can't see humanity in mutants."

The accusation stung, but Solari remained stubborn. "They aren't human; they're abominations. Unnatural."

"They are no more unnatural than you are with your three-fingered hand."

Solari recoiled from insult, taking no satisfaction in seeing Elysia's face drop and hand reach out in apology just seconds later.

"I'm sorry, Solari. I am, truly. That was insensitive."

Solari remained silent, kept her hands firmly by her side.

"In truth, they are no different from us," Elysia murmured. "There are good ones, bad ones. Mutants that are lazy, enterprising, radiant, scared, innocent, beautiful, murderous…Some have blue eyes, some have green. Some have scales where you have skin, or an exposed spine where yours remains hidden."

Solari glanced towards the storage room, picturing the cowering mutant inside. "They caused the war," she snapped. "They changed everything. Turned everything to shit. Without them, you wouldn't be living in a shanty town and I wouldn't be sitting here with no family and no fingers."

"Oh, Lareya—you know that's not true."

Maybe. There was a seed of doubt buried within that conviction fighting to put down roots and germinate. She pushed it aside; just because blaming the mutants was easy, didn't make her statement untrue.

Elysia peered at her. "What do you know of the mutants? The wall? The war?"

Just what everyone else knows.

Not that there was much to know. The mutants had emerged in the years just before Solari's birth. The early ones were curiosities. Freaks. And then the population numbers exploded—children born with three arms, mothers sprouting tails. But only in the South.

Later came the realisation that it was the radiation streaming out of the hole in the ozone layer. It had been there for decades, growing inch by inch until it split wide open. Gaping over the southern end of Tasmania, the hole birthed a whole raft of mutations. Mutations that never emerged in the North and that were later quarantined in the South behind an impervious wall.

Solari hated the border wall. Hated it in the way that only an inanimate object symbolising all that was fucked up in the world could be hated. Hated it more than the wealthy and educated technocrats who had constructed it to ensure no undesirables followed.

Safe and secure behind their barrier, with their science and commerce and governance, the rich and powerful had left the South to falter and implode. And it had. Spectacularly. All because of a wall, built because of mutants.

"It has been a while since you last visited," Elysia murmured, breaking into Solari's thoughts.

It was a strange pivot away from the talk of mutants and the wall.

Elysia patted Solari's hand and stood from the table. Solari watched as she disappeared into the small bedroom next to the storage room and returned carrying a large, leather-bound book.

"What is your first memory of me, Lareya?"

Solari frowned at the tremor in Elysia's voice, at the way the healer avoided her gaze and kept it firmly on the book. "I remember Papa bringing Denavim to you when he first got sick." It surprised her how clearly the memory appeared. She had been five and her brother, only three years' older, was firmly cemented as her hero.

Elysia's face softened. "Ah, Denavim. He was such a sweet

boy."

She opened the book on the table, pushing it closer to Solari so that she could view it easier. Inside, faded photographs filled the pages, glued beside scribbled notes and carefully inked dates.

Denavim stared back at her, a chubby toddler face with rosy cheeks. Solari glanced up at Elysia, confused. Elysia kept her head down and turned the page. A young woman, almost familiar, stood cradling a swaddled-baby. Beside her, the same chubby-cheeked toddler with rosy cheeks stood beaming up at her.

Solari glanced at the date printed next to the photograph. Twenty-six years ago. Under the date, in Elysia's spidery script, were three names: Denavim, Solari, Christianne.

Christianne.

Her mother.

FIVE

"That's impossible." Solari was unable to draw her gaze from the photograph. "She died in childbirth."

It had been the story her father had hated recounting, no matter how many times Solari begged him, no matter how many drinks she plied him with. Difficulties had emerged in the third trimester; Solari—the name her mother had given to her unborn child—was not positioned right. Pain turned her mother weak, listless. Anxious. When the due date arrived without any signs of labour, her father had wanted to take Christianne to the hospital, but she resisted. *"All will be well."*

When contractions started eleven days later, they had come on strong. For eighteen hours, Christianne had laboured; delivering a baby girl who entered the world fragile and blue. Christianne did not see it. Her final push to deliver Solari had taken with it her final breath.

"Your mother didn't die that day," Elysia murmured. "Although, I suppose, her life did end."

Solari shook her head, unable to comprehend what Elysia was telling her. For years she had mourned a mother she had never known, and for many more she had raged against a mother who had left her burdened with the tragedy of her brother and father. Adoring and hating a woman she had never met.

Wrinkled hands turned pages of the book. The next

photograph was smaller than the others, but it sat alone on the page. Solari's mother stood on a beach, pebbles scattered around her, frothy waves lapping at her feet. She stood with her back to the camera, but looked over her shoulder—away from the endless to who? Solari's father? Elysia?

She looked beautiful. And tragic.

Her perfectly-structured face was painted with sadness and longing. And yet, something worse lingered in the picture. The photograph was grainy—at a glance, the abomination could be mistaken for dark shadowing. Solari looked closer.

No, there was no denying it. The left side of her mother's face was covered in a thousand glittering scales.

"This was the last day she spent with us." Elysia's voice crashed through the whirl of Solari's emotions.

Solari glanced at the date. One month after she had been born.

None of it made sense—the date, the photograph, the tenderness in Elysia's voice.

"The mutation appeared towards the end of her pregnancy with Denavim," Elysia continued, her fingers resting lightly against the fragile pages of the book. "She was one of the first—at that stage, talk of mutants was nothing but a whisper. A fairytale absurdity.

"We thought it was a skin condition, brought on by a hotter-than-usual summer and the difficulties of a third trimester. It was only a small patch and it seemed to fade after Denavim was born. And then she fell pregnant with you. We couldn't take her to the hospital for fear they would turn her away, or worse, turn her over to the mobs. The extermination pogroms were starting up. We feared she would be discovered."

Elysia's words spun out faster and faster. Solari's hands ached, desperate to reach up and block her ears from the sound, to rip the photograph from the book and tear it to shreds.

"I delivered you myself in the kitchen of your childhood home. We hoped it would get better like it had after Denavim's delivery. But it got worse. Became more prominent, harder to hide under layers of makeup."

Elysia's words faltered. The two of them sat in silence, staring at an old photograph of a dead woman. *A dead mutant.* Her mother.

The quiet became too much for Solari. "What happened?"

She wanted to know, and yet her heart raced with the fear of what she would learn. She had made peace with her dead mother so many years ago, this new revelation felt like the tearing of scar tissue. Losing her, finding her, losing her anew.

"We heard word of an enclave established near Miena. There was talk of a secret community that would keep them in hiding during the day, transport them at night. Moving them along until they reached the enclave.

"But Christianne was stubborn. She wouldn't leave her children. We begged and pleaded with her, but she refused. She loved you and Denavim so much." Elysia's voice broke.

Solari looked up with eyes blurred with tears. Elysia, too, was crying.

"She was his wife. My baby sister. We needed her to survive."

Elysia's relation to her mother, to her, would have been a shocking disclosure if not for the king tide of uncovered secrets already drowning Solari.

"So your father held her down while I administered the sedative. The courier came that night. We never saw her again."

***

An hour later, the clanking of little feet across the steel balcony interrupted the silence. The boy, Matteo, strode in proudly, holding aloft Solari's satchel, his hands and face coated in fine, white dust. Elysia thanked him with handful of sweets and a ruffle of unkempt hair, but Solari remained motionless.

There had been no word from her mother in twenty-six years. With non-mutants strictly excluded from the enclaves, it was impossible to know whether the silence was from anger or death. Whether she had abandoned those who had betrayed her, or had died anyway, despite their efforts to keep her safe.

A surreal energy floated around Solari. Her father's suicide, a year after they buried Denavim, was once unforgivable, but now…

"We could have saved him." Solari's voice was husky, her throat raw from fighting the sobs that had threatened to escape.

"She could have been a match."

Elysia shooed the boy out of the container and locked the door behind him. She looked over at Solari, her face crinkled. With pain? Regret? Shame? "We tried everything to heal Denavim."

There was truth in what she said; Elysia, Solari, her father— they had all fought to keep her brother alive. Sacrificing everything. Sacrificing too much. Maybe if there had been more time, if they had been less desperate. But the disease didn't afford them the luxury; arriving quickly and spreading rapidly, it attacked Denavim's organs and set his bone marrow like concrete. He needed a transplant, but neither Solari, nor her father, nor Elysia were compatible donors. Neither were their friends or colleagues or neighbours or random candidates they had bribed with pieces of Christianne's jewellery.

Her father had taken Denavim regularly to Elysia for alternative treatments, and when those failed, Solari began to venture into the Fringes looking for more radical options. Her father spared no expense, selling the family home and everything in it to pay for tests and medicines and therapies. And when the money ran out, he turned to DuPlessis.

Her father had promised the world in return for DuPlessis' help, and the crime lord had agreed to the terms. His help extended Denavim's life sixteen months beyond prognosis, but the next month he sent his heavies to collect on the debt. With a broken leg, cracked ribs, and a twenty-five percent interest rate, her father negotiated a three-day extension. The next day he killed himself.

Solari had found him swinging from a lonely tree growing outside the industrial sector. DuPlessis, unperturbed, had merely transferred the debt to Solari.

She raised a hand to touch the scar at her cheek, pain rippling along the knuckles of her deformed fingers; the tonic was wearing off. Ignoring the pain, she grabbed the satchel from Elysia. With her good hand, she rifled amongst the vials and notebooks until she found her phone. All the confusion and helplessness and victimhood made her sick. And angry. Punching in the numbers, she clenched her eyes shut and waited for the call to connect.

"Details." A female voice. Bored.

It was a stark reminder that not everyone's life had been turned upside-down that day.

"Solari Peterov. ID 161115. Precursor Manufacturing. Address for tetrahydron pick-up has changed. Five shards will be ready by sundown tomorrow at the eastern entrance to the gypsy quarter. And tell Jerath I want the permanent solution."

Ending the call, she opened her eyes and looked over to Elysia. They shared the same almond-shaped eyes, Elysia and her mother. How had she not known they were related? All those years, wasted years, one betrayal after another.

"I will transport your mutant," Solari said, flat and cold.

Elysia opened her mouth to say something, but Solari stopped her with a shake of her head.

"I will do it as payment for your help tonight and for letting me sleep here and for all you did for Denavim. I will do it because I do not want to be indebted to you. I want to owe you nothing. And after this, I never want to see or hear from you again."

She waited, watching pain flit over Elysia's face. Finally the older woman nodded.

"I will come for him after sundown," Solari said. "Have the truck ready."

And with that, she turned and strode into the bedroom. She dragged the sheets and blankets off the bed and threw them to the floor, fashioning a pillow with her flak jacket. She didn't want to smell Elysia's sweet, sea-tinged scent, didn't want to be confused by the comforting familiarity.

Hugging her wounded hands to her chest, Solari lay down on the thin mattress and closed her eyes.

SIX

The sun was a fiery, orange ball low on the horizon when Solari caught the first glimpse of Jerath's motorcycle cresting the hill of the gypsy quarter, his form hazy in the sea spray that hung heavy in the air. He pulled to a stop a few metres from where she stood waiting for him. The arrogant bastard just sat there, hand outstretched, waiting for her to go to him.

She sighed, her sleep-deprived mind wanting to pick a new fight, her sense of self-preservation winning out.

Jerath frowned, clearly unimpressed, when she deposited the crumpled plastic bag in his hand. His eyes slowly moved from the product to the bandaged-covered, malformed hand that had held it.

"Worcsulakz won't be impressed with any compromise to quality."

"Good thing there isn't any."

Wrinkling his nose, Jerath tucked the bag and its shards away in the bike's saddlebag. "I got your message about the permanent solution."

Solari stilled. With her mind still at war over the news of her mother, she hadn't been inclined to think about Anders and his fate.

"Are we still doing that?" He watched her closely, hand resting casually on the bike's handlebars.

Solari nodded.

"You'll need to ramp up production," he said. "Double in the first three months, triple for the following nine."

It was an outrageous demand. Keeping up with the current quota already stole most of her hours. Accepting the new contract would effectively mean giving up her life for an entire year.

A year without Anders. A forever without Anders.

"OK."

Jerath nodded. "Well, that's done then. Next collection—double quota—in five days."

The rev of his motorcycle was like a vice gripping her brain.

"And, since your ex will no longer be a problem, I expect to pick it up in the normal place."

The dust that flew up as Jerath took off should have been the final insult—but she still had to collect the mutant.

She trudged back to Elysia's container, ignoring the children skipping about her, avoiding the bonfires, the food vendors, and the stray dogs. The truck, a heavy and battered model, sat where Elysia said it would be. Solari walked to the back wheel on the passenger side and reached under the mud flap. Ripping the tape, she liberated the keys from their hiding place and walked back to the front of the old beast.

She paused, resting her palm against the cold metal of the door. It would be a simple trip—the Second Enclave was situated in the old township of Ellendale, a three-hour drive from Hobart. The path would skirt the edges of the Fringes and, at this time of dusk, be clear of traffic. A simple journey.

And yet, it felt momentous—marking the line that would separate her older life from her new. A life without Anders and Elysia. A life at the mercy of Worcsulakz and his insatiable demand for precursors.

Fear and anxiety gnawed at her heart. But there was nothing for it now, her words had condemned her to this new path. She would follow it and survive—like she always had.

Solari opened the door and slid into the driver's seat. Rustling sounded behind her and she looked over her shoulder to find the mutant boy cowering in the back, head bent and eyes wide. His life would never be the same either.

"You might want to brace yourself; the road will get bumpy."

He squinted at her and frowned, as if weighing up whether to trust her or not. She shrugged and turned back to the front. Not her problem. She was to deliver him, not mollycoddle him.

Turning the key, she startled as the engine roared to life; she hadn't expected the rust-bucket to have such lungs. She needed to be more careful. In the early evening there was the risk of prying eyes and suspicious minds, curious children who would speak to bored adults, enterprising adults who would trade rumours and information to the highest bidder.

Solari maneuvered through the back streets, her hands tight on the steering wheel. The gypsy quarter's container stacks and humpies receded in the side mirror. She glanced again over her shoulder, finding glittering scales and fearful eyes. Shaking her head, she tore her gaze away and focused on the road; it was difficult to look at the mutant boy and not think of her mother.

As a child, Solari had stared at the mothers of other children, wondering if her own would have held her hand like that or combed her hair with the same gentle hands. Now she avoided looking at a terrified mutant boy, unable to keep her mind from wondering whether her mother had also cowered in the back of a battered truck, if she made it safely to the enclave, if she still lived…

Taking a hand from the wheel, Solari reached for the blanket lying on the floor of the passenger seat. It was scratchy, it stunk of diesel, and was sticky with a hundred stains of unknown origins. She threw it over her shoulder into the back of the truck, glancing behind to see the boy grasp at it greedily and wrap it around his shoulders.

***

The journey passed in silence as the night crept up on them and turned the road ahead dark. Solari was too pre-occupied with thoughts of her mother, with surreptitiously glancing at the boy, to see the ambush on the road ahead. By the time she caught the flash of white, the contact of the truck's headlights on steel, it was too late. She pulled at the steering wheel, the vehicle swerving violently, but still the road spikes caught the front, right-hand wheel. The truck lurched, the boy waking with a yelp.

Solari pulled again at the wheel, the truck careening towards the thick cluster of trunks at the edge of the Fringes. Her eyes flitted between the oncoming trees and the sight of three black-clad bandits emerging from the shadows.

Fighting instinct, she let go of the steering wheel to lock the two doors, jamming down the hard plastic pegs jutting from the door frames. The truck collided with a tree, knocking her forward and slamming her head against the steering wheel. Pain exploded behind her eyes.

Through the fuzz of confusion, her brain registered gratitude at the absence of glass shattering. She peered into the side mirror, catching sight of the blood streaming from a cut above her eye. Memories of sharp steel slicing along her face distorted her vision and panic rose thick and fast up her throat.

She shook her head and tried to refocus, a vague urgency tickling at the back of her fractured mind. And then she saw them, the black-clad figures with their faces hidden beneath woollen balaclavas advancing on the truck.

Behind her, a low moan rose above the ringing in her ears; the boy lay splayed on the metal floor, grasping at his head.

"Get under the blanket," she whispered fiercely, training her eyes back to the advancing assailants. "Don't move. Don't make a sound."

He moved too slowly, the figures growing larger in the cracked side mirror.

"Quickly! They'll kill you if they find you."

The bandits were almost at the driver's seat door. Her instincts screamed at her to climb into the back of the truck, with no windows to be smashed and more room to retaliate, but she just sat there. Almost as an afterthought, she scanned the driver's cabin for a makeshift weapon—anything she could use to defend herself— knowing it was useless, that all the tools were in the back with the boy.

The crash of the crowbar against the window shattered in her ears, glass fragments disintegrating and falling about her like snow.

She grabbed her satchel and held it out. "Here! Take it. Take what you want."

The laugh that followed was cold and menacing. But not so terrifying as the clang of metal at the back of the truck. In the side mirror she saw a leaner bandit reappear with a crowbar in their hands. Solari forced her gaze back to the bandit at the driver's side, lest her eyes betray the boy hiding under the blanket and pressed up against the back of the truck in the only blind spot available.

"What's in the back?" the bandit asked, his voice low and gravelly.

"I'm on my way to pick up medical supplies," she said quickly, her voice shaking as her hands trembled in her lap. "For the gypsy quarter." A cold sweat broke along her skin, making her hands clammy and her forehead slick.

The figure at her door rifled in her bag, pulling out her wallet, her phone. Solari looked past him to the third figure—shorter than the others, female?—who stood a short distance away, scanning the road for other vehicles, other victims.

"She'll fetch a nice price," the reedy one said, materialising at her door. "Even with the scar."

So, not just bandits. Slavers. Solari's gut clenched.

DuPlessis had introduced her to the racket just before he gave her the scar. Selling slaves for work and sex beyond the wall was good money. Worcsulakz had thought it *distasteful*. DuPlessis had no such qualms.

"You work for DuPlessis?"

The name was a circuit-breaker, causing the two men to pause and look more closely at her.

"That, little girl, is not a name you should speak lightly." The larger bandit wrenched the door open and pulled Solari from the driver's seat. She fell to the ground heavily, grunting. A swift kick to her abdomen left her breathless and scrambling in pain. The same mirthless laugh ricocheted around her. "A name like that can get you into trouble. Real, *painful*, trouble."

She rolled onto her side, desperate to avoid another blow. There was a flash of movement behind the leaner bandit. His eyes widened, his mouth caught in a silent scream. The burly bandit was too focused on lining up Solari for another kick to notice. Only when the thud of his companion dropping to the ground cut through the air did he turn around.

The mutant boy raised the pistol gleaned from his victim, pointed it at the bandit, and pulled the trigger.

The *crack* exploded into the evening quiet, blood pissing out of the bandit's throat. He dropped to his knees, clutching at the wound. The smaller bandit, alerted by the noise, came running from their lookout position. Another *crack* was followed by a shrill scream; the approaching bandit fell and clutched at their leg.

The boy walked over, his hand shaking as he trained the pistol on their writhing body. Evading the fumbling attempts to strike at him, he raised the gun again and fired.

Solari turned away, only to be confronted with the sight of the burly man bleeding out at her feet, his body still, his hands limp beside him. She turned back to the boy.

"We need to get out of here."

SEVEN

The boy disposed of the bodies in the Fringes while Solari changed the truck's tyre. The headlights illuminated a small crescent around them and she watched silently as he dragged the bodies, one by one, along the ground. Behind him, a glittering black trail lingered, as if a giant, mutant snail had slithered their way. Every now and then, their gazes locked on each other's—a quiet communication, a shared nightmare—but neither of them spoke aloud their thoughts.

When they finally pulled back onto the road, it was late. The shattered window provided easy access for the chilling breeze and Solari snuggled into the warmth of her flak jacket. The boy sat next to her in the passenger seat, the blanket wrapped around his shoulders and a black balaclava covering his scales. Looking at it made Solari shiver, so she kept her eyes on the road.

Forty minutes later, the makeshift walls of the Second Enclave loomed before them, bright with a score of industrial-grade spotlights. Solari pulled the truck to a stop a hundred-or-so metres from the nearest wall and killed the engine. The metal beast shuddered and fell silent.

Safe havens for mutants like the boy, the enclaves did not let others inside. Not without a fight.

She looked over at the boy. He pulled the balaclava from his face and stared at her. She had forgotten how green his eyes were. How perfectly they matched the verdant scales trailing down his cheek.

"I should go," he mumbled.

Solari nodded, a knot forming in her stomach at the thought of his uncertain fate. With the guilt of abandoning him after he had saved her.

He clambered out of the truck, shutting the door gently despite its beaten chassis. Passing by her window, his lean frame backlit against the onslaught of white light, he shuffled towards the enclave without looking back.

"Wait," she called after him.

The boy stopped and turned around. Rummaging around in her satchel, Solari's hand tightened around the lumpy protein bar that languished at the bottom.

"Here." She tossed it to him, the boy easily plucking it from the air. He smiled, the gesture lighting up his face. The knot in Solari's stomach loosened.

A rectangular light appeared in the wall. Solari watched as the boy approached and then disappeared through it. She sat there, long after the door closed, staring at the wall and letting the spotlights bathe her vision.

When the cold became too much even for her butchered hand, she turned the key to start the truck's engine. The beast coughed and hacked, but didn't start. She tried again, her hand singing with pain and lacking the strength to push the engine over.

It was too late and she was too tired; she would rest and try again later. Grabbing the blanket from where the boy had left it, she wrapped it around her shoulders and scrambled into the back of the truck. The scratchy material protected her a little from the cold metal of the truck's floor. She pressed herself against the cushions of the cabin seats, seeking more insulation from the chill that poured in through the shattered window.

This close to the Fringes, she could hear its nocturnal rumblings; the night-time calls of its nightmare monsters. She turned her back on them, pulling the blanket up around her chin and curling in on herself. The tightness of her heart and tremors of anxiety threated to keep her awake, but the call of sleep was persistent. Each blink lasted longer, her body promiscuous in its desire to succumb.

Warnings, fuzzy under the weight of oncoming sleep, pushed against her weakness. But the sandman would not be kept waiting, and he stole wakefulness from her even as she resisted.

***

Solari woke with a start, unsure of whether she had been asleep for minutes or hours. A scratching at the truck's metal shell sounded as if it were directly behind her. The surge of fear evaporated any remnants of sleep.

Light from the enclave-wall spotlights spilled into the truck, casting long shadows. The scratching sounded again, a jarring melody to the beat of blood in her ears. Solari sat rigid, unable to move, unable to look anywhere but to the jagged shards that framed the broken window of the driver's side door.

Scratch, scratch, scratch. The sound made her heart stutter.

And then the sound materialised into something tangible, scrabbling up to peer inside the truck. And her heart seized.

Thylacine.

Black eyes glittered in a narrow face above a slender snout. The beast let out a rapid-fire snarling, scrabbling to keep purchase on the chassis. Its wild gaze eventually found Solari, and the snarling quickly turned to a hacking bark full of crazed and hungry desperation.

Teeth gnashed at the window, dark blood spilling from the beast's mouth. The thylacine rippled with the trademark stripes of the Tasmanian Tiger, but the animal was mutant; a row of fang-like protrusions erupted from its fur along the spine. With a single, powerful leap it launched on to the hood of the truck and pawed at the windscreen, Solari firmly in its sights.

Shaken from her stupor, Solari tore her eyes away and scrambled into the driver's seat. She fumbled with the keys, wrenching them from the pocket of her jacket and jamming them into the ignition.

The pain in her hand still flared as she tried to get the engine to start, but the adrenalin surge dampened its heat.

Start, damn you.

At the sound of the truck spluttering, the tiger leapt back to the ground. It appeared at the driver's side window; teeth gnashing, dark blood spilling from its mouth, spine fangs shimmering. She dropped her hand from the key, leaning away from the abomination trying to tear its way into the truck.

Her hand shook as she tried to reach for the key, darting back and away as the tiger snapped at her with its razor teeth. With each lunge, the beast pushed further into the breach. Desperation, thick and bitter on her tongue, drove aside her fear and she lunged for the key, hand clamping on it tight and twisting it with all the strength the adrenalin would lend her.

The truck roared to life, drowning out the guttural hunting call of the tiger. A flash of white heat exploded in her forearm, the tiger's fangs penetrating her flak jacket as easily as a knife would. Pain moved in waves up the rest of her arm as the tiger took hold, its fangs tearing at the limb as it threw its head side to side.

Screaming against the assault, Solari forced her free hand to push the gearstick into drive and slammed her foot down on the accelerator. The tiger maintained its grip and Solari swerved wildly, feeling her flesh peel away in shreds with every wild swing of the truck.

Finally, the tiger released her, its head thudding against the window frame before it fell back to the ground. Eyes flashing to the side mirror, Solari watched in horror as the beast faltered back onto four legs and attempted to give chase. She pressed harder at the accelerator, her gaze caught between the road ahead and the terror behind.

She needn't have worried—the thylacine was slow, unable to gain on the truck with its stiff and clumsy gait. Still, she didn't release the pressure, dust flying up as the truck transitioned too quickly to the hard surface of the road.

In her mind's eye she could see globules of Thylacine DNA amassing under the skin of her forearm. A new panic sharpened the old and she pressed her foot heavier against the accelerator. She would not survive Anders only to die from a mutant infection.

***

The township of Westerway was dark and silent when Solari reached it twenty minutes later. In the glare of the headlights, she could make out the rows of apartment buildings, the empty squares and their crumbling archways. It all swayed and swam before her eyes.

It was too hot in the truck.

No, that couldn't be right. *The windows. The cold.*

It was too hot and yet she shivered.

The truck lurched dangerously, veering sideways on the straight road. Solari clutched at the steering wheel, desperate to correct the trajectory. Her mangled hands slipped uselessly against the hard plastic.

The pain in her arm was like acid burning through muscle, sinew, and bone. It screamed at her. She tried to raise her hand back to the wheel, but her arm refused to obey the commands of her muddled brain.

A wall loomed ahead, aglow with the full brunt of the truck's headlights.

It was too close. And getting closer.

Pins and needles sung through her left hand as she desperately gripped the steering wheel.

Brake. Brake.

The addled thought came too late; the collision a dance between brick and metal in slow motion.

***

"Hey, stormgirl." The voice came to Solari in a dream. Something cold and wet rested against her forehead. She swiped at it, hearing it fall with a dull thud.

"Now, now," the voice admonished. "Don't be getting feisty on me."

Solari opened her eyes, the lids crusted with sleep. A female, maybe her age, maybe a few years older, perched on a battered stool. Muted sunlight filtered into the room. Morning? Afternoon?

Shaking her head to lift the persistent fuzziness, Solari tried to make sense of her surroundings. The room itself was small. Crooked venetian blinds hung skewed against the only window. And a wash basin—its porcelain, stained and cracked like everything else in the world—stood in the corner.

"Didn't your mother ever teach you good manners?"

Solari grimaced and sat up. Black spots bloomed in front of her and she clamped her eyes shut to kill them. "I didn't have a mother." Her voice was hoarse, scratching along a dry and sore throat.

"Pity," the other woman said. "Looks like you could have used one." Her gaze tracked over Solari's scars, from her face to her forearm to her hand. Solari followed it, startling when she realised she was naked from the waist up, save the bandage that wrapped the entire length of her arm and across her chest.

"To slow the blood flow," the woman explained. "What bit you?"

The memory came back to Solari in half-formed flashes. Something big. With fangs. And stripes.

Thylacine.

She stopped short of saying the name aloud; it would have only invited more ridicule. Thylacines were urban legends that parents told their children to scare them from venturing too close to the Fringes.

She shook her head, the tiny movement sending a series of twinges through her upper body. The same blinding pain that had plagued her before the collision had evaporated.

"Well, whatever it was, it did a number on you." The woman stood up from the stool and walked towards the door. "The infection was already in your chest by the time Scotty found you."

She leant against the doorframe, watching Solari closely. "We pumped you full of alijeah; there's a bottle on the nightstand."

Solari eyed the bottle of pills sitting on the table next to her. As a biochemist, she was familiar with a lot of chemical compounds, even more so with antibiotics for mutant infections, but she had never heard of alijeah.

"Scotty took the gun hidden in the back of the truck as

payment for the first bottle, but we'll need cash next time you visit."

"What makes you think there'll be a next time?"

The girl laughed, a tinkling of glass shattering. "There's always a next time with alijeah."

"Where's my truck?"

"Where you left it—broken against the wall."

Solari groaned. More delays. More problems with Worcsulakz.

She swung her legs over the bed, immediately regretting the move. Nausea welled in her belly, and she gripped the bed to stop swaying.

"Easy, stormgirl. You haven't eaten in days. Get your energy up—and then move." The woman winked at her and exited.

Haven't eaten in days. Days. She had been gone too long. When had Jerath scheduled the next pick-up? Five days? Five days for a double quota?

She needed to leave. But her truck was wrapped in a wall and her chest in a bandage.

***

The room was just one of many crowded around a narrow landing. With the pills tucked safely into her jeans' pocket and her bandages hidden under an unfamiliar long-sleeved shirt that smelled of citrus and mint, Solari ambled down the flight of stairs. The murmuring of indistinct voices drifted up to her, gaining volume and clarity as she descended.

Avoiding the sound of laughter and music, she turned towards the chill sneaking in under the exit door. The cold outside held a stronger bite, easily penetrating the thin material of her shirt. In that moment, Solari felt the loss of her flak jacket more keenly than she did her wounds.

The street was as quiet as most small town roads were, and completely normal in its presentation—the shuttered windows, the ozone-bleached paint, the crushed metal perishing against a nearby wall. Everything normal, and devastating in their own way.

Three men were stripping her truck for remaining parts, their hands full of tarnished steel and blackened hose. She waited for them to leave, unable to stop them and unwilling to walk into another fight she couldn't win. Minutes later she shuffled over, ignoring the debris scattered around the street.

The truck sat awkwardly on the cracked bitumen, dispossessed of its tyres. The bonnet was an empty shell, as was the truck itself—the steering wheel, the gear stick, the pedals and seats; it had all vanished. Urban carrion to enterprising predators.

There was nothing to salvage—her flak jacket and satchel were gone along with everything else—so she headed back inside the hotel, striding towards the light and laughter and voices. The pub inside was like every other that Solari had visited—dark, noisy, and suffocating with the stench of sweat and stale beer.

Solari took a seat at a table in the corner, the soles of her boots grabbing at the sticky carpet. In spite of the foul smells, her stomach rumbled and she thought wistfully of the protein bar she had thrown to the mutant boy. She wondered if he was faring better than her.

Glancing around, she sized up potential targets—someone who was alone, even if just for a few minutes, or someone who was too drunk, too distracted, too overconfident. She didn't have to wait long; a lanky man at a nearby table leant drunkenly towards his friend and stood up, leaving his wallet entangled in a jacket on the vacated seat.

"Mind me stuff," he slurred loudly.

His friend, a burly looking man with a straggly beard, nodded absently, too busy with the three twenty-something girls that hovered around the table.

"Oi. Mind me stuff," he slurred again.

"Alright, alright," his friend shouted, scowling at him before turning back to the girls.

Solari waited until the lanky one was halfway to the bathroom before she stood up and walked slowly towards the bar. She turned her body to block the view as she reached down and nabbed the wallet. Maintaining her pace, she strolled to the bar, lifting half the cash stuffed in the wallet's crease.

She'd seen people lift the whole stash, or take the entire wallet, but that was stupid or lazy. And Solari was neither.

"What can I get you?" The tall, redhead behind the bar didn't bother looking up as she wiped down the countertop. *An exercise in futility.*

"Chips and gravy. And a beer."

The bartender nodded and started pouring the beer. "Hey Scotty! The keg needs changing."

A dark-haired male, not much older than Solari, popped his head around the corner of the bar. Tattoos ran from his skull to his bare shoulder. A stained white singlet showed off muscular arms, the dirty fabric cinched at the waist with a familiar grey, flak jacket.

Her flak jacket.

Hello Scotty.

"I'll grab one from the van when I get a chance," he yelled back, disappearing again behind wall of bottles.

"Your beer," the bartender said, pushing a chipped glass full of dirty liquid towards Solari. "I'll bring your chips over when they're ready."

"Thanks." Solari handed over some cash and walked back towards her table. The stench of the beer made her stomach roil. *God-awful stuff. Who would drink this shit?*

The man with the straggly beard was where she had left him, still captivated by the girls who all took turns leaning in a little closer, cozying up a little tighter. At the last step, Solari pretended to stumble, tipping her glass and spilling the beer over one of the girls.

"I'm so sorry! So sorry!" Solari put the empty glass on the table and reached for the jacket still sitting on the chair. Replacing the wallet, she haphazardly dabbed at the girl with the ugly fabric.

The girl looked at her in horror, her friends and their paramour in fits of laughter. No, Solari was not stupid. The girl grabbed the jacket from Solari's hands, the wallet falling conspicuously to the floor.

"Hey, watch it!" the man cried, rescuing the wallet and grinning up at the other girls.

Solari retreated to a table further away, watching as the beer-soaked girl hurried towards the bathroom, running into the lanky drunk making his way out. He groped her on the ass as she squeezed past him.

Pig. He deserves to be robbed.

She felt for the wad of notes tucked beside the pills in her pocket. Not enough to get her back to Hobart, but enough to bide her time while she figured out a plan for Scotty and his van.

EIGHT

"Hello, Scotty." Solari's voice was a soft purr.

She had watched him for the past five hours, the last three of which he'd spent drinking with the redhead whose shift ended when a boy no older than fourteen arrived to take her place.

He turned to look up at her, grinning as recognition flitted across his face.

The scar. Everyone always remembers the scar.

"You're awake," he said, voice deep and gravelly with too much beer.

"Yeah, I hear I have you to thank for that." *And for stealing all my shit.*

His face broke into a leery smile. It was that easy.

Solari knew she should not be surprised—her voice was a weapon, her sex was a weapon—and yet, she was.

"And how would you like to thank me?"

The redhead sighed and stood up from the table, fixing Solari with a glare as her parting gift.

I'm doing you a favour.

"I'm sure we can think of a few ways."

His smile widened. He would be attractive if he wasn't so repulsive. She trailed a finger along the ink on his skull. He laughed, deep and throaty. It made Solari's skin crawl, but she managed to gift him a smile.

He stood up and grabbed her hand, too tight; he was trying to intimidate her, to sound her out. Solari didn't flinch or grimace. He thought he was menacing, but compared to Anders he was just a pre-teen high on ego and not much else. Laughing louder, he pulled her towards him. "Let's go, buttercup."

He led her to the back of the bar where the cellar was full of large, metal kegs, and pushed her forward. She stumbled a few steps, gaze drawn to the exit door less than a metre away, and then turned back to Scotty.

"Now, let's get to thankin'," he said, throwing her flak jacket to the floor and pulling his pants down to reveal a flaccid penis.

Solari schooled her face—careful not to laugh, or roll her eyes, or groan at the sheer idiocy of the man.

The pants jangled as they hit the polished concrete. She smiled. It was the sound of her escape.

Sauntering towards him, she let her hips promise something she had no intention of giving. He reached for her head.

"Unh-uh." She shook her head slowly. "Trust me. It's better with no hands."

He laughed again. "You're a fucking dirty little girl, aren't y—" His drunken growl erupted into a groan of horror as Solari's knee came up with full force into his unprotected groin. He fell to his knees, clutching at his crotch and writhing in pain.

Moving quickly, Solari crouched down and grabbed the keys from his pocket, evading his flailing legs as he struck out at her. Without a backwards glance, she grabbed her flak jacket and pushed open the exit door.

A grey van with battered panels sat parked out front. But there was nowhere to drive it. The loading dock was a secure laneway, gated and locked.

Shit.

She looked down at the half-dozen keys cradled in her palm, trying to figure out which, if any, would open the gate. Cursing under her breath, she looked over her shoulder and back into the cellar. Scotty was still where she had left him, but it wouldn't be long before he recovered from his pain and came after her.

The van key was easy to locate, shaped in that unusual way of all car keys. She unlocked the driver's door and climbed in, her gaze constantly shifting back to the cellar, her body on high alert.

Hands shaking, Solari turned the key in the ignition, rejoicing when the engine roared to life with no hesitation. Her eyes shifted from the gate ahead to the rear-view mirror as she sped towards the end of the laneway. Just as she braked metres before the gate, Scotty appeared in the laneway. He stumbled towards the van, yelling something incoherent.

Solari pulled the key from the ignition and fumbled through the others attached to the keyring. Ignoring the racing of her heart, she jumped out of the security of the van and ran to the gate, hands reaching for the padlock and jamming one key after another into the bulky metal.

Scotty was getting closer, his curses louder. She needed to hurry—he would eventually attract attention and she was not equipped to take down two assailants, no matter their drunken state.

The click of the lock sounded bright and sharp against the thudding of her heart and Scotty's garbled curses. Solari tore it away from the chain and pushed fiercely at the gate. It swung in a broad arc and caught on the uneven bitumen, grinding to a halt with the scraping of metal against rock. Cursing, she looked over her shoulder. Scotty was too close.

Her arm throbbing with the exertion, Solari climbed awkwardly back into the van and locked the doors. She struggled to find the van's key and insert it into the ignition, her fingers trembling with fear and exhaustion. The rumble of the engine was quickly followed by a loud bang. In her side mirror, she could see Scotty hammering his fists on the van's metal skin.

Solari jammed her foot down on the accelerator, twisting the steering wheel to put the van in the trajectory of the half-opened gate. The collision shuddered up her arms, sending new waves of pain crashing through muscle and radiating through her chest. Memories of the other collision flashed in her mind, melding with the present. She grit her teeth against the disorientation and gripped the wheel tighter.

In the end, Scotty was much easier to evade than the thylacine.

Solari allowed herself a victorious laugh as she watched his tattooed skull disappear from her vision.

***

The first thing Solari noticed when she returned to her apartment three hours later was that the power was back on. The kitchen light flickered over the destruction she hadn't cleaned up after Anders' last visit. Fragments of glass and splintered furniture sat like eerie sentinels while her pedestal fan rattled away in the corner.

The power was a good sign.

Maybe my luck is starting to come good, after all.

She headed towards the bathroom, her mind already on the task of pulling together a double-quota stash of tetrahydron in forty-eight hours. Thoughts of snowrock swirled in and amongst thoughts of Jerath and Anders and Scotty. So preoccupied and tired, she walked past the small, gift-wrapped parcel sitting on the kitchen benchtop.

The bright yellow ribbon registered in her mind a moment later and she backtracked to the kitchen.

Elysia. It was typical of the old woman to send a peace offering.

She debated whether to open it; memories of their fight were still rough whips over raw skin. But curiosity wrapped its seductive fingers around Solari's mind—taunting her to find out what meagre gift Elysia thought could soothe the betrayal.

The expensive paper fell away to reveal a small, cardboard box. Solari lifted the lid, recoiling from the contents and dropping the box. It bounced off the benchtop and tumbled to the floor, spilling the two fingers.

Solari gagged. The digits were waxy looking with dark, black spots where the blood had congealed. Panic slowed down time and sped up her heart rate. Her brain stuttered at the thought that Anders was still alive, that he had escaped Jerath's permanent solution; that he had come back for her.

The terror stole her breath, her gaze never wavering from the fingers. Her fingers.

Except…

Except they were longer. Too large to be a pinky and ring finger. The knuckles were too prominent, even counting for swelling.

Only then did she see the piece of paper that had also fallen loose from the box. The script was neat, its large loops and decisive strokes filling the page. The gift was not from Anders.

Your permanent solution, as agreed. The price, however, will need to be renegotiated… Dispatch will arrive in three days to collect you.

She dropped the note and looked around. Even amongst the debris, she could see that things had been moved. Rearranged. They had been back to collect her. Were waiting for her.

Crap.

There wasn't much worth taking and she didn't have time to think about it. The photo of Denavim was still where she had left it, an island in the only cleared patch of carpet in the room. Picking it up, she folded it in half, pressing the crease between her and her brother.

Solari on one side. Denavim on the other.

She pushed it deep into her flak jacket pocket before the emotion took over. Racing to the air vent, her fingernails scratched at the loose screws, twisting and pulling until the grate released.

Impossibly-bright notes sat stacked in neat piles, their polymer sticky with the residue of past cooks. She grabbed at them and stuffed them into her pockets. Not a fortune by any stretch, but enough to get her away. To try her luck somewhere else.

Heart in her throat, Solari took one last look around her trashed apartment and zipped up her jacket.

Time to go.

Her feet crunched on the broken things she was leaving behind. It wasn't much of a home, but when she didn't have much of anything, it was something.

Taking a deep breath, she turned to grab the van's keys on the countertop. And came face to face with Jerath.

"Hello, Solari. Going somewhere?"

NINE

Jerath and his equally brutish friend kept silent as they drove Solari through the night-time streets of Hobart. The sound of gunfire transformed into dull pops as it reached the bulletproof glass of the car.

Solari sat in the back seat, staring out the tinted windows that made the night seem darker and the streetlights dimmer. It was disorienting, which was probably the point. Only when the car entered a brightly-lit garage was she able to make out her surroundings.

The space was cavernous and filled with rows of heavy-duty cars. Ice filled Solari's chest and sunk to her stomach. They hadn't brought her to a district Captain or even a Deputy. She would be meeting with Worcsulakz himself.

The journey from the garage to the penthouse passed by in a blur of lush carpets and priceless artworks. Reaching a pair of immense timber doors, Jerath rapped twice and stepped back. The seconds stretched into eternities.

"Enter." The thick Polish accent broke through the heavy doors.

Solari's fingernails dug crescents into her palms. Pushed from behind, she fell into the room wide-eyed and off-balance.

An older man, late-forties with streaks of grey in his hair and closely shaven beard, sat behind a large, timber desk, dressed impeccably in fabric straight out of a snowrock dream. He didn't look up as Solari stumbled into the room, just sat there ignoring them. Keeping them waiting, again.

Arrogant prick.

The sentiment held no heat—the harshness of the words was lost in the thundering of her heart and the wet slick of her sweaty palms.

Solari used the time to study the man, the legend that was Worcsulakz. He was more refined than she had anticipated. She had expected him to look more like DuPlessis—an ugly, crass man with crime lord written all over him. Instead, he looked more regal—the silver spike to DuPlessis' iron rod.

"You kept me waiting." His tone was dark, the threat subtle but clear.

"She was trying to escape, sir," Jerath's colleague said, and scowled at her. Solari remained quiet and didn't offer any excuses. Her story was not one she could tell and, in any case, would not assuage their...*inconvenience.*

"So, this is the girl?"

"Yes, sir," Jerath said beside her.

Worcsulakz looked her over slowly—not with the lecherous attention that DuPlessis once had, but with the no-nonsense appraisal of someone deciding the value of an item they wished to purchase, or sell. As if she were a piece of snowrock, and he was searching for flaws, impurities, blemishes. Solari dipped her head; she had her fair share to offer.

"I don't remember you," he said matter-of-factly and leaned back into his chair. "I thought I would—it's not often I have the pleasure of stealing one of Pierre's treasures from him. How long have you been working for me?"

"Eight years," Solari said. "Of a nine-year contract."

Worcsulakz thinned his lips. "I'm told your product is the best in the Southern Reaches." He flicked his gaze to Jerath, who nodded. "I don't touch it personally," Worcsulakz continued. "You don't need to touch a fire to know it's hot."

He leaned forward and propped his elbows on the desk, lacing his fingers together and scratching at his chin with his thumbs.

"You've been quiet these past eight years," he said. "I'd almost forgotten about you."

That was the plan.

"Shame," he said quietly, the word lacking any kindness of pity, "that your…troublesome ex…well, that he proved more troublesome than I would have liked."

Worcsulakz cold, flat stare was unflinching. She should look away, demure to his ice-cold assessment, offer some act of contrition—even if it wasn't genuine. But Solari had always been more defiant than demure, and there wasn't many opportunities to be defiant in this world. So she kept his gaze.

His lips thinned again. In Solari's experience, powerful men did not appreciate the defiance of powerless girls. Worcsulakz smiled, the gesture as benign as it was terrifying.

"The old terms of our agreement are no longer valid." He flicked his hand in dismissal. "Jerath, Zjelko—show her to the new terms."

There was no recourse. Jerath pulled her back through the double doors, Worcsulakz's head already bent back over his desk, Solari and her defiance forgotten.

Jerath and Zjelko dragged her along the corridor, their pace and her confusion tripping her feet. *What new terms? What is happening?*

Elevator doors slid open and Jerath pushed her inside. The metal cage whirred almost silently as it made its way down through the levels. Solari focused on the LED numbers flashing on the display screen, a new anxiety worming its way into her mind.

What if the electricity shuts off? What if the elevator stops? And we are stuck?

She dismissed it quickly; Worcsulakz was too rich to be affected by electricty outages. The sort of power that Worcsulakz wielded protected him from most problems. It was the sort of power that created immunity. Invincibility.

His generator is probably the size of my apartment.

The thought was reassuring but Solari's stomach still fluttered as the elevator continued without pause. P1. P2. B1. B2. B3. The shift into subterranean levels sharpened her fear to a finer point. They were not leading her back to the garage and the car and her apartment on the other side of the conflict zone. They were leading her somewhere else, to a new stage of this dark nightmare.

The elevator slowed, came to a stop, and exhaled softly as its doors opened. Solari exhaled her own shaky breath, and then drew it in sharply.

Beyond the doors, stretched a metal cavern. Stainless-steel benches sat in rows from windowless wall to windowless wall. Everything gleamed in a too-bright, white fluorescence. A metal railing ran like a snake across the ceiling, dripping long chains to the floor.

Dread, cold and relentless, washed over her.

"Welcome to your new terms, Solari." Jerath's voice held little humour, but his mate laughed. The sound echoed against the tile and steel and concrete. Solari recoiled—not at Jerath, or the insane cackling, but at the thought of one of those chains clasping around her neck and tethering her to the endless line of benches.

"For how long?" Her voice pitched too high, betraying her panic.

"Three years."

The proposition was ludicrous. And horrifying.

Three years locked away in a basement. Three years making snowrock twenty-four seven. Three years being chained like a mongrel dog, sleeping on a manky bedroll, showering in a cold, sterile shower.

Her body crumpled in on itself as she fought the desperate need to collapse to the floor and howl.

"Why?"

"Your boy Anders was a pain in the ass, that's why." Jerath pulled up a sleeve to show an ugly gash, red and angry. "He brought a few mates to the fight and those mates were very well connected. Worcsulakz doesn't like treading on DuPlessis' toes for the fun of it."

Anders, the bastard. It was all his fault. He was still making her life hell, even from his grave.

"He was working for DuPlessis?"

"Yeah. He didn't tell you that?"

No. He didn't tell me that. The no-good sack of shit.

God, she wanted to cry. She could feel her lips tremble and her throat ache with the effort of holding back the sobs bubbling up from her chest.

"I hope you made it worth it," she whispered hoarsely.

Jerath smiled, a hard and uncompromising twist of his lips. "The present I left you was only the beginning."

Her mind skipped through scenarios of Anders' grisly demise. But there was no comfort in it, no sadistic joy. The claustrophobia was strangling her thoughts and sending everything into a shattered kaleidoscope.

"Enough chat," Zjelko interjected. "Time to get working."

He pushed her towards the benches, unmoved by her protests and struggling. "I don't have my stuff."

"We have stuff here," Zjelko replied.

"Not the stuff you need to make my kind of tetrahydron."

"Where is it?"

"Back at my lab."

"We'll get it for you."

Panic and frustration set her fingers tingling.

"You don't know what I need."

"You can tell us."

"They can't be transported together."

"We'll transport them separately."

"You'll mess it up," she screamed desperately.

Jerath clamped a hand down on her arm. "What do you need?"

Her mind worked furiously, trying to keep her story straight. Convincing.

"There are vats of different chemicals back at the lab. They can't be moved as they are and they can't be moved together."

Zjelko scowled and muttered something under his breath. Jerath silenced him with a look.

"So?" he said, turning back to her, the frustration building on his face.

"So, I need to decant them. Some need to be decanted into

glass with porcelain stoppers, others into heat-resistant plastic, others into—"

"Yeah, yeah. We get the idea."

"But that's just the beginning. Some can't be moved in more than fifty mils of volume, others need to be stabilised with secondary chemicals before they can be moved at all."

"Okay, Solari. I get it. We'll escort you to lab."

"She'll just try to escape," Zjelko spat in protest.

"Of course she will," Jerath said, turning his cold gaze back to Solari. "But she knows that any attempt will result in more missing fingers, doesn't she?"

Solari nodded silently. Jerath smiled, pleased with himself. He thought he had cowed her. He didn't know she would risk more than fingers to avoid spending the next three years in that oversized metal coffin.

***

There were no prying eyes peeking from behind closed curtains when Solari led Jerath and Zjelko into her lab. The two men flanked her tightly, bumping against her with each step. Zjelko openly scowled, clearly disapproving of the situation, but Jerath maintained his typically cool demeanour.

"Wait here," Jerath said, gripping her shoulder and scanning the lab. "Zjelko, check it out."

The broader man canvassed the space, bending under benches and looking in lockers, confiscating anything that could be used as a weapon. He pulled at the fire blanket stashed on the bench and tore at the tape that bound it.

The moth wings.

Memories of finding the mutant insect in the Fringes floated to her hazy and fragmented. Time had taken on a surreal quality in the days that had since passed.

The iridescent wings fell crumpled to the floor under Zjelko's rough hands. Solari grimaced.

"Don't try anything, Solari," Jerath said, leaning in close. "It won't end well for you."

She glanced down to her damaged hand. Jerath wouldn't be as frenzied as Anders. Wouldn't hack maniacally. No, his torture would be calm and calculated.

"I need the passcode," Zjelko yelled, pausing at the door to the coolroom.

Solari stepped forward, but Jerath gripped her tightly and pulled her back.

"Where do you think you're going?"

"To give him the passcode."

"Unh-uh. Call it out from here."

"So everyone can hear and break in later?"

"Change it afterwards."

Damn it. Every attempt to gain some leverage came to a dead end.

"5129-1018."

Zjelko disappeared into the coolroom, returning a few minutes later empty handed. "We're clear."

"OK," Jerath said, releasing his grip on Solari. "Get to work and make it quick."

Gritting her teeth, Solari stepped forward. She needed to play it smart. Her mind rattled, working through a quick inventory of the chemicals in the coolroom, mentally ticking off the ingredients she needed. Some chlorine and methylchloride, some corralina seaweed and that small batch of *hypnea spinella* algae she had hidden away.

"We need to make the room smaller," she said, indicating the partition-wall track overhead. "The chemicals react to oxygen, we need to limit the volume."

Zjelko yanked the partition door across the floor of the lab and pulled the complex locking mechanism into place, effectively sealing them in a two-by-three metre space that backed onto the coolroom.

Solari stepped towards the coolroom, again running into Jerath's frame.

"I need to get the chemicals."

"Nope. Tell him what you need."

Saying the names of the chemicals out loud was too risky. Jerath was not stupid and she didn't want to risk the chance of him figuring out her ploy.

"He'll be too slow to find it. Can I at least point them out to him?"

"From the door."

Jerath escorted her to the coolroom entry and stood beside her, blocking her in between himself and the frame. Under his watchful eye, she directed Zjelko to the vials and containers, her heart hammering at the thought of Jerath figuring it all out too early.

Zjelko placed the last of the jars on the benchtop and Jerath closed the coolroom door, the click almost lost beneath the sound of blood in her ears. They both watched her closely as she stepped up to the bench and began working.

She focused on the simple things—decanting, pulverising, soaking, slicing—some of it necessary, all of it distracting. The two men were wary at first, standing silent with arms folded across their chests, squinting at every vial, every movement. Slowly, they began to relax—confident that she was obedient, that they were in control, that nothing was amiss.

Zjelko was the first to break, boredom and frustration opening his mouth. Inane comments eventually shifted to easy chatter, the two of them organising the rest of the shift around a brothel that needed to make a protection payment and preparing an ammunition shipment that was due the next week.

Seeing her chance, Solari began the real work. With steady hands, she swapped out the steel pot on the stovetop for a clean one and added the seaweed and algae that had been soaking in the chlorine. Slowly she poured in the methylchloride and fastened the lid to the pot.

Blue flames erupted to life and licked the bottom of the steel.

"We'll take it from here," Jerath said, pulling Solari away.

"You need to keep it at a low heat," she replied, her voice calm and steady—nothing to betray the maelstrom within.

"For how long?"

"Twenty minutes."

It took every ounce of self-control and self-preservation to keep from looking at her two minders, to keep her hands from trembling, to keep her stance relaxed. The conversation around her lost definition, became a mumbling of low-pitched sounds; all of her focus on the pot.

The minutes stretched interminably. *Please let this work.*

And then, against the drumming of her heart and the drone of conversation, came the whistling of pressure escaping from the pot.

"You need to turn the heat off," she said, too loudly. "And pour it into the glass beaker near the sink."

Jerath nudged Zjelko forward.

"Which one is the beaker?" Zjelko asked.

"Watch the girl," Jerath said. "I'll do it."

Solari took a deep breath and held it as Jerath pulled a beanie from his pocket, wrapped it over the pot lid handle, and lifted.

A cloud of high-potency, volatised chloroform billowed into the constrained space. Jerath turned wide-eyed to Solari. Zjelko reached for her, but she stepped back and watched him stumble, the toxic vapour already working its magic.

Breath still caught in her chest, Solari raced around the benches, moving to the farthest corner of the lab. Black spots bloomed in her vision, her brain screaming for the chance to exhale. But she held fast; this wasn't the first time she'd had to ignore her primal instincts in order to survive.

Zjelko was at the coolroom door, pushing uselessly against the keypad, his addled brain unable to remember the passcode. Jerath was on his knees, suffering more for being closer to the pot when the chloroform released.

Just another minute.

Her lungs close to breaking point, she stared at the men from her corner, willing them to pass out, denying her body the same luxury.

She needed to breathe. Oh God, she just needed to breathe.

The loud thud was Zjelko falling to the floor, his head hitting the tiles with force. Jerath was curled in on himself against the bench and she was unable to see if he was unconscious or just biding his time and prevailing in survival mode.

She couldn't wait any longer.

Hands shaking, she fumbled at the partition lock and wrenched the dividing wall open. Still holding her breath, she stumbled through into the front part of the lab and slammed the partition shut behind her, daring only to open her lungs when she heard the wall click back into place and the lock mechanism reset into position.

The sweet scent of chloroform hit her immediately, her brain already vulnerable from the lack of oxygen. Clamping her mouth shut again, she raced for the exit, tripping at the last minute and crashing to the floor. She gasped, swallowing another lungful of diluted poison. Scrambling to her feet, she caught sight of the fire blanket and the psychedelic wings peeking out from under its coarse fabric.

Grabbing both the blanket and the wings, she pushed towards the exit, breaking into the fresh air and sucking in lungfuls of untainted oxygen. The blanket she would use as shelter or disguise, the wings she would sell the first chance she got.

She moved fast; half-running, half-stumbling down the streets, her ragged breath burning along a scorched throat, never stopping, never looking behind her until she saw her old apartment block loom ahead and the streetlights glint off Scotty's van.

They didn't know she had the van; wouldn't notice it missing, wouldn't know to look for it.

She raced up the apartment buildings stairs two at a time. Jerath and Zjelko had stripped her of the money she had stuffed into her pockets—"finder's fee," Zjelko had quipped—and there was nothing left inside of any value. Anders' fingers lay black and rigid on the threadbare carpet where they had fallen; she kicked them away as she stepped to the countertop and grabbed the keyring she had stolen from Scotty and the small collection of loose notes she kept stashed under the cutlery drawer.

There was no pause this time, no hesitation or moment of nostalgia. Without a backward glance, Solari raced down the stairs to the van. Depositing the wings behind her on the back seat, she turned the key in the ignition and gunned the accelerator. The night sky of Hobart flashed in the rear-view mirror as she sped towards the highway, heading as far away as she could from Worcsulakz and the terrors he would inflict on her if he ever found her.

TEN

Towns passed by in a blur; each one just another dot on the highway, another place Solari couldn't stop to seek haven in. Worcsulakz tentacles were long. And persistent.

She scanned the van for potential weapons, eyes darting from the road to the empty bottles on the passenger side floor and the mostly-empty jerry can bouncing around in the back. Still gripping the steering wheel, she opened the glove compartment and rummaged around, delving past the crumpled receipts and empty cigarette packets. The pens she liberated, imagining stabbing Jerath in the jugular with a particularly slender one.

But it was still not enough.

She would be able to use the tyre iron that was no doubt stashed under the floor in the back. And, maybe, if she was lucky, there would be a can of WD40 she could brandish in a pinch. But all of her options relied too heavily on luck—on being close enough to her attacker to use them, on being strong enough to overpower her attacker or fast enough to then outrun them, on the attacker not holding a more sophisticated weapon.

Because a pen was no match for a gun.

Where would Scotty hide a gun? Somewhere within easy reach...

She shut the glove box and reached under the driver's seat, cringing as her fingers brushed against squishy lumps of god-knows-what. She searched the edges, looking for a panel that lifted up. *Nope.* And the underside, hoping for the cool touch of solid metal. *Nothing.*

If Scotty had a gun, he hadn't left it in the van.

Doubt started to niggle in her mind; the further she travelled away from Worcsulakz's reach, the closer she came to DuPlessis'. Heading north was just trading one nightmare for another. With a face like hers, there was no way for her to blend in, nowhere she could hide. Instinctively, she turned the van west, towards the untamed wilderness.

Her foot flicked between the brake and the accelerator, her heart racing and stuttering in sympathy with the car, indecision clouding her mind. The Fringes may have been the only place where neither crime lord had ascendancy, but its monsters hunted indiscriminately in the wild space and there was no way she could survive even a week in the dark heart of Tasmania.

Solari screamed at the top of her lungs and bashed her good fist on the steering wheel. She was out of options: south led her to Worcsulakz, north the DuPlessis, and west to the Fringes. There was no direction that would lead her to safety, allow her to disappear.

Thoughts of Elysia leapt to mind, crashing through her rising panic; memories of disappearing from the container's living room and hiding in the storeroom as a child. Just as the mutant boy had. She glanced in the rear-view mirror, remembering the way he had cowered in the back of the truck—silent and stoic and scared. But there was no mutant boy behind her now, just a half-empty jerry can and a fire blanket.

Solari slowed the van, ready to backtrack to the Gypsy Quarter, to push aside her hurt and hide her wounds. Perhaps she could forgive Elysia, perhaps Elysia would forgive her. She could hide in the Gypsy Quarter, lay low for a while, bide her time until she could figure something out…

Despair gnawed at her insides. She was deluding herself, and making a poor attempt of it. It would never work—too many people would recognise her, would sell her out to Worcsulakz at the first flash of money. There was nowhere she could run, nowhere that would hide her from the crime lord's reach, nowhere where she wouldn't be recognised and hunted.

Hunted.

Slowly, the tiny seed of an idea started germinating in her mind. Perhaps there was one place…

Shaking aside her earlier indecision and anxiety, she pushed her foot hard against the accelerator. Turning the van north, her mind swirling with thoughts of the mutant boy and her mother, Solari raced towards the First Enclave.

***

It was in the early hours of morning that Solari pulled off the highway. Tyres crunched on loose rocks as she maneuvered the van into a sparse thicket at the edge of the Fringes. Like the Second Enclave where she had deposited the boy, mutants had built the First Enclave close to the Fringes to isolate it away from the people that hunted and brutalised them. Its wall was less than a kilometre away, but the encroaching wilderness would hide her and the van from view.

On unsteady legs, she exited the van, her footfalls soft against the grass spiked with frost, the metal shell of the van cold to her touch. With tired muscles she wrenched the side door open, bracing against the beginnings of a breeze that rushed into the new void. Dawn light filtered its way through the gaps in the tree canopy overhead, alighting on the trembling moth wings and making them glitter.

The colours weren't as vibrant as they once were, and the wing roots looked dry and fragile, but, when she gently poked at them, the fibrous ribbons shivered and rippled.

Still alive. Just.

Working quickly, she scoured the Fringes boundary for the elyxier weed that grew wild in disturbed soil. She had experimented with the mutant plant back when Denavim's condition had become desperate, when her fight switched from finding a donor to making her stem cells good enough. Of all the exotic, untamed, largely-poisonous species she had tested and manipulated, the elyxier weed had given her the most hope; its black sap part immunosuppressant, part parasite.

Back then, she had hoped it would facilitate engraftment, help her stem cells invade Denavim's body and force it to accept them as its own, allowing them to replicate and grow new cells. It hadn't worked; her brother, her hero, was just too different from her.

Fingers black with sap, she returned to the van with her harvest, internally berating herself with every step. She was being stupid or irrational or delusional. *Or desperate.* Using one of the empty bottles, she bashed at the elyxier, watching its life force run like congealed blood onto the metal floor of the van. Glass fractured as she smashed the bottle against the towbar and ran its jagged edge along her palm, gritting her teeth as the skin screamed and then throbbed.

What's another scar on a mangled hand? And besides, the bigger pain was still to come.

Mixing the blood with the sap created a small pat of dark, funky-smelling paste. She loosened it with as much saliva as she could generate, and, with hesitant fingers, applied it to the tips of the wing roots, watching in relief and horror as their rippling morphed into violent twitching.

There was no time to waste, yet her body went still. Time passed in every convulsion of the wing roots. *Enough, Solari. Just get it over with, already.*

She looked down at the broken bottle, its glass already tinged with blood, and shrugged out of her flak jacket and shirt. With trembling fingers, Solari unwrapped the long bandage wrapped around her arm and chest. She rolled it up carefully, savouring its softness, and laid it on the seat next to the wings.

Naked from the waist up, her body shivering from cold and fear, she picked up the bottle in her damaged hand. Reaching up behind her back to her left shoulder, she pushed the jagged glass deep into the flesh below her shoulder blade.

A deep-throated cry pulled free from her lips, even as the rest of her body stiffened. Her hand threatened to lose its hold on the bottle, so she forced herself to grip it tighter. And then dragged it down through the muscle and sinew of her back.

What she wouldn't do for a shard of snowrock. Her mind swam with the pain and a cold sweat broke out on tormented skin. In the chill of dawn, she felt aflame.

Blood, wet and warm and sticky, dribbled down to the small of her back, pooling where her jeans sat snug against her waist. Her hands were shaking violently now. Trying to force composure on her ragged breathing, Solari transferred the bottle to her left hand and dragged it down the other side of her back.

Every millimetre of torn flesh sent a bolt of lightning through her body, scrambling her thoughts until there was nothing left but the sensation of white, hot pain.

She was gasping now, the breath coming in too fast, burning her throat. Nausea rolled over her and a shrill, piercing whistle erupted in her ears. Black spots distorted her vision, turning everything to static.

No, no, no.

Solari shook her head in a desperate effort to stay conscious. Her hand dropped the bottle and distantly she heard it shatter anew. She scrabbled for the wings and brought them closer to the edge of the seat. Their roots pulsated and wrapped with determination, with *hunger*, around her fingers.

Snatching her hands away, she turned away from the wings, presented her flayed back to them, and slowly lowered herself down on them.

The assault on her body knocked away what little breath she still held. An icy torrent raced through her body, only to be incinerated by waves of fire. The pain left her gasping for air; her mouth locked wide and taut, her lungs unable to give voice to the scream.

She needed the antibiotics, but her hands disobeyed the tiny voice of reason languishing under the weight of her terror. Her body was convulsing, resisting the insistent burrowing of the wings.

Unable to bear the burden of pain, her body slipped from the edge of the seat to the floor of the van. The shock of the impact and the cool of the metal stilled the thrashing of the wings, and in that moment of clarity Solari's brain regained control.

Sobbing, she reached into the pocket of her jacket, fingers scrabbling past the glossy feel of the photograph that Jerath had allowed her keep and wrapping around the bottle of alijeah pills. Her hands shook, the pills rattling against each other in their glass cage, but managed to twist the plastic cap away.

Shots of fire, like contractions, began building in her back. She tried to bring the bottle to her lips, grunting in pain and frustration as the pills skipped over her face and clattered to the floor.

Just one. She just needed one. Ideally two. But one would help to keep her alive.

Her teeth clenched the bottle's lip, chattering against the glass. Her tongue tickled with pills; one, two, five? She didn't care. She swallowed hard, forcing them down her throat.

The bottle dropped from her mangled hand and she surrendered to the growing onslaught.

ELEVEN

The shivering woke Solari; her body fever-riddled—too hot, too cold. The wing roots still twinged in her back, but the pain was dull—like a slab of concrete crushing down; heavy, dense, oppressive, but dull.

Her hands roamed the cold floor around her, searching for scattered pills, finding only dirt and glass. The curse came out garbled against a dry and scratchy throat. Desperate, she dragged her arms around in wide arcs, crying hoarsely as each sweep pulled at the raw skin of her back.

The torture was rewarded with a cluster of pills near the door. She swallowed them greedily. Her body shivering, she reluctantly lifted the soft, downy material of the wings and folded them around her.

***

It was darker the next time she woke. With a start, she remembered that she was near the Fringes. Trees loomed in the dusk shadows, their thick trunks and spindly branches like the skeletons of long-forgotten giants.

Solari shifted her weight against the floor of the van and waited for the pain to assault her body. But it never came. She grunted as she sat up and pulled her legs into the van, her body protesting as she scrambled from the floor to the seat and pulled the door shut.

The wings folded and twitched around her, their rippling against her skin a source of disgust and comfort. Body numb with the cold, she curled up in the foetal position on the long bench seat and shuddered as the wings fell over her like a blanket. With the van now barricaded against the monsters that roamed nearby in the dark, she closed her eyes and drifted in a different kind of nightmare. One where monsters stalked her inside the van.

***

Solari exited the chrysalis of the vehicle on shaky legs. The bandage that once criss-crossed around her chest dragged under the weight of the wings, but she had tied it tightly and, for now, it kept them in place.

She walked with an awkward gait, her jeans pocket bulging with the bottle of alijeah pills salvaged from the van's floor. Her body shivered beneath the flimsy cotton of the t-shirt, her flak jacket left languishing on the back seat of the van. She felt vulnerable without it, but it had been hard enough retrofitting the shirt to accommodate the wings. Instead, she clutched tighter at the fire blanket and draped it further over her shoulders to stave off the pre-dawn chill.

The wall of the enclave loomed as soon as she passed the tree cover of the Fringes. In the grey light, she could see the spotters atop the wall, their torchlights sweeping the area in wide arcs. If not for the alijeah, her heart would have turned somersaults in her chest.

Stupid. Stupid, stupid, stupid.

It was a stupid plan. They would never fall for it.

The wings fluttered — in the breeze? Because of her anxiety?

Keep walking.

It was the only option left. *And if it fails, so be it.* Dying at the hands of mutants couldn't be any worse than dying at the hands of Worcsulakz, or DuPlessis, or the wild things of the Fringes.

The spotters called down to her, their voices garbled under the haze of alijeah. She walked closer. Their yelling grew louder and more agitated.

Breathing became difficult. The wings seemed to drag heavier. She stumbled.

Just a few more steps.

A crack echoed in her ears, the sound of the sky fracturing. She looked up, the world tilting. Vaguely, she was aware of falling. She twisted, felt her knee cry out, the pain muted under the medication to a dull roar.

The ground swelled up towards her in slow motion, everything appearing in surreal detail. Her arms reached out to break the fall, one thought clear in her mind.

Protect the wings.

***

"Easy, Lepidopterae." The deep male voice came to her muffled through clouds of cotton and fur.

Solari tried to open her eyes but they remained shut, her eyelids glued together with the remnants of sleep. Panicked, she tried to sit up, to force her weak body to move. A hand pressed down on her chest.

"Easy. You're safe." The voice was clearer. A deep rumbling of thunder. "Rest. Recover."

Confused, Solari tried to shift from under the gentle weight, but the hand didn't move.

The thunder rumbled again. He was laughing.

She tried to open her eyes again, to lift her arms, to strike out. Her hands grazed something soft. *So soft. Impossibly soft.*

There was nothing in the world that could be that soft.

And, yet. A memory tickled in her fuzzy mind. She had felt something like that before, somewhere dark, and isolated. *The Fringes.* And it had been soft. And beautiful. Bright colours swirling like a kaleidoscope, her hands sinking into soft fuzzy fur, fingers stroking downy wings.

Wings.

It all came rushing back to her—Anders, Elysia, the mutant boy, Scotty, Jerath. She pushed harder against the infuriating half-sleep, against the weight that held her down. Still it contained her and kept her prisoner.

"Rest, Lepidopterae. You are safe."

But, Solari had never been safe.

TWELVE

The enclave was bigger than Solari had imagined. Walking the perimetre made her tired—her shoulders ached, the wings throbbed, and her legs seized in unforgiving cramps. But, she felt too vulnerable lying in the arrivals tent day after day. So, she moved.

The spotters had pulled her from where she'd collapsed outside the enclave walls. Like all new arrivals, she had been taken to the small cluster of tents near the gate, where medics had assessed her and patched her up.

It was confronting to see mutants with old stethoscopes draped around their necks and thermometres poking out of their pockets. With each touch, she had shivered, and then worried that her recoiling and shuddering would betray her. But to everyone else she was just another brutalised mutant; her shuddering a symptom of her torment. If she hadn't shivered they would have been suspicious.

That was a week ago, give or take a couple of days; the painkillers at the enclave were just as potent as the alijeah pills that still bounced around in her pocket and robbed time of any clarity. Since then, she had been visited by many. *But, not the man with the voice like thunder.* They had checked her, settled her, screened her. Soothed her. Healed her.

There had been a lot of questions, on both sides, but not many answers. At most, she had learned that no-one ran the enclave and there weren't many rules. Everyone who entered its gate was free to keep what they had brought with them and contribute or trade what they liked, and there was no leadership or administration—mutants organised themselves loosely into a cooperative of sorts and naturally divided into smaller cliques, seeking out friends and allies that gave them strength and comfort. Some mutants, Solari learned, had lived in the enclave for a decade or more, becoming the oracles of enclave life. Much like Elysia in the Gypsy Quarter.

The thought of Elysia was always bittersweet; always accompanied by the residual anger of their last meeting, but softened in the light of all that had transpired since—in the greater violence, in the reluctant knowledge that she might be the only family Solari had left.

In many ways, the enclave was like the Gypsy Quarter—a chaotic, unstructured, almost *organic*, mass of lean-tos and humpies that surged with, and spilled, all forms of life from their bellies. The breadth of phenotype diversity was breathtaking. And chilling. Scales, feathers, furs—some mutants were more animal than human, others bore mutations that were more curiosities than deformities.

In each face, Solari searched for the one that had peered from Elysia's photograph. The intervening twenty-six years would have aged her, but Solari clung to the irrational belief that a child would always recognise the face of their mother. And that a mother would never forget the face of her child.

"Watch it, Lepidopterae!" A smaller woman, with a row of spikes running down her shaven skull, glared at her.

Lepidopterae. The strange word was now familiar; it was how they classified each other—*Lepidopterae*, scale wings; *Osteoclasta*, reformed bone; *Reptilia*, reptile-like. There were hundreds of classifications.

"Sorry," Solari mumbled to the Osteoclasta and stepped out of the way.

Like the Gypsy Quarter, the First Enclave housed its veterans at the centre point, but here there were no stacks of containers, only rows of basic brick cottages. Solari trailed her hand along their facades, relishing the rough texture as it scratched along itchy palms.

The medics had been outraged at her mutilations, quick to assume the same tormenters that had carved her face and cut off her fingers had tried to hack at her wings. It was easy to explain the bloody gashes and bandages as her poor attempt to salvage the mutant appendages.

They had done as much as they could for her—stitching the rough gashes, disinfecting the wounds, medicating for the pain and infection—but ongoing treatment was still required. To 'regain maximum function'. It was a wasted effort, but Solari needed to maintain the cover and so she trudged along the muddy avenues of the enclave towards its centre.

She stopped at the main intersection to scan the doors, finding the healer's sign on a small, white-brick house. Weaving in and amongst the throng of mutants around her, she came to a pause at the front door, her mangled hand resting against the brightly-painted heart. Anders had once told her the healer's symbol, in ancient days, had been a snake—but that was Anders, a lying sack of shit to the end.

The rush of blood pushed her to rap harder on the door than she should have, the vibrations felt in the stumps of her missing fingers. An elderly woman opened the door, white haired, wrinkled, and scowling.

"Yes?" she asked impatiently, waving her hands about in the air.

"I was sent here for healing," Solari said, eyes fixated on the woman's hands. Embedded in the back of each one was a perfect eye; one green, one blue. Quickly, she peered up at the crone's face, expecting to see the same mismatched irises but finding them to be a very normal brown.

"Well don't just stand there. Do you need healing or not?"

Solar mumbled some nonsensical sounds and followed the crone inside.

"Never seen an Occularaxis before, ey?" The woman fiddled around with some jars, glancing sporadically over her shoulder at Solari. "You Lepidopterae aren't common around here, either."

At the thought of her wings, Solari felt them shudder around her. It was a strange sensation, having the monstrosities keyed into her emotions.

"Can you see with them?" she asked, turning her thoughts back to the Occularaxis' eyes.

"Of course I can see with them," the woman said, turning around with her hands full of creams and ointments and salves. "What? You think they're there just for decoration?"

"But, how does it work?" Solari asked, ignoring the woman's ire and genuinely confused about the mechanics of it all. "I mean, what do you see? What your face is pointed at or what your hands are pointed at?"

The woman sighed and flipped her hands over and back in a rapid, rolling movement. "I see both, you stupid girl. What an ignorant question. It's like asking 'do you see what your left eye is pointed at or what your right eye is pointed at?'"

Solari frowned, not understanding the explanation but not wanting to pursue it. *It's not like I can wave my left eye around one way, and my right another.*

"What's wrong with you anyway?" the old woman snapped.

Lost for words, Solari held out her brutalised hand, her wings rustling with the annoyance that flared in her belly. The woman leant in, her long white hair falling about her like wild epiphytes. She peeled back the bandages and inspected Solari's hand, frowning as she pawed at the rough skin.

"Well, there's not much I can do with *that*. You're missing two whole fingers." She threw the hand back, the stubs twinging as Solari wrapped the bandages again. Wings fluttering, Solari glared at the crone.

Like a snake striking at prey, the woman flicked a skinny arm out her and grasped Solari's good shoulder with surprising strength.

"Now this," she said, twisting the shoulder until Solari turned. "*This* I can work with." Bony fingers poked at the raw skin below her shoulder blades and then trailed down the wings. Solari felt each stroke as she would from a lover bringing her to climax.

"How long?" the old woman demanded, turning her back around.

"How long, what?"

"How long what?" the woman mimicked, derision thick in her voice. "How long since the *attack?*"

Solari stood up and swatted away the hand that reached for her, the dregs of her patience exhausted.

The chuckle that erupted in the space was low and guttural. "You remind me of someone."

It was enough to halt Solari in her tracks. She ignored the cackling and stared at the crone.

"Sit down, stupid, stubborn girl," the Occularaxis said, waving about her eye-embedded hands, "and I will tell you who you remind me of."

THIRTEEN

The old crone's hands were tough and unforgiving as they prodded at the junction where the mutant ended and Solari began. Waves of heat radiated from Solari's shoulders to her waist, and her wings fluttered and shivered with each burst of pressure.

The Occularaxis prattled as she worked, reminiscing about the early days of the enclave. "It was supposed to temporary. Not permanent. Not forever." She stabbed a finger in Solari's back, causing her to cry out.

"Shh, girl, I'm trying to tell you something." She frowned, the deep crevasses of her face catching the afternoon light. "Hard to move on, though, once you're safe. When you're protected; protected from the monsters out there." She flicked her head, indicating the world past the enclave borders, and then turned back to Solari.

"You have the same eyes," she whispered harshly, staring into Solari's eyes, not flinching away from the left with its ugly white scar and ruined iris. "She was a Reptilia, yes? Ah, but they are all Reptilia. So many of them, with their scales, and snouts and…" She waved her hands around to make up for the words that eluded her.

"Her name was…was…"

Solari became still. Not even her wings trembled.

The crone shook her head violently, as if shaking it would uncover the layers of dust and debris that had accumulated in the years of eking out a miserable existence in the Southern Reaches.

"Christianne." Solari whispered the name; a supplication, a wish.

The crone laughed, the cackling a hot brand along Solari's nerves. "Christianne, Christianne." She mangled the name, sharpening all its soft edges, muffling the tender vowels. Her mother's beautiful name sounded like a curse from the crone's wretched tongue.

"Your mother, yes?"

Solari didn't answer, couldn't look at the woman with her wild hair and crazy eyes. "Where is she?"

"She wasn't happy with being protected. With being safe. No. She wanted more. Your mother, she wanted more. She wanted out. She wanted to be free."

The crone was prodding again, her fingers smearing pungent ointment over Solari's back. "She was a little mouse when she came here. Tried to claw her way out. Didn't believe the big, bad wolf was there outside the gates. She scampered away quickly that one. Didn't last two weeks."

Solari pulled away from her touch. "What does that *mean*?"

The crone rolled the eyes in her head. "It means she got out." She spoke the words slowly and deliberately, as if to a simpleton.

"But to where?" Solari snapped, her wings shivering.

Cackling. Loud, maniacal, infuriating. "Only the Fixer knows where. Only the Fixer knows for sure."

Bony fingers reached for Solari, but she pulled away; she'd had enough. Throwing down a red twenty-dollar note in payment, she stormed out. The laughter followed her all the way to the door and down the street. Walking through the uneven, haphazard dirt roads of the enclave, she could still hear it—even though its sound had died blocks earlier.

***

The wall of the First Enclave was massive. In the northern corner, where the ground was dark and marshy, it dominated the quiet and barren surrounds. Solari's legs propelled her towards the massive structure, heavy and wobbling and sore. She fell against it, the concrete and wire grazing palms already tortured.

She stood there, hands resting against the cold façade. And threw her head back. The scream was an awakening beast—tearing her throat and ripping from her lips.

On and on she wailed, beating bloodied fists against the wall, raging against the world, her mind, her memories. The screaming was endless—it siphoned from her soul and poured, uninhibited, in a steady stream of agony. The wall swam before her eyes, tears streaming down her face in currents.

A tightness in her chest threatened to cut oxygen and reduce her wail to a hoarse whisper. She sank to her knees, the cold and damp of the ground soaking through her jeans, the chill burrowing to her bones.

Slowly, the intensity of emotions leached out of her, leaving her only with the memory of Elysia's words. *Christianne was stubborn. She wouldn't leave her children. We begged and pleaded with her, but she refused.*

She refused. She loved you and Denavim so much.

The words merged with the crone's cackling. *She wanted to be out. She wanted to be free. Only the Fixer knows.*

The Fixer. The Fixer.

Tiredness, like a leaden weight, settled upon her. The wings, her awful, unnatural wings, fluttered insistently, enveloping her shaking frame and protecting her from the cold as she sunk down to the ground. She shivered and curled up on herself, wakefulness slipping away from her like mist in a storm.

FOURTEEN

"You are a feisty one, Lepidopterae." Thunder rolled through her dreams, bringing her back to consciousness.

Opening her eyes, Solari expected to see the green canvas of the tent that had been her home for the past week. Instead, she was confronted with dirt walls lit with incandescent bulbs, the warm light throwing long shadows over everything.

The shadow that fell across Solari was attached to a lean Metallicari. Large iron plates ran from his shoulder to forearm, glinting in the soft light and setting a stark contrast to the dark skin of his face and torso.

It was hot in the small space; the humidity clung to her, amplifying the smell of soil, making it cloying. Sweat settled between her shoulder blades, itching the place where the wings had burrowed beneath the skin.

"Don't scratch, the infection is bad enough already." His hand pushed her arm back down, metal scales rippling as his wrist flexed.

She bristled against the touch, pushing against the hand in an effort to sit up. He pushed down harder—a cat paw on a mouse tail. The usual frustration at defeat tingled inside Solari, but then it flared. A nuclear rage exploded within her. She was not going to let it happen again; would not allow another man to hold her down, lock her away, *whittle* her away.

Lashing out, her fingernails clawed at his naked chest, leaving red, angry tracks in their wake. He moved quickly, his arms shooting up to block her attacks, deflecting rather than counter-striking.

When strong hands bound her wrists, she twisted her body around, stumbling from the simple, raised mattress to the dank earth. She didn't fight to reassert her balance, instead used the movement to kick out at her captor. The Metallicari groaned, dark eyes flashing with danger. Still, she kicked, her whole body flailing, wanting to do damage.

One of her kicks found its target, slamming hard against the Metallicari's shin. He grunted, then roared; the sound ricocheted around the room, causing her heart to stumble, giving her the briefest pause. His hands came up and she braced for the inevitable blow, the one that would silence her.

Desperate, she threw her fist towards his throat, the only vulnerable piece of flesh he offered her. Metal shuddered and rattled as his fist engulfed hers, stopping the punch from landing. His grip tight, he spun her away, pulled her arms down to trap them against her body, and flicked a leg around her own to diffuse her attempts at kicking and stomping.

"For the love of humanity." His lips brushed against her ear. "I. Am. Not. Going. To. Hurt. You."

Solari squirmed and roared, but his grip held firm. Her thrashing grew weaker, the charge of the situation dissipating in the light of her futile efforts.

"I am going to let you go," he said. "You can leave if you want. Do not try to hit me again."

Slowly, his grip on her lessened, gradual and understated like ice melting or shadows growing. Only when her body had completely separated from his did she exhale. Her blood thrummed with liquid fire, but she remained rooted to the spot; unable to move for fear of collapsing.

Trying to compose herself, she looked around the room, the space appearing blurry in the haze of her rage and frustration. As her vision cleared, she noticed the room was sparsely decorated. A lopsided, wooden chair—hand-made?—sat in the corner, covered by a drab woollen blanket and an assortment of books. The books, paper-bound and curled at the edges, looked ancient and well-loved; relics from an ancient time…before the gangland war, before the mutants, before the hole in the ozone layer.

The bed, jammed up against the wall, was in disarray—evidence of the tussle written all over it. Clean sheets lay wrinkled, exposing the thin mattress beneath. And on the wall above the bed hung a sheet stretched and framed by slender tree branches. The fabric was marked into four quadrants with dotted lines in dark ink.

She stared at the patterned mural, tried to make sense of the annotations. A large blot in the bottom left quadrant was marked as *'Helios'*. She saw it replicated in the next quadrant, but slightly offset. Glancing at the other two quadrants, she found it there also, but again in a different location.

Soft footfalls sounded as the Metallicari stepped closer. His arm came up slowly, his finger pointing at the blot in the bottom right quadrant. "*Helios*, the morning star. It's low and bright on the horizon during spring, moves higher as it cycles through the rest of the seasons."

Solari tracked her gaze over the rest of the ink markings, taking in the unfamiliar names. *Hermes. Aphrodite. Cronus.* It was hard to believe they were stars. In Hobart, the stars appeared to Solari as jealous lovers, only ever peering out of the night sky when the power cuts had silenced the other, brighter lights.

Curiosity getting the better of her, she glanced surreptitiously at the Metallicari. His long, dark hair was tied back, accentuating the angles of his face. With his right side blocked from view, he appeared free from mutation. Lean, muscular, relaxed. A sated predator.

Except he hadn't predated on anything. No blow had been struck, no injury dealt, no damage exacted. He wasn't like the others; not like Anders or Jerath or DuPlessis. With them, she would have walked away from the fight with bruises and cuts, or broken bones and missing fingers. If she could have walked away at all. With them, she would not be standing there intact.

And yet, here she was; her body tired, but unmolested. There was no remnant of urgency left in the room. No threat of danger.

"Who are you?"

He turned to face her, his mutation flashing in her vision.

"Just another Metallicari." He spoke without irony.

"What is your name?" she persisted.

"My name is Alcaeus."

Alcaeus. The name was soft and hard at the same time. Exotic and familiar.

"And what of you, Lepidopterae—what is your name?"

She paused, trying to come up with a false name, something she could hide behind. But her brain was too slow and her tongue stepped in to betray her.

"Solari." She sighed. *What does it matter that this mutant knows my name? There's nothing he can do with it.* "My name is Solari."

"So, Solari," he said, his voice skipping around her name like he was tasting it, "why are you looking for the Fixer?"

Her heart lurched. She had thought the Fixer was just another mad rumbling of the crone.

"You know the Fixer?" The tremor in her voice betrayed her emotion.

"Unh-uh." Alcaeus shook his head slowly. "My question first."

"The old woman. The Occu—, the Occularaxis." She threw her hands in the air, frustrated that she wasn't making sense, that the words were tripping over themselves. "The old healer with the eyes in her hands. She said that only he knew where the mutants went when they escaped the enclave. Where they ended up."

Alcaeus frowned. "Why do you care where other mutants went?"

"Not other mutants. Just one." A small part of her, the part that was buried deep under all her survival instincts, wanted to open up to him, to just unload, to let someone in. But it wasn't the time. And Alcaeus wasn't that someone. "How do you know the Fixer? How did you know I was looking for him?"

His face was grim, his eyes piercing hers. Searching for something—a hidden motive?

"I found you slumped against the wall, shivering. Your hands were bleeding. I thought you were dead, and then I saw your wings flutter. Your lips were moving—I thought you were gasping for air, but, when I bent down, I could hear you; you were saying the same thing over and over. *The Fixer. The Fixer.*"

He frowned again, the deep furrows making him seem older than the thirty years she had picked him for. "It's not a name that is uttered lightly around here. Conscious or not."

"But who is he?" Solari asked, impatient, not caring about the rules of enclave or about the consequences of uttering a dangerous name.

Alcaeus shook his head, a rueful smile returning the youthfulness to his face. "She. She is the Fixer."

Excellent—I don't have another shit-for-brains male to add to my list of monsters.

"She's—" He ran his hand down his arm, metal plates rippling under agitated fingers. "She's the one who knows there's a third alternative. It's not just a choice between being abused on the outside or being captive on the inside."

His words found the soft spot of her heart and twisted. He could have just as easily been describing her life. Her choices.

"What's the third alternative?"

"The Northern Zone. The Fixer couriers mutants beyond the Border Wall."

***

Solari felt sick. Memories of DuPlessis and his sexual slavery racket broke through the carefully-constructed walls of her mind. Her hand flitted to the scar that split the right side of her face, but she pulled it back before it could touch the ridges of dead skin.

She perched on the edge of the bed, careful to keep her distance from the Metallicari who sat beside her. The energy of the earlier fight had completely dissipated, a tepid flush of tiredness numbing the fear and frustration that had raged less than an hour ago. And yet her mind still raced, struggling to make sense of all she had learned.

"Why?" She clenched her hands by her side, her heart racing in anticipation of the answer.

"Why does she take them beyond the wall?" Alcaeus clarified, frowning in confusion.

Solari shook her head, frustrated and anxious. "No, not why. Not why. For what?"

Alcaeus frowned again. "I don't understand."

Her stomach twisted itself into a mobius strip. *What isn't there to understand? Only two things pass from the Southern Reaches to the Northern Zone: drugs and people. Drugs travel clean. People travel dirty.*

There were only two uses for Southerners in the Northern Zone—slaves for labour or slaves for sex. Or, if you were particularly unlucky, slaves for both.

"I thought the North hated mutants. Isn't that why they built the wall?"

"They don't hate us. They just don't want to be swamped by us. Or *infected* by us."

He laughed—a beautiful, deep rumbling; rich like the earth around them. He found the idea ridiculous. Solari didn't find it as funny; as a child, she had thought you could catch a mutation just from passing too close to a mutant on the street. Even now, she worried the alijeah wouldn't be enough to hold off infection before she could escape and tear the wings from her back.

"But, they *are* intrigued by us," he continued. "To them, we are…exotic. And the fact they fear us makes us all the more interesting."

It was Solari's turn to be confused. "I don't get it."

"We are unique specimens." He ran a hand down his metal plates. "Rare." His hand reached out to trail the lightest of fingers across her wing. A burst of electricity sprung from his touch, shivering up through her shoulder blades and tingling at the nape of her neck. "And unique, rare specimens attract collectors."

Visions of hacked wings, disembodied plates, and flayed scales swirled in her thoughts, making her head hurt. She imagined them crushed for medicines so that men could have longer erections or reassembled into fashionable jewellery for bored socialites. Pulverised, blended, burnished, broken.

"They harvest mutations?"

"No, they collect mutants."

We are unique specimens. We.

"Why?"

Alcaeus shrugged. "Better than killing us."

And, in a way, Solari understood — for years, she had traipsed through the Fringes, exploring mutations and collecting specimens that she could manipulate, that displayed the right properties or were a useful means to an end. But, when she had cut the wings from the moth, she had not only been thinking of precursors. She had been mesmerised by the horrific beauty of them.

She recalled the photograph of her mother; a beautiful woman with scales trailing down her cheeks. *A unique specimen.* Someone worth collecting.

Only the Fixer knows. Only the Fixer knows for sure.

"How do I find the Fixer?"

Alcaeus paused, his frown deepening. "You don't find the Fixer. She finds you."

"But, you know her. You know who she is."

"Maybe."

Solari sighed and tightened her fists, fingernails driving deeper into palms already soft and tortured. She forced herself to slow her breathing, to stay calm. She needed him. She needed his answers.

It hadn't been important earlier; all she had wanted was a temporary safe-haven from Worcsulakz, a place where she could plan her next step without worrying about the consequences of her last. A refuge that didn't mean risking DuPlessis or the wild things of the Fringes.

And she had that. Had found it in the enclave.

It should have been enough. It would have been, if not for the reminiscing of Elysia and the maniacal cackling of the old crone. She had never known her mother; her father had refused to talk about her and, with his death, Solari had thought she'd lost the final link to the woman who had brought her into the world. Knowing that she had been alive all those years ago, had made it to enclave…*Could still be alive.*

It changed everything.

"Help her find me."

FIFTEEN

Two days later, Alcaeus came to the arrivals tent. Perched on her bed, Solari watched him as he weaved easily around the rows of bunks, pausing to chat to new arrivals and pulling faces at the children playing a simple game of hide and seek. Their giggles swelled in the too-quiet tent and pulled at Solari's lips. It had been forever since she had genuinely smiled, and yet here she was, sweating under a nylon canvas roof, surrounded by mutants, and grinning at a Metallicari pulling faces.

"You ready to get out of here, Lepidopterae?" he called, approaching her with a comical swagger. She smiled wider despite herself. With his metal plates hidden under a long-sleeved t-shirt, it was easy to forget he was a mutant; easy to think he was someone in disguise, just like her.

"Where are we going?" she asked, standing up before hearing his answer.

"You can't stay here forever. And no-one will find you if you do." He reached her bed and paused, casting his gaze around the nearby space. "Is this all you have?"

His puzzlement was understandable. Most new arrivals she had seen had come burdened with everything they could carry through the enclave walls—bags filled with clothes, food, and various survival items (torches, batteries, knives, rope). But some, like Solari came with nothing but the clothes on their back and a few trinkets stuffed in their pockets.

"Yep, this is it." Her mind flitted briefly to the boy she had dropped off at the other enclave and she wondered whether his chances at surviving in the Second Enclave were any better than in Hobart.

The Metallicari shrugged in the way of those who had learnt to make do with what they had. "At least you have your strength."

She opened her mouth to scoff and then caught herself. She should have felt weak by now. It was close to a fortnight since she had grafted the wings to her back, and even with the alijeah and first-aid, infection should have been setting in with the continued presence of mutant DNA, should have been slowing her down. But the Metallicari was right; she felt strong. Maybe the alijeah had done its job.

He led her out into the enclave beyond. None of the other mutants paid them any mind as they pushed their way into the crowd that had gathered at one of the few clearings.

"The enclave works a little differently than the outside," he said loudly, leaning closer to her to be heard above the dense chatter of voices. "There's a limited supply of free communal goods—urgent medical care is donated by volunteers, the community garden grows some yams, zucchini, and maybe tomatoes every now and then, and there's a scrap heap on the other side of the arrivals tents you can use to build or fix your humpie—but if you want something beyond the basics, you're gonna have to trade for it."

The crowd jostled, endlessly moving and shifting around them. Solari bit down hard against her rising revulsion. Alcaeus grabbed her hand and she let him drag her to the front of the crowd. In the middle, a space had opened up to reveal a middle-aged Arichnidia, her chelicerae twitching in sagging jowls, standing over a tattered blanket and two small tins of food.

"Someone to repair my humpie," she called above the noise, waving one of the tins above her head to attract attention.

"Five hours," a young Reptilia shouted beside Solari.

"Six hours," someone else shouted from within the mass of bodies.

"Seven," the Reptilia countered.

And so it went until the young Reptilia walked away with the prize for twelve hours of work fixing the Arachnidia's humpie.

"Where do they get all this stuff?" Solari asked Alcaeus, her gaze flitting past the mutants to the raft of treasures they bartered and auctioned.

"Some of it they brought with them," Alcaeus said, leading her back through the crowd. "Some is dropped off by old friends and family who still care enough to check in on them. And some is couriered in by soft mutants."

"Soft mutants?" she asked, once they were back in the clearing.

"Mutants like me," he explained. "With mutations that can be hidden. Every now and then they head out and beg, buy or steal things they know can be traded on the inside."

"Why would they come back to the enclave if their mutations can be hidden?"

The Metallicari didn't change his pace, but his postured straightened and his shoulders squared. "Just because they can be hidden, doesn't mean they'll stay hidden. Eventually, the truth comes out. Easier to run snatch-and-grab missions than spend the rest of your life running and hiding."

"So what happens if you have nothing to barter or trade?" she asked, thrusting her hands in her pockets and running her fingers over the alijeah pills, what was left of her money, and her beloved photo of Denavim—nothing she was keen on parting with.

"You can always beg," he said, inclining his head to the edges of the scrap heap where a few mutants sat hunched over with palms outstretched.

Solari shook her head and looked back to Alcaeus.

"Or," he said, and fixed her with a grin, "if you're willing to risk a little, you can gamble for it."

***

The brick cottage at the centre of the enclave was almost identical to the crone's. Bad memories flocked to forefront of Solari's mind and a fluttering came over her belly. Alcaeus' orientation to the enclave was helpful, but what she really needed was an introduction to the

Fixer.

"Alcae—"

The Metallicari rapped on the door, oblivious to her hesitation. The strange rhythm was answered by a blue-eyed, olive-skinned boy whose beauty caused Solari to flush. Belatedly, she noticed the rows of jagged ribs that fanned out from his chest like bony fins.

"Alcaeus," he said, his voice low and husky. "You come to clean us out again?"

"Nah," the Metallicari said, slapping the boy on the shoulder as he stepped inside. "Just want to show my new friend the lay of the land."

"Ahh, the Lepidopterae," the boy said, flashing Solari a grin. "I heard there were some exotic arrivals lately. Didn't know you were a card shark."

"I'm—"

"She's not going to give away her gameplay to you, Emir," Alcaeus interrupted, nudging her with his hip. "But, nice try."

The boy grinned wider. "Alright, alright," he said leading them down a carpeted hallway. "You know the drill. Twenty dollar or equivalent buy-in. There's already two full tables, but the third will have the minimum number of players if you both join."

He opened a door at the end of the hallway and ushered them in. The room felt crowded with four makeshift tables taking up the entire space. Two of them were fully occupied by a dozen mutants, each nursing a hand of cards and wearing expressions that ranged from boredom to barely-suppressed anxiety. The third was empty, and the last hosted an overweight Tripex whose three arms sat braided over the table, and a scowling Pellis whose tawny fur tufted up from her collar like an expensive stole.

"Alcaeus," the Pellis murmured as the Metallicari took the seat next to her.

"Hello Bettina," he said, throwing two twenty-dollar notes onto the table. "Frank out working today?"

Solari smiled despite the unease pooling in her stomach. If not for the metal plates and thick layer of fur between them, the conversation could have just as easily been another mundane round of small talk in the hallway of a Richmond apartment block.

"No, just sleeping off a hangover. Who's your friend?"

"Bettina, meet Solari. She came in a couple of weeks ago."

The Pellis nodded politely at her but turned back to Alcaeus. "Does she know how to play?"

"We'll soon find out," he replied, winking at Solari.

"Enough chit-chat," the Tripex said, his third hand tapping impatiently on the table, while his other two shuffled a faded deck of cards. "Let's play."

***

"How long have you been in the enclave?" Solari asked, pulling up the edges of her two cards to peek at their undersides and schooling her face to calm when the king and queen of hearts greeted her back. It wasn't as if she had ever played poker before, but she had watched enough late-night games on television while pushing to meet a tetrahydron deadline to pass as capable. The reasonable stack of chips in front of her reassured her that her confidence wasn't all delusion.

"I came here ten years ago," Bettina said, moving a small stack of garishly-painted wooden chips to the centre of the table. "Frank had been here a few years before me. He's an Osteoclasta, has bone spikes running up and down his legs like hairs, but they're thin enough that he can file them down. He could have stayed on the outside, but fate brought him here. He's my third husband."

"And your best," Alcaeus interrupted, pushing his own wooden rounds across the table.

"If you say so," Bettina replied, winking at him.

It was all so normal. And even with Bettina's thick layer of fur, Solari found herself enjoying the woman's stories.

"What about you, sweetheart?" Bettina said, eyeing the equivalent stack that Solari pushed to the centre. "Did you chase someone here or leave someone behind?"

Solari smiled, amused at the obvious match-making interrogation. And then the Tripex next to her pushed his own stack of chips across the table with his third arm, and she remembered that these people weren't her people, and her smile faded.

"My ex," she said, her voice cool and detached. "He hacked at me like I was a rancid piece of meat, so I left him behind."

In her peripheral vision, she saw Alcaeus twist to look at her, but she kept her focus on Bettina. The Pellis was a few years younger than Solari, but the sympathy that softened her face seemed to come from a similar life-experience.

"They're not all like that," she said, drawing up the sleeve of her dress to show thick white lines of scar tissue on pink skin untouched by fur. "My second husband was a piece of shit who wielded a knife only marginally better than he wielded his man parts. Tried to carve the fur from me like he could sell it as a pelt.

"After him, I thought I would never find a man worthy of me. I never wanted to even think about another man touching me. And then I found Frank. Alcaeus wasn't lying when he said he is my best; he's a goofball who drinks too much after a long shift, but he gives me the best parts of his hauls and his blanket when it's extra cold."

"Enough with the fucking chit-chat," the Tripex said, tapping again on the table. "Can we just get on with the game?"

Bettina shot him a filthy look, but fell quiet, pushing another stack of chips forward to meet his raise. She smiled softly at Solari and gave a wink. Solari offered her own small smile back; it was hard to despise someone who showed so much sympathy and solidarity.

***

"All-in." The Tripex called, using all three hands to push the rest of his chip stack to the centre of the table.

"Call." Solari pushed the vast majority of her chips in to join the already massive stack.

Two hours later and it was just her and the Tripex left. Alcaeus had bowed out first after a run of bad cards and luck. Bettina had lasted another hour, but both Solari and the Tripex had worn down her stack. It surprised her how fast the time had evaporated. How she had let herself relax a little more with each new hand, each bout of good-natured ribbing, each eye-roll from

106

Alcaeus and Bettina at the snark from the Tripex who still hadn't introduced himself.

The Tripex grinned and flipped over his cards. The ace of diamonds and jack of clubs made a pretty accompaniment to the two aces and jack already laid out on the table. But they were no match for the two tens that mirrored Solari's hand to create four of a kind.

Alcaeus immediately broke out into a deep, rumbling laugh and Solari grinned widely as she plucked the eighty dollars from the pouch in the middle of the table.

"See?" Bettina said, winking as the Tripex stormed away from the table. "Bad luck can't follow you forever."

"What are you going to do with your winnings, Lepidopterae?" Alcaeus asked.

She threw a red twenty-dollar note his way and fanned out the other three in exaggerated swagger. "What feast can sixty dollars get us?"

Bettina laughed and shook her head. "Not for me, sweetheart. Frank will be waking up soon, and I want to catch some of that sugar before he disappears off to work again. You two enjoy yourselves." Blowing a few kisses their way, she stood up from the table and made her exit.

"I know a place where we can get spiced chicken, roast corn, and vodka that doesn't burn the skin from your throat," Alcaeus whispered conspiratorially after she had left.

"Sounds like my kind of feast," Solari replied, surprised at how much it really did.

"Then let's get out of here."

The olive-skinned Osteoclasta grinned at them as they made their way back to the front door. "I knew she was a card shark," he called.

"Yeah, yeah, Emir," Alcaeus called back, opening the front door for Solari. "Maybe next time she'll teach you a few tricks."

"I think I'd enjoy that," Emir called, winking again at Solari.

Solari laughed and stepped out into the heat of the midday sun.

"I think you've seduced our very own blue-eyed Don Juan,"

Alcaeus said, settling into a casual pace along the hard-packed road.

She laughed again but shook her head. "No, he's not my type."

"Oh yeah? What is your type?"

It would have been easy for her to spin a flippant reply, something exaggerated or ironic. Instead she found herself answering with the truth.

"I don't know," she replied, keeping her gaze ahead. "I'm still trying to figure that out."

***

Solari's mind hummed with the vodka and heat. She and Alcaeus sat next to each other on white plastic chairs, mopping up the roast chicken juices with soft flat bread that still raised the hairs on Solari's neck with just how delicious it was. This was a world away from the soybeans and rice that had been her staple for the last five years.

Overhead, a broad canvas umbrella protected them from the worst of the sun's heat as they ate and watched life in the enclave pass by.

"Good, hey?" Alcaeus said around a mouthful of corn and bread.

"Mmm," she replied, tongue tingling with the shock of vodka.

He had been easy company—the meal had been devoured mostly in silence, occasionally punctuated with a casual observation or laughter about something they had heard or seen earlier in the day. But mostly, they just sat there, enjoying the meal and the view and the rare opportunity to just enjoy life.

"My mum used to cook meals like this when I was a kid," Alcaeus confided.

"With the vodka?" Solari asked, surprising herself with the teasing tone in her voice.

"No," he said, his lips twitching into a smile. "But, I used to sneak some afterwards." He leaned back and smiled wider. "We lived out near Bridgewater and there was an old Italian nonna who lived next door. Her children and grandchildren had moved on, her husband had died years ago, and she was just straight-up lonely. I'd sneak over to her place all the time and we'd sit on her back porch drinking vodka and just talking. Well, she did all the talking. I just sat there knocking back shots and listening.

"That's all she wanted. Someone to listen. She would have sold all of her belongings to have someone who would just sit with her and let her reminisce about a time when she was happy."

Solari's bread turned to a lump of ash in her mouth. Because there was a part of her who would have done the same thing.

"Mum couldn't understand why I'd always return so sleepy—she was convinced Mrs Girolami was getting me to do all her yardwork and household chores."

He laughed—that rich, deep rumbling that called to a part of Solari untouched by her own trauma. She stared at him, smiling despite herself, and felt her wings ripple along her back.

***

The walk to the arrivals tent passed by in a blur. Solari's belly was full, her tongue still tingled with the taste of spices and charcoal, and her mind hovered in that pleasant state of inconsequence, still fuzzy under a haze of too much vodka.

"We were supposed to start building your new digs," Alcaeus said, pointing to the scrap heap beyond the line of canvas peaks.

"We got carried away, huh?" she said, her voice sounding distant to her own ears.

"No harm in celebrating some good luck. We'll start building tomorrow."

Solari slowed and looked closer at the Metallicari, shivering as her wings ruffled against the small of her back.

"Why are you being so nice to me?" It came out as an accusation.

He fixed her with a mock frown. "You're the one who shouted me lunch. Why are you being so nice to *me*?"

He drew to a stop at the edge of the tent, the late afternoon sun softening the angles of his face and turning his skin golden. It was distracting. Why had she spent so much time with the

Metallicari?

"You were going to help me find the Fixer," she said, stepping into the shade of the tent.

"I told you, Solari." His voice was light, sing-song and shimmering with vodka. "You don't find the Fixer. The Fixer finds you."

SIXTEEN

Orange flames licked the night sky, the bonfire sending a steady plume of smoke to the stars. Solari sat on an old pallet, the fire blanket across her knees and her wings wrapped protectively around her chest. Around her, mutants danced in the firelight, twisting and twirling, their mutations illuminated by the fire in one moment and hidden by the shadows in the next.

Solari's eyes drifted easily to Alcaeus, his arms flashing gold in the firelight as he twirled a young Osteoclasta in tight circles, faster and faster. She was a pretty thing—lithe and graceful, with thick hair that tumbled to her waist. Pretty despite the rows of bony protrusions that ran like tiny bumps down her arms.

Alcaeus laughed, his head thrown back, entirely lost in the moment. He was strong and wild. And free.

As free as you can be in a cage.

Still, that was more than Solari had been in years. Here in the enclave, she could walk where she wanted without fear of bullets, or fear, or enslavement. As much as it galled her to admit, the mutants she despised just weeks ago had created a safe, functional, sustainable environment free of fear and oppression. A place where she could be happy.

Could I?

Happiness was an elusive concept; she had craved it as a child, debated its existence as a teenager, and decried it as an adult.

Happiness was for others; for Northerners, for people of the past.

Alcaeus grinned at her, was showing off. She laughed, despite herself. It was easy to forget he was a mutant—the mutation seemed to disappear from her vision, overshadowed by the sheer magnitude of his personality.

It had been his idea for her to come along, to join the revelry of the summer solstice. *"It's an opportunity to be seen by the Fixer,"* he had said. *"And, besides, you need to loosen up—you're like a hungry animal ready to pounce."*

Arriving at the bonfire had been overwhelming; despite her daily forays around the enclave, she had not anticipated the sheer number of mutants. Any hopes of finding the Fixer had been quickly dashed, lost among the sea of faces.

"Cheer up, Lepidopterae," Alcaeus had said, tapping her under the chin. *"It's a party."*

"I'll never find her here," she had complained, contemplating the long walk back to the tent where it would be calmer and quieter.

"You are a slow learner, Solari. You don't find the Fixer."

"Yes, yes," she said, rolling her eyes. *"The Fixer finds you."*

And he had laughed at her again—which did nothing to wash her irritation—and then winked.

She looked at him, still dancing with the Osteoclasta, his abandon and his joy intoxicating. There was something about him; something so different to what she had found in others. He was infuriating. And yet, she found her thoughts drifting to him and her eyes seeking out his presence.

A subtle shadow fell over her. A woman, maybe a decade older than Solari, came to stand in front of the pallet and face the fire. Backlit as she was, it was difficult to identify her mutation, until she turned and looked down at Solari. Two small horns pierced through short, curly hair.

"Mind if I sit down?" she asked, indicating the ample space on the pallet.

Solari bit down on a flash of irritation. She wasn't here to watch Alcaeus dance, or enjoy the fire, or meet random mutants; she was here to find the Fixer. Or be found by her.

She peered closer at the new arrival. She was…*What? Too*

young? Too unobtrusive? Too softly-spoken? Solari had pictured the Fixer as someone old and battle-scarred and rough. And the mutant before her was not that.

Probably because she's not the Fixer.

The quiet had stretched for too long and the Osteoclasta, seemingly taking Solari's silence for assent, sat down on the pallet beside her. She shifted to get comfortable, brushing against Solari's wings and sending them rustling. Solari quickly stilled them, but the unease dragging at her core didn't dissipate. It was hard to tell what she hated more; her wings, or her inability to control them.

With the view clear again, she found Alcaeus. Just minutes ago he was a whirling mess of vitality and joy, now he stood rigid among the throng of mutants around him. He stared at her, his broad frame burnished by the glow of the fire, his eyes communicating an intensity despite the distance.

Solari glanced over her shoulder, seeking the hidden danger he had found.

"So," the Osteoclasta said beside her, the words almost inaudible above the music and mayhem. "Alcaeus tells me you've been looking for me."

Where Alcaeus' laugh was deep and rumbling, the Osteoclasta's was light and tinkling. "The reaction is always the same. Expecting some ogre, were we?"

Solari stared at her, Alcaeus forgotten for the moment, her thoughts a jumble, her lips unable to form a response.

"It's unusual for someone so new to the enclave to already be seeking a way out."

Like mother, like daughter…

"Wait," Solari said, shifting her body to face the Osteoclasta. Her mind was ticking over, trying to hold to a puzzle piece that threatened to slip through her grasp. "You can't be the Fixer," she said slowly, looking from the mutant beside her to Alcaeus and then back again. "You're too young—my mother left this place twenty-six years ago. You would have been, what? Ten, eleven years' old?"

The Osteoclasta's smile faded, her gaze dropping from Solari's.

"That will be all, Hyacinth." An older woman, early-fifties, materialised from the shadows behind them. Dark-skinned and dressed in black, she seemed more a manifestation of the night than a mutant. Whatever her mutation was, it was hidden by the layers of fabric that left only her face and hands uncovered.

The woman placed a hand on the Osteoclasta's shoulder, but kept her gaze firmly on Solari. The younger mutant removed herself without a word or backward glance, melding into the crowd and disappearing from view. She drifted past Alcaeus, who ignored her or didn't see her; he was so still…If only Solari could see his face.

"You say your mother left here?"

Solari turned to the older woman. In the firelight, she could see black spider webs tracing their way underneath her dark skin.

"Christianne. Her name was Christianne."

Was. Is.

"What was she?"

She was my mother. "A Reptilia." The words came out devoid of any emotion. Part of her still struggled to believe it was true; her mother, a mutant.

"Scales? Blood? Tail? –"

"Scales."

The woman huffed and shook her head. "Too many. Too common." She cocked her head to the side, reminding Solari of a raven. "But, you…" Her voice was low and slippery. "You are not common. We don't see many Lepidopterae anymore; you are only the second I have *ever* seen."

Solari tore her gaze away, sucking in a deep breath as if she had just surfaced from underwater. Ahead, beyond the bonfire, Alcaeus still stood rooted to the spot, a sentinel in a sea of dancing mutants.

"It is…*unusual*… for a Reptilia to beget a Lepidopterae." The woman's voice was like glass shards along Solari's spine. "The genetic markers are not…*compatible*."

Solari shrugged, unconcerned. Mutations were random and inexplicable; there was no logic to their targets or patterns. Just because one old woman hadn't seen something, didn't mean it wasn't possible.

"Where do you take them?"

"To the North," the woman replied, seemingly unfazed by the shift in topic.

"Do they all make it?"

"No."

"And the ones that do?"

"They survive."

"As what?"

"You ask too many questions. You remind me of him." The woman inclined her head towards Alcaeus. "When he was young and stupid."

Solari ignored the insult. What did she care for the prattling of a nameless mutant? It was a hollow thought, though; the nameless mutant was the only real lifeline Solari had to her mother.

"What life is there for them beyond the wall?" she asked.

The woman laughed. It was strange to hear so much laughter amongst the damned when it was the rarest of all commodities in the Southern Reaches. "Here, we are reviled. There—" She waved an inky hand in the general direction of the North. "There, we are *revered.*"

"I need to know where she is." Solari caught herself, hearing the irrational present tense for a woman who, even if she did make it out of the enclave, was undoubtedly long-since dead. "I need to know where she went."

"Then follow her, Lepidopterae. *Follow her.*"

The music around them had grown louder, the dancing more frenetic. Alcaeus was no longer visible, the Metallicari's reassuring form lost amongst the revellers.

"You are a rare specimen," the woman crooned. "You would be highly sought-after. Yes. Men would fight for you and women would weep because of you."

"And what would be your cut?" Solari asked, standing to face her directly, abandoning her search for Alcaeus. She towered above the smaller woman, but the woman did not shrink away.

"What does it matter?"

And she was right. It mattered nought.

"Not interested," Solari replied, turning back to the fire and the crowd.

Not entirely true. She was interested; but, the woman didn't remember Christianne and the only thing to suggest Solari's mother had ever made it to the enclave, let alone left it, was the mad cackling of an old crone with eyes in her hands. It had been a fool's dream to think she could find her mother.

"Suit yourself," the woman said, turning away. She disappeared without hesitation, much the same way as she'd arrived, slinking back into the shadows until there was nothing to see but that part of the night that remained untouched by the bonfire.

Solari bit down hard on the inside of her cheek. What was she thinking? She had just been offered a way out of the enclave and the Southern Reaches, and she had turned it down. All her adult life, she had dreamt of escaping to the North, and now, in a moment of stubborn defiance, she had rejected the first chance of making that dream a reality.

She turned around quickly to peer into the darkness, trying to locate the Fixer, but finding nothing but endless shadows. *Stupid, Solari. Stupid, stupid, stupid.* Regret and despair grew in her belly.

Closing her eyes, she took a deep breath; the smell of damp earth and bitter smoke filled her nostrils. Exhaling, she opened her eyes and let the movement of the crowd file down the spikes of emotion. Mutants pushed and crushed against one another, garish in the yellow light, caught in an insistent feedback loop of energy and abandon.

They were all strangers to her. And, for the first time in her miserable life, Solari felt the truth of what it meant to be genuinely alone.

***

Avoiding Alcaeus after that night was easier than Solari anticipated; he was always early to rise and late to return. She found herself staring at his place from the small patch of earth she had claimed as her own, wondering about the events of the summer solstice.

The Fixer, too, had not been seen in the week since the festival, though Solari had looked. At times it seemed the summer solstice festival was just another fever dream.

Shaking her head to clear the tangle of thoughts, she turned her attention back to her lean-to. Physical exertion was the only way to exorcise her inner demons, and for the last few days she had pulled and twisted and repositioned the materials of the once-shaky structure, determined to turn it into something habitable.

Muscles complained as she made her way back to the front of the enclave to look for more materials. The scrap heap beyond the arrivals tents was small and haphazard, but there was an enterprise about it, a hopefulness and economy that she admired.

Her fingers burned as they raked through jagged slices of glass, uneven sheets of steel, and rough-hewn slabs of timber. Slowly, a small pile of usable materials grew by her feet. Memories of her Hobart apartment kept her distracted—the faded carpet, the peeling wallpaper, the cracked tiles. She had hated it then; now it appeared in her memories as a palace.

A palace in the middle of a war zone.

It had been impossible to think her life could be more miserable, and yet here she was—hiding among mutants with nothing to her name except a fire blanket and scraps of rejected building materials.

Her gaze drifted to the north and her thoughts drifted to what life beyond the wall might look like, the life the Fixer had promised her, the life she had turned down. She imagined her mother dressed in finery, gazed upon by privileged Northerners, scales glittering under lights dripping with crystals, fingers plucking at fruit and cheese served on silver platters.

She laughed, the sound scaring away the ravens that picked at the food scraps nearby. That image of the North was the same one DuPlessis had taunted her with; yes, she would have lived in luxury, would be tended to and sheltered, would have drowned under the desirous stares of men and women—but that vision had been only a half-truth. Yes, they would have coveted her, before they had taken her, manipulated and raped her. She would be desired, and she would be owned.

The sharp sting of metal slicing through skin brought her back to reality. Crying out, she looked down at her hand, blood blooming and dripping onto the pieces of scrap at her feet. She kicked at them in frustration, sending them clattering to the ground. With the shock of the cut subsiding and the pain now throbbing, Solari balled her hand up in the hem of her t-shirt. The fabric was filthy, unrecognisable from the clean cotton that had once smelled of citrus and wild mint.

Cursing, she abandoned most of the afternoon's findings, picking up a small sheet of rusty corrugated iron and dragging it behind her. It would suffice, for now.

Mutants avoided making eye contact with her as she strode along compacted dirt streets. As the only Lepidopterae in the enclave, they knew her, were intrigued by her. None, however, approached her. There were no mumbled greetings or generous smiles; they were wary of her. It was an aversion she had cultivated with her dark scowls, her shudders, her hurrying past with her head down. Other new arrivals were welcomed into the enclave, their building efforts aided by dozens of helpers, but Solari walked alone. Was alone.

Alone was Solari's default state, and she had finally come to embrace it.

Today, she didn't hurry as much. Her gaze passed over the mutants on the street and searched the shadows between the houses and tents, seeking out the Fixer or her Osteoclasta proxy.

The corrugated sheet slipped from her hand. She swore and picked it up, only to drop it again seconds later, the metal now slick with condensation. Her fingers ached as she tried to maintain purchase on the sheet, dragging and dropping it, dragging and dropping it, all the way back to her lean-to.

Bracing it against her hip, she shimmied it up the rickety structure, cursing the mangled hand she needed to use to angle it into place. It was useless—the piece was too small. Even if she secured it to the structure with the barest of overlaps, it would pull everything else out of alignment.

Overheard, dark clouds amassed in the sky. It would be nightfall soon and she needed to secure the lean-to if it was to weather the impending storm. There was no time to venture back to the scrap heap, so she turned her attention to the northern wall;

perhaps there would be more fallen debris from the Fringes there.

Her journey took her past the wilder part of the enclave. Sounds of parties and violence regularly drifted from 'the Dregs', the name the other mutants gave to the ramshackle collection of over-crowded humpies. Ahead, a group of four mutants sat around on old crates and rusted barrels, their faces animated with the drugs and alcohol smuggled into the enclave by soft mutants or sympathetic couriers.

They watched her as she approached. A tall, reedy male, his face normal except for its startling blue tinge, called out something unintelligible to her. The others laughed—a row of dominoes falling. They reminded her of the junkie mutants that used to wash up in the neighbourhoods around Hobart's central boroughs when their supply got low; all scabbed up and itchy, smelling of piss and reduced to mumbling and maniacal messes.

"Are you deaf, winged bitch?" a Tripex with three arms shouted at her. "He said take your skanky, dust-slaking wings back the way you came."

The cackling rang out again. Solari paused. She should turn around and head back; if she hurried, she might still make it to the scrap heap. And yet, it galled her to give in to those…those *abominations*. The familiar slur lacked its usual strength; worse, it came tinged with shame. It was harder to indiscriminately hate them all, now.

She took a step back. The mutants were still laughing at her; except the Tripex, who just stared at her, scowling. It unnerved her—she had seen that look too many times before. The look of a predator, of promised violence.

The Tripex folded her arms across her chest, the three limbs wrapping in a loose braid. She was bigger than Solari. Broader. But it wasn't the physicality of the mutant that was menacing, it was the way she held it; like a weapon.

Solari turned from her and the other mutants; the evening had not yet turned dark, there was still time to salvage what she had started.

Something hard ricocheted off the back of her skull and she stumbled forward. Her hand reached up to where the pain was radiating. It came away red and sticky. She turned, groggily, spying the rock that assaulted her. Before she could look up to see who threw it, another sharp burst of pain exploded at her temple.

White, blinding light rendered her blind. The world went silent, pressure building in her ears as she fell. A high-pitched whistling built around her. Her eyes fluttered, her vision briefly clearing. Shadows were moving towards her.

Her hearing returned with a faint pop, the subsequent whistling replaced by laughter and catcalls. A shiver ran through her body. She tried desperately to move her limbs, but they were slow to respond. She struggled to sit up, to pull herself from the ground.

A kick to her abdomen left her gasping for air. Her eyes widened, pupils dilating to take in more light, more details. The boot inched towards her head in slow motion. She rolled, her left hand reaching out and yanking at the calf in motion, her right snagging the rock still wet with her blood.

Her assailant, off-balance, fell heavily to the ground. She expected it to be the Tripex, but instead was confronted by a face full of scales.

The mutant snarled at her, grabbing at her legs. She kicked him away. Yelling, he launched at her again, tackling her to the ground and pinning her there. Her thrashing achieved nothing, the Reptilia laughing as he scrambled on top of her, bearing down on her with menace.

The others called out, encouraging him, excitement and derision in their voices. He turned to face them, grinning wildly. Solari didn't hesitate. With as much force as her body could generate, she slammed the rock into his temple. He wobbled above her. The laughing escalated; the others didn't realise she held the rock.

She kept hitting, ignoring his grunting and groaning, the rock smashing into his cheek and nose. Scales and blood rained down on her. Hysterical screaming filled her ears.

The mutant slumped down on top of her. Thrumming with adrenalin, she pushed him off and frantically cast her gaze around for the others.

They were walking towards her. The Tripex frowned at the unconscious Reptilia and began to run. The screaming, Solari's screaming, grew louder. She scrambled up, blood pounding at her temples.

Shaky steps launched her into a wobbly run. A blow from behind sent her crashing to the ground, the rough surface tearing up newly-healed skin. Arms wrapped tightly around her legs and didn't let go, even as she kicked out and thrashed wildly. A hand gripped her hair and yanked her head back.

"You fucked up, Lepidopterae." The Tripex spat the name like an insult. "There's no way you're walking back to your humpie alive."

The pressure on Solari's throat choked her of words and air. Static crackled before her eyes, clouding the dusk sky above her. Her thoughts slowed down and every sensation sharpened in clarity. She could feel the ragged edges of skin where it peeled away from her palms and the indentation of the Tripex's fingernails where they dug into her neck. The sound of footfalls and heavy breathing tickled in her hearing and her nose stung with the scent of dirty moonshine and the rich musk of wet soil. The last sensation was a familiar one; it took her back to Alcaeus' room, with its dense walls covered in maps and—

The Tripex grunted and relaxed her grip on Solari's hair. A different kind of pain shattered through Solari's skull as her head crashed back to the ground. The pressure on her legs relaxed and, only then, did she realise the absence of laughter.

A strong hand gripped her shoulder. She swiped at it feebly, the tiny action sending shivers of pain down her arm and into her chest.

"Easy, Lepidopterae."

With surprising gentleness, she was pulled to her feet. A metal sleeve braced her right side, a cooling salve to her bruised flesh.

Alcaeus. The name whispered through her consciousness, softening the jagged edges.

The Tripex lay motionless on the ground, the faint movement in her chest confirming she still lived. Ahead, the Osteoclasta from the festival, her tiny horns poking up through dark curls, walked towards them.

"The Reptilia's dead," she announced flatly, glancing briefly at Solari before turning back to Alcaeus. "If you and the Lepidopterae want to live, you'll have to get to the escort. Tonight."

SEVENTEEN

The basement, though larger than what Solari would have thought possible, was cramped. Boxes, rolls of fabric, and shelves of curiosities filled the space and lent it a musty scent. Solari and Alcaeus sat side-by-side, their bodies pressed lightly together out of necessity. They hadn't spoken since arriving at the Fixer's house.

"Don't say anything," Alcaeus had said. *"Keep your head down and your mouth shut."*

"But—"

"There's no debate, Solari. Either you take what the Fixer offers, or you die here—at the hands of a lynch mob from the Dregs."

And so she had kept quiet while the two of them were marched down the small stairwell to the basement. Quiet while the evening hours ticked by. Quiet while the Fixer, Hyacinth, and Alcaeus discussed her fate.

The last convoy of mutants had left for the Northern Region two days ago and the next one wasn't due for another month. But, if Alcaeus could get her to the first rendezvous point, she might be able to link up with the others already on their way.

"It's a two-day journey," Alcaeus had said.

The Fixer was unmoved. "Make it in one. Hyacinth will come and get you when it is safe to leave."

And then it had all turned silent, with nothing to break it but the nervous rustling of Solari's wings. God, she wanted to get out of that basement. Why was Alcaeus just sitting there? How could he be so still?

She struggled to not fidget, to keep her legs from twitching. Metal scales, cool and hard, pressed against her arm, and the tips of her wings tingled where they brushed against the concrete floor and Alcaeus' back. The feeling travelled up the spine of her wings, ending in pins and needles at her shoulders blades. She shivered.

Desperate for a distraction, she looked to the shelves and scrutinised the things kept there in jars and pressed in frames and pinned to boards. It reminded her of her lab's coolroom, and the familiarity brought comfort. Her gaze wandered from shelf to shelf, her mind silently reciting the phylum and class. *Fritallaria pontica.* Its pale-green, bell-shaped flower has kept its purple blush, preserved against the silent weathering of time. *Phylum: Tracheophyta. Class: Liliopsida.*

Not that everything on the shelves was organic. A bright blue stone flecked with gold pulled at her attention. *Lapis Lazuli.* She remembered a pendant, set in gold, that had sat on a dresser in her father's room for years. *"It reminds me of your mother's eyes,"* he'd said when Solari had asked him about it as a child. The pendant was Christianne's, a wedding gift from an adoring beau to his one, great love.

Later, her father had sold it to an unscrupulous lender operating out of a rundown, concrete bunker on B Street for one-tenth its fair value. Sold the last link to her mother so that he could pay for DuPlessis to save his only son.

The rock looked heavy. Solari imagined gripping its rough edges, and then immediately thought of the dead Reptilia. His face had changed in those final seconds. Not from the rock that had bashed in his temple and sent blood rushing down to coat her hands, blood that she still wore on her t-shirt. No, his face had changed from something within; the realisation of his impending death? Surprise at dying at the hands of a pathetic Lepidopterae? Relief at escaping this hellish life of misery?

Her hands shook at the memory and she clasped them tightly in her lap. It was hard to remember the bloodied scales of his face and not think of her mother. Was that her fate as well? To end up dead on an unforgiving patch of dirt?

She shivered again, her wings rustling more visibly. This time, Alcaeus reacted. Metal plates clattered softly as he lifted his arm and wrapped it around her shoulders. The gentle act of reassurance surprised her and she stiffened. He didn't react and, after of a few seconds of indecision, she relaxed into his side.

How long had it been since she'd been touched without violence? A wave of electricity ran through her body, leeching the tension and pain from bones and tissue. The lump in her throat grew heavy and she bit down on her cheek to stop the tears, ignoring the burst of metallic bitterness on her tongue as teeth punctured skin.

Whereas once the touch of mutated metallic plates would have had her skin crawling, now they were a comfort. It was easy to think of them as an immutable barrier between her and the person they were attached to; something that allowed comfort but didn't demand intimacy.

Her body trembled; at first, tiny spasms—a heart skipping a beat, a record player jumping a groove. She clasped her hands tighter, but the spasms grew more violent, until her entire body was shaking.

Alcaeus pulled her closer, her head resting on his broad chest.

"I'll take the pain away. Sleep, Lepidopterae."

Pressure built in the soft spot between her neck and shoulder. She didn't pull away from his fingers, just let the pressure and pain ratchet higher until it obliterated everything else and ushered in the darkness.

***

"Rise and shine, Solari—it's time to leave." The voice pulled her from sleep, bringing her back to the small, cramped basement. The lights had been switched off, the only illumination coming from the battery-powered torch in Alcaeus hand. He stood over her, the stream of photons creating a pool of light at her feet.

"Why can't we just stay here?" It was a stupid question. She knew it before she asked it, and yet part of her still hoped it was a possibility.

"Our fates are tied, now, Lepidopterae. We'll both hang for the murder of that Reptilia, regardless of whether he deserved it or not, unless we leave this place."

She ignored the hand he offered and pushed herself up. "Lead the way, then."

Up the stairs and through the house, all was quiet except for their hesitant footfalls.

Outside, Alcaeus shut off the torch, their steps now guided by the meagre light of a thin crescent moon and the warm glow of distant fires. The Metallicari's feet beat out a steady rhythm, moving down side streets and avenues, shunning the places of light and noise for the silent and dark pathways.

He moved too slowly. Solari walked faster, pacing ahead before the light became too dim and she had to slow down for him to catch up. In the darkness, the twists and turns disoriented her. A rumbling drifted in the cold air, growing louder.

Solari looked to Alcaeus, but he didn't seem to react. Her foot struck an invisible obstacle and she stumbled, her ankle flaring in pain. Slowly, details began to emerge in the night, introduced by a soundtrack of shouting, laughter, music, and fighting. The Dregs.

"We can't be here," she whispered fiercely.

"Shh. Trust me. I live, you live."

She scanned the road ahead, pushing her eyes to see beyond the places where dark grey shifted to black, searching for a lump in the road. For the fallen body of a dead mutant. With every step, she expected to see it. To smell it.

"It's not the same road." Alcaeus' voice floated to her in the darkness. "And they would have removed the body by now. They've probably been dancing around the funeral pyre for the last hour."

Her heart rate slowed and she relaxed back into a natural walk. "Why are we here?"

"There's a gap in the wall, not far from here."

"That's our way out?"

"We couldn't just waltz through the gate."

Loud voices cut through the night. Alcaeus' gripped her

shoulders and pulled her to the ground.

"Fallon said it was the Lepidopterae bitch. The one whose head is so far stuck up her—"

"There's only one Lepidopterae, you fucktard, I know who she is."

"Well, Fallon said she killed him."

"Yeah, well, Fallon is a low-life, three-armed loser, who…"

The voices drifted away. After a while, Solari and Alcaeus stood up. The Metallicari continued towards the wall, but Solari paused, looking over to where the bonfire danced in the far distance.

"You coming?" Alcaeus murmured.

"Let's go," she said, pushing past him. "But no more dawdling."

He chuckled, a low, deep rumbling. "OK. No more dawdling."

They walked side by side, setting a brisker pace than before. The night returned to quiet, broken only by the soft humming of Alcaeus. The tune was familiar. Ancient. The lyrics whispered in her mind.

Waltzing Matilda. Waltzing Matilda. You'll come a waltzing, Matilda, with me.

She glared at him, futile in the dark, but still satisfying.

They reached the wall not long after, Alcaeus careful to only switch the torch on in short bursts as they walked the perimeter. The marker was a scattering of fallen branches, piled haphazardly against the wall. Alcaeus pulled them away to reveal the breach; a metre wide hole in the reinforced concrete. Beyond, barely illuminated by the torch, rustled the dense thickets of the Fringes.

"No need to be scared, Lepidopterae, it's just the Fri—"

Solari strode past him, crouching low and squeezing through the space, her wings brushing against the jagged edges. She *was* afraid of the Fringes, with good reason. But being afraid had never stopped her from entering it.

*****

With every rustle of leaves, or crunch of feet on undergrowth,

Solari's chest tightened. Walking slowly, she ignored the darkness wrapping itself around her like a blanket and instead focussed on the pool of light at her feet. Alcaeus moved quietly beside her, sticking to the edge along the wall. It would take them longer to exit, but Solari was grateful for his caution—the real nasties of the Fringes tended to stick to the darkest centre.

As they walked, Solari's mind raced with options for their next steps. She recalled the van she'd abandoned just off the access road. "There's a—" She stopped; the van would be the easiest way to the rendezvous point, but revealing it would mean revealing who she was. No mutant would have a vehicle at their disposal.

"There's a what?"

"Nothing."

"There's a nothing?"

"No. I mean, there's…I thought I heard something."

Alcaeus laughed softly. "A little scared are we?"

She rolled her eyes, grateful for the darkness that hid the gesture. And then she did hear something. A low, deep growl.

"Alcaeus," she whispered fiercely.

Alcaeus stopped walking, his torch making a long sweep through the nearby bushes. Solari's legs cramped with the strain of staying still when the safety of the Metallicari was so close.

The growl sounded again. As the torchlight skittered between them, Solari could make out Alcaeus stretching his arm out towards her.

"Solari," he whispered, low and urgent. His fingers flickered, beckoning her closer. "Slowly. Slowly, slowly."

The space between her shoulder blades itched—the place where her mutant wings buried deep into her flesh. In the fragmented darkness, everything seemed so much more ominous. And menacing. Her body ached with the need to stay still and the desperation to run clear.

"Solari," Alcaeus whispered again, louder.

She took a step forward. The growl was louder this time; closer. Too close. The torch light moved erratically from one spot to another, catching on branches, vines and rocks, and bringing them into clear focus before plunging them back into darkness.

Two bright eyes shone in the shadows. The roar that accompanied them hit like thunder a second later.

The torch sailed through the air. It landed awkwardly against a nearby rock, casting a strange beam of light up to the canopy. The high-pitched wail that ripped from Alcaeus' throat shattered her calm. A feral energy rose within her and she dashed to the torch. Spinning around wildly, the light picked up an impossible battle; the Metallicari wrestling with a nightmare abomination. Fur and scales and muscular forelegs danced in the unsteady light, claws seeking to rip and shred and maim.

Frantically, she looked around for something that could serve as a weapon, her brain a mess of unfinished thoughts and urgency with no clear direction.

The rock. The rock.

She cast the light around, finding the rock the torch had landed on just moments ago and racing to reclaim it.

Alcaeus' screams were hoarse, now. Grunting, panting, growling, wailing—it all mixed together in a macabre melody. Desperation, thick and insistent, sang in her veins. Solari dropped the torch, struggling to gain purchase on the rock. It was heavy and coarse against her fingers, and its jagged edges bit into palms recently healed, recently shredded.

And then it was gone, released with a force spurred by panic and desperation and pure need, thrown down onto the beast's back with every shred of power she held.

The spasms and groans ceased. In the surreal light of the discarded torch, all she could see was a mass of metal, scales, and fur. Her fingers scrabbled at the unnatural entanglement, siezing as she heaved the mutant off Alcaeus.

She waited for his reaction, her ears straining for the sound of a gasp or groan. An invisible hand clutched at her heart. *Please, live. Live, Damn you. Live.*

Her hands were sticky. Wet with what could only be blood. Of the monster? Of Alcaeus? She reached down and grabbed under the Metallicari's arms, struggling to lift him. Swearing and grunting, she resorted to dragging him along the underscrub.

Damn it. You will *live. You will live.*

EIGHTEEN

The road was quiet. Even the van moved quietly—a low, constant hum that did nothing to hide the silence that surrounded the lifeless body in the passenger seat.

Every few minutes, Solari reached out to touch Alcaeus' chest, but couldn't feel anything through her own trembling. Blood stained his clothes, seeping through the worn cotton, and ragged trenches mauled his flesh, terminating only where they hit impervious metal scales. Vulnerability and invincibility coexisting uneasily on the ravaged Metallicari.

She needed to ditch him. Transporting a mutant, even a dead one, *especially* a dead one, was a bad idea.

Gripping the steering wheel with one hand, she used the other to prod at his exposed shoulder. Fingers pressed into his muscled flesh, blood oozing out of gaping wounds. But still no response. Dead or dying, it didn't matter—nothing good could come from keeping him.

This close to the Fringes, she could just pull over and leave his body in the thickets. He would be safe from the random glances of passing cars.

But not from the monsters.

Her imagination painted a vivid picture of mutant beasts ripping at brutalised flesh, tearing off metal plates in chunks that pulled skin and tendon with them.

She glanced again at the motionless Metallicari and kept driving. Their fates were tied, now.

She headed north, seeking out the border wall. Without Alcaeus to guide her, there was no way of knowing the rendezvous location, but if there was a way to the Northern Zone, it would be through the wall.

The tension building in her shoulders and neck slid down to her wings. Cramped against the tattered vinyl seat, they twinged in sharp bursts of pain. She shook them out a little, the left wing brushing against Alcaeus and leaving a faint trail of technicolour dust along his arm.

Swathes of wild space slowly transitioned to the beginnings of urban life. The scar on her face itched, little bursts of static flickering on and off. She didn't need to see the orange anchors to know that she was in DuPlessis' territory, now.

Beside her, Alcaeus groaned softly. Solari's chest tightened and then flooded with relief, tension escaping from her wings in a rush of shivers. She glanced from him to the road and back again. The groans grew louder.

She reached for the bottle of alijeah pills in the door beside her, the tiny capsules threatening to skitter to the floor as she tried to open them while maintaining control of the truck.

"Here," she said, shaking out a couple of pills and pressing them into his palm. "Take these. They will help."

Alcaeus was quiet again and seconds passed without him moving. Her fingers trembled, the steering wheel shaking in her grasp. She gripped it tighter, forcing down her rising anxiety.

"Alcaeus? Alcaeus!"

Finally, the man beside her shifted, a hoarse cry pooling spittle at the corners of his mouth. She guided his hand up to his lips.

"Take the pills. You need them."

Blessedly, his lips parted and the pills disappeared into his mouth.

"We're heading north." She spoke loudly, desperate for him to hear her. To understand. "But, I don't know where the rendezvous point is."

Alcaeus was quiet again.

"You need to tell me where the courier is."

It was useless; the Metallicari had slipped again from consciousness.

***

When the first purple bruise of dawn appeared on the horizon, Solari pulled over. The immense height of the border wall loomed ahead, a black shadow that cut the sky in half.

She glanced at Alcaeus. He had woken twice during the journey, and each time she had fed him more pills. Occasionally, he had thrashed, sending blood trickling from raw wounds; but, mostly, he was quiet, save the rare groan or unintelligible whisper. Now, he was still and silent; the shallow rise and fall of his chest the only sign that he lived.

Solari hesitantly reached towards him. Her breath caught and she paused, briefly, before letting her fingertips drop to the cool, metal plates of his arm. Something about seeing her tortured hand against his invulnerable armour comforted her.

Reluctantly, she pulled her hand back and turned her attention to the view outside. The border wall was still over a kilometre away; close enough to walk, far enough away to not be spotted by whoever stood on the ramparts. It was only the third time she had laid eyes on it: The first, after it had gone up, cradled in her father's arms, the actual memory forgotten but the story told a hundred times during her childhood; the second, after Denavim had been diagnosed, their father desperate to commute the death sentence and find miracle workers in the North who could help.

It was still intimidating—full of impossible promises and shattered dreams. Even though she was too far away, she could visualise the rows of wooden crosses that picketed the ground along the three pm shadow-line.

In the early days, many had tried to breach the wall, contriving daring escapes that defied imagination and sense— catapults made of scrap; trucks kitted up with high-octane fuel; homemade explosives; DIY hovercrafts—each one more ridiculous and just as unsuccessful as the last. Gunned down or pushed over, the deserters all fell. And never got back up.

Her father had stared at the crosses. She had watched him, seen in his eyes the conflict between recklessness and responsibility. How close had he come to his own harebrained scheme?

"Solari?" Alcaeus sat up slowly, straightening from where he had slumped against the passenger-side window. "Where are we?" He grabbed at his abdomen, fingers pressed down on the torn and bloodied fabric of his shirt. "What happened?"

Solari pulled his hand away. "Don't touch it." She handed him the alijeah pills. "Here, take these. They'll help with the infection. And the pain."

He eyed them warily before throwing his head back and swallowing two.

"I didn't know where the rendezvous point was," Solari said. "So, I just drove north."

"How did you get the van?"

"I stole it."

His eyes widened a little at that.

"So. Where is the rendezvous point?" She was relieved he was alive, but she was still tired and cold and ready for this part of the nightmare to be over.

Alcaeus shifted again in his seat, bending to look at his wounded midsection. "About fifteen kilometres north of the enclave."

Solari looked over at the wall. They had travelled four times as far. "You said it was a two-day journey."

"It typically is." He groaned and leant back in the seat, still clutching his middle. "Sometimes it can be done in one, if you risk the more dangerous areas of the Fringes."

She stared at him. "You courier mutants through the Fringes?"

"I don't courier anything. But it's not like they can be couriered along the highways is it?" Alcaeus exhaled and let his hands drop to his lap. "There's an old access road that starts west of the enclave. It runs up to a place called Liawenee—an old, inland fisheries site—and then further north to the wall.

"Liawenee is cold as fuck and barren and dangerous, but the old buildings still hold up and can house around thirty mutants at a time. It's possible to fend off the nasties of the Fringes for a couple of days in the old town, but any longer and the odds shift."

"So, let's go to Liawenee," Solari said, fingers gripping the keys still in the ignition.

Alcaeus laughed, then grunted, pressing his palms against his abdomen. "It's not that easy, Lepidopterae. We'll need to drive south along one of the most dangerous highways in the Southern Reaches, in the day. We'll need to ditch the van at the Fringes and make our way on foot through the dark heart and, even then, we'd have lost half a day. The convoy would have left already; we'd be stuck at Liawenee for a month."

"So, what do we do then?"

"We survive in the outside world for a month and try to catch the next convoy."

"That's not an option."

"It's the only option."

"For you maybe."

They sat staring at each other.

A life outside, caught between DuPlessis and Worcsulakz—each with their own reasons to track and kill her, or worse, enslave her—was what she had been trying to escape when she entered the enclave.

"I will leave you here if you want," she said. "I will even drive you back to the town we passed two hours ago. But, I will not be waiting around a month for my ticket out of here."

"What will you do, Solari? What are your options?"

He wasn't irate; didn't raise his voice, or frown, or show any indication of frustration or derision. Just sat there, calmly waiting for her answer.

Except she didn't have one. Not yet.

I need to get to the rendezvous point. No. *I* need *to get to the* North.

"DuPlessis," she said, the name like acid on her tongue. "He runs a slavery racket, sending girls to the Northern Region."

"And?"

"And, I can guarantee you—he doesn't need to use an old road in the Fringes to move them."

NINETEEN

They took the back roads to Blackwood Creek, trading the better roads to the east for the privacy of the crumbling roads near the Fringes. The van rumbled and shook as Solari navigated the deep holes and crevasses that had eroded the surface. Her hands ached from gripping the steering wheel and she cringed at every groan from the vehicle and the passenger beside her.

An hour later, she pulled the van over on a stretch of dirt road near a rusted-out water tank on the outskirts of the township. Alcaeus was frowning, but he had stopped voicing his objections to her plan. He looked down at the flak jacket that Solari reluctantly handed over.

"It will cover your plates *and* your wounds," she said, frustration tightening her words. "Just walk into the corner store, buy some food, and leave. You don't need to speak to anyone, and in a town this small, with DuPlessis running the area, they won't be asking questions."

"You seem to know a lot about DuPlessis."

"Just get the food." She pulled out some sticky, plastic bills from her jeans pocket and handed them over.

"You are full of surprises, Lepidopterae."

You don't know the half of it.

The door creaked on its hinges as he opened it and stepped out. The early-morning sunlight glinted off his metal plates and bronzed skin. He shrugged into the jacket, grunting as his arm bent back to fill the last sleeve. Shutting the van door, he paused and leant on the window sill. Her jacket suited him.

"If I'm not back in forty minutes, drive. And don't stop until you reach the Second Enclave."

It was their Plan B. Alcaeus had argued that it should be their first plan of action, but Solari had less confidence that life in an enclave would turn out well for her. Besides, her secret would not hold in the Second Enclave. *Maybe.* The mutant boy she had couriered from Elysia's would know her true identity, but there was some hope he would also protect it.

Doesn't matter. We won't need a Plan B.

"Solari?" Alcaeus' voice pulled her from her dark thoughts. He was still leaning against the window sill, his arms folded and wearing a frown. With his plates hidden he was just another man.

No. Not just another man. He was different from all of them. From her lying, desperate father. From her shit-for-brains ex. From the sadistic DuPlessis, arrogant Worcsulakz, apathetic Jerath.

"Yeah, I heard you. Drive to the Second Enclave. Just get the food, alright?" It came out harsher than she intended. She softened her tone. "Don't keep me waiting, OK?"

Alcaeus straightened, rapped on the sill with his knuckles, and headed into town. The alijeah would mask the worst of the pain and give him a burst of energy, but it wasn't sustainable. She only hoped he made it back before the effects wore off; driving into town to look for him would draw attention they couldn't afford.

She watched as his broad frame grew smaller, and when it blinked out of view she pulled her gaze away and shifted it to the east, to Powranna. She had been seventeen when DuPlessis' cronies had tied her up with the other slaves in one of the warehouses out there. Seventy kilometres east and the only thing between it and Solari was the stretch of highway that DuPlessis used to run guns and money from the town's armament to the central point at Oatlands.

In her mind, she recreated the road and the warehouse in as much detail as she could remember. She could see the cages, smell the dank corridors, hear the cursing and the laughing and the fucking of gang members. Each remembered detail pulled into focus half-forgotten memories, and all the residual emotion attached to them. The desperation, the fear, the useless anger, the raging panic.

So, when Alcaeus returned thirty minutes later, grinning with his unlikely success and proudly brandishing a plastic bag full of tinned meat and old bread, she didn't return his smiles.

***

"I was fifteen when the first plate appeared."

Solari stopped chewing on the stale chunk of bread. It was an hour since Alcaeus had returned and the first time either of them had spoken.

"My dad was a pastor," Alcaeus continued. "The real deal— full-on religious, fire, brimstone, righteousness, revelation. He loved to preach about wickedness, and temptation, and the devil's abominations. *Then I desired to know the exact meaning of the fourth beast, which was different from all the others, exceedingly dreadful, with its teeth of iron and its claws of bronze, and which devoured, crushed and trampled down the remainder with its feet.* Daniel 7:19."

He reached up and ran a hand down the tessellated metal plates. "For a man of God, he had a wicked temper. I didn't wait for the second plate to appear. I threw some things in a backpack and left. No goodbye note. No farewell."

He stopped to scoop some tinned beef from the can resting on the dashboard. She wondered how he could be so calm.

"That was more than fifteen years ago," he said around a mouth full of food. So, he was older than her. But not by much. "Thing is, I didn't realise that strangers would hit harder and deeper than my father ever could."

He let the words hang in the space between them, but the subtle invitation went unanswered. Solari didn't want to share her story.

The bread was dry in her mouth, sucking all the saliva from her tongue to form on big lump that felt like a fistful of sand. He would have to go back to the store in the afternoon for water.

"We'll need to be close enough to see how DuPlessis is

moving them," she said eventually, unapologetic in shifting the conversation to the matter at hand. "But not so close that they'll see us."

Beside her, Alcaeus sighed and scooped another chunk of meat. "We'll need to ditch the van."

She nodded. "But where? Too close, they see us. Too far away, and we're sitting ducks if they spot us."

"I forgot," he said, grunting as he reached to the floor and retrieved her flak jacket. "I got you something."

He threw her the jacket and then reached for the bottle of alijeah pills in the centre console between them. Normally, she would have been pissed that he was stealing all of her good pills, but she hadn't needed to take any since…since?…she couldn't remember. *Definitely before the solstice festival.* And that seemed a lifetime ago. Her wings rustled in some subconscious response to the memory. She ignored them. "What did you get me?"

"Check the pocket."

Her fingers grazed a textured, crinkly material. Pulling it from the pocket, she could make out enough of the faded print for it to be legible. *Tasmania—Feed your curious.* It was an old promotional flyer, a relic from a distant past. Carefully opening it, lest the paper rend along its folds, Solari traced her fingers across the faded picture of Hobart before the wall and the war.

"Your gift is to remind me how shitty this paradise has become?" She scowled at Alcaeus.

He laughed. "Turn it over."

On the reverse side, in rich detail, was a series of maps. She pulled the page closer, squinting at the small, faded text, and trying to orient herself. A lot had changed since the maps were drawn and yet many of the town names remained the same.

"Here," she said, pointing to a small red dot near the green of the Fringes. "This is us. This is Blackwater Creek."

Alcaeus leaned closer, the metal plates of his arm rubbing against the thin cotton of her shirt and sending her wings rustling again.

"And this," she continued, tracing her finger along a winding road heading east and tapping the t-intersection at its termination point, "is Powranna. This is where DuPlessis has his northern armament. Trucks move the guns south to Oatlands and pick up slaves at Turnbridge, Campbelltown, and Conara on the way back north."

"How do you know all this, Solari?"

Because other slaves would talk. Because I ended up in one of those trucks before I got away. Part of her wanted to open up like he had, to tell her story, unload it all. It had been a lifetime since she'd had anyone to talk to, to trust with her secrets. Anders had once been that person. *The lying, barbaric piece of shit. I hope you're rotting somewhere in a shallow grave, you dog.*

"The drivers will change over at Powranna," she said instead, keeping her head down and eyes on the map. "That will be our chance."

Alcaeus was silent. When she finally looked up at him, she found him staring at her, his brow furrowed. Her avoidance of his question had not gone unnoticed. She wondered if he would make a deal of it, demand that she explain how she knew all of this detailed information about gangland operations and DuPlessis' racket.

Please let it go, she mentally whispered to him.

Finally he sighed and looked down at the map. "We could leave the van here," he said, pointing to a faded green patch near the highway. *Powranna Nature Reserve.* "If it still exists."

Smiling gratefully at him, she folded the map and returned it to the flak jacket pocket. "Only one way to find out."

***

Solari's anxiety coalesced into a dense rock that lodged in her throat. The 'nature reserve' they had passed minutes ago had been nothing but a mess of concrete and weeds. Worse still, the surrounding landscape was similarly flat and barren; nowhere to ditch the van, nowhere to hide from DuPlessis' thugs. It was dangerous being on the road for so long, so close to the armament.

"There," Alcaeus said, pointing to a ramshackle farm shed a few hundred metres off the road and partially hidden by overgrown shrubs.

She didn't hesitate, turning the wheel and pushing the van through wild grasses. The drought had turned the soil as hard as the bitumen of the road, but not as smooth. The van rattled and shook as they sped over uneven ground, the sound of rocks ricocheting off the vehicle's underbelly like bullets. Knuckles white on the steering wheel and cursing at the cloud of dust rising behind her, Solari accelerated towards the shed, swerving at the last minute to steer the van in behind the rickety, old structure. She slammed on the brakes once they were hidden from the road, and pulled the van to a halt.

In the new silence, she could hear Alcaeus groaning. He was pale, his face clenched and his eyes shut tight. His hands pressed down on the wound at his abdomen. In her haste to protect them from detection, she had forgotten just how badly he was injured and how quickly the alijeah would wear off.

"Are you alright?" She reached out to touch him, but pulled back at the last second. "Alcaeus?"

He mumbled something. She leant closer to hear it. He mumbled again, the sound a prelude to the stream of vomit that spewed from his mouth. She recoiled from it and then caught herself, recognising the repulsion for what it was—the natural reaction of anyone faced with the bitter smell of regurgitated meat and bile, not the skin-crawling aversion of someone hit with projectile mutant DNA.

There wasn't time to dwell on it; Alcaeus descended into a fit of hacking and dry retching. They really should have got some water back at Blackwater Creek.

"Hey, hey, hey," she murmured, reaching behind him and gently pushing him forward. She kept her hand there, the vibrations wracking his chest transferring along her arms to her wings. Slowly, they subsided, enough for him to lean back and open his eyes.

When he looked at her, his pupils were dilated, the brown of his irises washed out and grey. She needed to get him inside the shed.

Her legs shook as she stepped out and walked to the passenger side. Taking a deep breath, she pulled herself together and opened the door.

"Hey there, metal man." Her poor attempt at humour was rewarded with a weak smile. She smiled back and reached for his arm, metal plates rippling at her touch. Alcaeus groaned as he shifted in the seat and leant heavily on her to exit the van. She faltered under his weight, even though she knew he was holding back, taking on more pain than he should to make it easier on her. "Let's get you inside."

They stumbled as she led him to the shed, its rusted corrugated iron like a dirty sunset in a steel winter sky. The large sliding door was off its hinges and the interior smelled like stale piss and dead rats. Alcaeus gagged again, but gratefully didn't vomit. Solari looked around, searching for a better option, but finding nothing save the vehicle parked outside.

"Maybe we should spend the night in the van?" She tried to keep her voice light, though her mind raced with thoughts of all that had gone wrong, and could still go wrong.

Opening the back doors of the van, she helped Alcaeus inside, arranging the flak jacket into a makeshift pillow and sweeping out the coarse debris from the floor. The colour was returning to his face, his body now relaxed. She grabbed the bottle of alijeah pills, frowning at its depleted volume, and handed it to him. "No more than two, unless the pain gets really bad. And then only three."

Propping the back doors open, she crawled into the front cabin and wound down the windows, begging for any kind of breeze to whip away the building heat. The van was a metal cooker in the late morning sun, and the temperature would only climb as the sun scaled higher.

"I'm going to look for something to ease this heat," she called over to Alcaeus. "I'll be back in a minute."

Alcaeus remained quiet. He was doing his best to hide his pain from her, and failing abysmally. If things got any worse, she would have to chance going back to Blackwater Creek for more supplies.

Going back was too risky, staying was too risky. Solari's throat constricted, and she wasn't sure whether it was the heat or her dwindling options that was suffocating her.

***

Having sweated through the afternoon, it was a sweet relief when the weather shifted and dark clouds appeared overhead. While Solari's efforts to insulate the van with timber off-cuts, broken corrugated sheets, and a battered tarp had provided some relief, the swirling sou-easterly that skipped across the paddocks and through the van was like a kiss from an angel of mercy.

The breeze rippled through her wings and she fluttered them open and shut to maximise the cooling effect, smiling as the current ruffled Alcaeus' hair and swept the long trails of sweat from his face. He sat in the open doorway, legs dangling over the edge, laughing as Solari spun slowly in the breeze.

A loud crack overhead echoed and rumbled, and then another. The sky was a deep, inky grey, and the breeze no longer a zephyr, but a proper, raging squall. It terrorised the tarp tied to the roof of the van, twisting and bashing it against the hot metal chassis before ripping it from the vehicle and launching it out over the weed-infested paddocks.

The suddenness of it, the drama, stopped Solari in her twirling. She looked from the runaway plastic to Alcaeus, who sat with eyes widened and a perfect 'o' on his lips. She was the first to laugh, the sound strangled at first—like a little bird squeezing its way free from a death grip. The release in her chest from that discordant sound, of the tension she had held tight for so long it had almost been forgotten, was a revelation.

The laughter grew deeper, and louder, and brighter. And, suddenly, Alcaeus was standing there with her, the two of them laughing as the dark sky split open and let down the rain.

The hammering of rain on the van's naked roof built to a crescendo. Solari spun again, faster this time, revelling in the sensation of water hitting her wings like cool fingers against a timpani.

The rain fell heavier. Finally she slowed. Alcaeus stood before her, thoroughly drenched and with a look of such hunger it arrested her. In two strides, he was centimetres away. His hand reached for her, and then stopped, as if waiting for her to show him that his hunger was reciprocated.

And in that crazy moment, with the wind tearing across the barren land and the rain washing away past sins and bad memories, she smiled. Strong arms encircled her waist, lifting her up and spinning her around again; slower this time, deliberate, enchanted.

She looked down at him, drowning in his dark eyes. And, when the emotion threatened to unhinge her, she buried her face into his shoulder, cheeks pressing against metal plates cool and smooth.

The first kiss at her neck was soft and gentle. An invitation. With her head swept clear of anxiety, she surrendered to it, felt the heat build in her core as the kisses grew lest restrained and more urgent.

Her feet touched down on the damp earth and she turned to him, hands reaching to his face to turn his lips to hers. His hands skittered up along her wet shirt, only to cascade down her wings. If the rain on them had felt like a symphony, his hands on them felt like wildfire.

She pressed closer to him, lips so hard against his she could feel them bruising. He was moving, guiding her back until her legs hit the van and she fell inside. She pulled at his shirt as he moved them further inside the van, out of the rain and into their own private storm.

With hands gentler than she thought possible, he liberated her shirt, slowly pulling it from wet skin and soaked wings, until there was nothing but his skin pressing against her own.

The initial flare of passion was familiar. And welcomed. It had been years since a man had touched her. Since Anders.

She paused, looked at her hands pressed to his chest, at the ugly stumps where her fingers had been. How could he find her attractive? Even Anders had thought her damaged goods with the scar that trailed down her face.

Running her hand up to his shoulder, she shivered as the stumps met the plates. And, in that moment, she froze; the reality of her situation crashing louder in her thoughts than the thunder overhead.

Alcaeus sensed her shift in mood, his hand drawing her face to his, forcing her to meet his puzzled gaze. The moment broken, the full brunt of reality rushed in.

What am I doing? This is madness. He is a mutant. A mutant.

She turned her face from his, pulling her hand back and lying very still.

"Solari?" The confusion and tenderness in his voice caused her throat to tighten, but still she pushed against his chest and sat up.

Outside, the rain beat against the van, a storm of white noise and rage.

"I can't," she whispered, the words lost in the cacophony.

It didn't matter that he couldn't hear; she could see his realisation in the way his frown deepened, in the way he sat back against the wall of the van. He had no words and neither did she.

Her wings trembling, she shuffled out of the van and ran out into the rain.

TWENTY

The lightning flashed, an angry scar in a turbulent night sky. It was Solari's only aid in navigating the unfamiliar territory. She walked quickly, stumbling often, almost falling, to banish the messy thoughts that plagued her mind.

She headed east, seeking out DuPlessis' compound. The insanity of it made her laugh. The last time she had arrived at Powranna, it had been in a van crammed with a dozen other bruised and dirty bodies. All tired, hungry, and scared. Except Solari.

Oh, she had arrived tired—she hadn't slept properly since DuPlessis' thugs had kicked their way into her apartment and dragged her from her bed. And she had been hungry—the stale, mouldy bread the guards threw at their captives had been inedible. Others had been content to nibble around the edges, thinking Solari foolish to refuse it, only to have what little strength they took from it taken back and more when the inevitable bouts of vomiting and diarrhoea commenced.

But when the van unloaded all the other sick, tired, hungry, and foul-smelling prisoners at the warehouse, Solari had not been scared. She didn't cower or shiver like the others, hadn't kept to the shadows or avoided eye contact. Maybe she had started out scared, when they had first taken her, in the early part of the journey. But not when she arrived. Entering Powranna, she hadn't been scared. She had been angry.

She still was. That anger, which had started early in her life and built over years of brutality, was still with her. But she had since learnt that being angry was often the same as being stupid. And now, she had the scars to prove it.

So, how was it after all those years since escaping Powranna, she was walking back towards it? *Walking towards it or walking away from Alcaeus?*

Alcaeus. She could still feel his hands on her body, the warmth of his breath and his kisses. Could still see the look of confusion and hurt when she had pushed him away. Without doubt, she had been stupid with him—but less clear was whether she had been stupid to get too close to him, or stupid to walk away.

Focus, Solari.

The rain was easing, but lightning still crashed overhead. She pulled her wings tighter around herself to ward off the rain and offer some level of camouflage, their colour grey and dark to match her mood. Slowly, she crept closer to the road. It felt like she had been stumbling around in the darkness for hours, but a glance at her watch as the lightning illuminated its face told her it had only been twenty minutes. She should be close to the compound by now.

Looking behind her, she searched for any indication of an oncoming vehicle. While the storm would deter unnecessary travel—to pubs or whorehouses—it would not delay supply runs or shipments from nearby holding places. And there was no way to tell whether a convoy was due in the next day, the next hour, or the next five minutes.

She walked slowly, constantly looking over her shoulder before turning back to scan for the compound's perimeter. Ten minutes later, the road ended at a t-intersection, the eastern route transforming to a rough gravel road underfoot. Ahead, maybe six hundred metres or so, she could just make out the faint lights of what had to be the compound. Pulling her wings up and over her head, she crouched down and shuffled forward, ignoring the sting of loose rocks biting into her knees and shins.

The compound was massive and it took her the better part of two hours to circle it. Two hours to let the rain and shadows dismantle her confusion, regret, and shame. With the lights and activity inside the compound, she had been able to make out the key points of entry and scope the places of low surveillance. It wasn't a huge amount of information or a mind-bending revelation, but it was a start. Something she could share with Alcaeus, something they could build a plan around. And maybe bridge whatever awkwardness she had created between them

Back on the road, she moved faster, motivated as much by her continued need to remain undetected as her desire to get back to the protection of the van. And to Alcaeus.

The glow appeared on the horizon as a strange, golden translucence. Like a sunrise. Or a fire.

She thought of the lightning that had flashed overhead and of the long dry grasses turned brittle in the extended drought that had only just broken.

A new kind of panic assaulted her; visions of a burnt-out van and unresponsive Alcaeus spun in her mind and spurred her into a run. So fixated on the distant glow and what it could mean, Solari forgot to move away from the roadside.

At first, the dim lights of the oncoming truck seemed to be just another bright spot in what was now easily recognisable as a growing fire. Only when the glow of the fire glinted off the truck's side panels did she truly see it and threw herself to the ground. The earth, though saturated, was still hard; Solari felt the jolt of the collision all the way up to her shoulder blades, her wings fluttering protectively around her before she could consciously demand they hide her.

The truck slowed, its loud roar softening to a low rumble. Solari buried her face deeper into the wet ground, resisting the urge to pull her wings tighter around her, resisting the urge to peek up as the rumbling grew louder and the truck closer.

They've seen me. I should run. I need to run.

Fighting the rising panic in her chest and the insane beating of her heart, she forced her body to be still and her wings to fall quiet. With the blood thrumming in her ears, she couldn't tell if the truck had passed.

The chitin layers of her wings tingled as she tentatively pulled away her camouflage. The street was dark, devoid of any lights or presence save the orange mist of the blaze and the acrid smell of smoke.

Despite the exhaustion in her legs, she ran the rest of the way back to open fields where she had left the Metallicari and the van.

"Alcaeus! Alcaeus!" She was shouting too loudly, her desperation to find him outweighing her fear of being discovered.

The chill in the air turned her soaked skin frozen. Thick sheets of rain stung her eyes and obscured everything save the ever-present glow of the fire. She craved the hard surface of the road, but the vehicle had spooked her, so she stumbled along the uneven ground of the paddocks, her wings like a cloak wrapped tight around her. Lightning raced across the sky, the air booming when it spiked downwards.

The fire was still ablaze when she arrived back at the dilapidated shed, burning through a patch of grassland a couple of acres away. The van was still where she had left it, but the tyres were slashed and the fuel line cut. Alcaeus was nowhere to be seen.

Solari ran to the shed, oblivious to the rancid smell made worse by the rising damp. Her eyes searched frantically for the glint of metallic plates, but found nothing. Bracing against the rain again, she paced a hasty perimeter around the shed, hoping to find Alcaeus hunkered down in a hidden culvert or hastily dug ditch. The farther she travelled, the more desperate she became.

"Alcaeus!" The rain drowned out her voice. He would never hear her.

Because he is not here.

It was a realisation that should have come earlier. Would have come earlier had the panic and desperation not burned so bright in her chest. Solari stopped walking, stopped shouting. Collapsing to the ground, from the exhaustion, the cold, and the fear, she wrapped her wings around her to stop the shivering and tried to order her thoughts.

In the end, she came to the only conclusion that made any sense. Alcaeus had been taken.

She wondered if the truck that passed her on the road had held him captive. The fire would have drawn it from the road and towards the shed, and the van. If Alcaeus had passed out on the alijeah pills, he would have been an easy bounty.

Slowly, she pushed herself up from the sodden ground and walked to the van. Whoever had vandalised it had done so to ensure no-one else could steal it. They would be back to salvage what was left; but not tonight, not in this weather.

With tired arms, she pulled open the back door and rummaged around for her flak jacket. Her chest flooded with relief when she found it stashed under the passenger seat. The map was still tucked away in one of the pockets, as were the alijeah pills. It was a small relief, one that paled in comparison to the realisation there was no blood on the floor, no signs of violence.

Unless it happened outside. And the rain washed all the signs away.

Fear and nausea swirled in her belly. She needed to stay calm and clear her mind, to figure it all out.

If Alcaeus was alive, there was only one place he would be taken to—DuPlessis' Powranna compound.

With a heavy heart and her mind still reeling with worst-case scenarios, Solari folded her wings tight against her back and pulled on her flak jacket. The wings bristled against the dense fabric as it weighed them down and crushed them. She ignored the discomfort and continued rummaging in the van.

To find Alcaeus she would need to get past the compound's perimeter. She reached under the seats again, grabbing glass bottles and pens from the debris and stashing them in the deep pockets of her jacket. Makeshift weapons were better than no weapons. Rolling back the thin carpet at the back of the van, she pulled at the panel to expose the spare-tyre well. Stashed beside the tyre was a collection of old porn magazines and a long, leather pouch. *Please let the tyre iron be inside.*

A sharp tug at the pouch liberated it from the well. It was heavy and her fingers clutched at the long, solid item hidden inside. Relief surged in her belly and she quickly opened the pouch. The tyre iron sat heavy and snug against the leather, but her eyes immediately fixed on something else. Nestled beside the tyre iron was a semi-automatic pistol and three cartridges.

Bless you, Scotty, and your dirty, tattooed skull. You may have just saved my life.

TWENTY-ONE

Solari hid in the shadows just beyond the compound's perimeter. Her wings tensed under her jacket and she desperately tried to calm them. While the spotlights on the fence would not pick up on the wing's dull colours, the lights would catch movement. Just as they did the movement within the compound.

It was busier than what she had seen during her reconnaissance; more activity around the front gates, more bodies in motion. Ten minutes into her surveillance and her plan of going in gun blazing had washed away with the rain.

It had been a stupid plan, but it had made her feel not so damn helpless for just a little while. She grit her teeth against the disappointment and sat back on her haunches. It was good to be courageous, but now she had to be smart.

Slowly, she crawled away from the lights of compound, standing only when she was clear of any sight lines. And then she ran, backtracking along the road she had just journeyed. Reaching the intersection, she wasted no time getting to work. There were a few fallen branches littering the road, but she needed more. She raced back and forth across nearby paddocks, gathering as many fallen branches as she could, dragging the heavier ones until her muscles tired.

Her gun was never going to be enough to take out a whole compound, but one or two supply runners was a possibility. And maybe a vehicle was a better weapon to get to Alcaeus than just a gun. Eventually, someone would have to drive into or out of the compound, and no matter where they were going or where they were coming from, they would have to come through the intersection.

She scattered the branches haphazardly, positioning the larger ones on the eastern road to the compound. It wouldn't be enough to stop a vehicle—even a small car would be able to get around the debris—but it would be a distraction. And that was all she needed, just one vehicle to slow down.

Retreating to a nearby culvert, she pulled the pistol from her pocket and jammed in the clip. It was years since she last held a pistol, even longer since she'd fired one.

Don't fret. It will be just like riding a bicycle. Except, she hadn't ridden one of those in over a decade, either.

Lying on her belly, she propped herself up on her elbows and looked around. From her vantage point, she could see the intersection clearly. She would have a clearer shot at vehicles coming from the compound or from the south, but even those coming back from a supply run would give her a chance. The only risk was a vehicle approaching from the north—but that was the least likely possibility.

Three out of four isn't bad.

Everything was ready; now she only had to wait. Despite the discomfort of the ground, and her sodden clothes plastered to her skin, the exertion of the day and the warmth from her wings threatened to pull the alertness from her. Even with hidden rocks pushing into her skin and the constant rumble of thunder overhead, sleep was singing its siren call. Solari dozed involuntarily, startling each time she woke, only to drift off into half-sleep again.

In that limbo of semi-consciousness, she dreamt. Of Alcaeus and the cool touch of his metal plates, of fires that burned through rain, of light that exploded into a hundred fragments and fell around her like bullets.

She woke with a start. Headlights pierced the darkness, growing larger as the vehicle advanced from the west. A returning supply run. Adrenalin bursting in her chest, Solari reached for her gun.

Her heart was thrumming, her grip shaky. She was second-guessing herself. Maybe she should wait until a van came from the compound, until she had a better shot.

No. It would be too heavily armed with more bodies inside. Too many variables, too many risks. This was her chance.

Hands shaking, she aimed the barrel low. She just needed to take out one tyre. Just one. If she could disable the vehicle, she could subdue the driver, replace the tyre, and advance on the compound.

She gripped the gun tighter, clenched her eyes shut, and fired.

***

The urge to retch obliterated any feeling of relief, and Solari scrambled to a half-sitting, half-crouching position, gripping her stomach and struggling for breath. Just metres away, the van had rolled off the road and into a ditch, twisting the chassis away from her view.

The flickering of the intersection lights echoed on the street, refracting off puddles and shattered glass but doing little to illuminate whether her shot had missed, maimed, or murdered.

Solari tried to filter out the white noise—the blood in her ears, the static of rising panic. It was no use; any sounds from the van, moans of desperation or desperate scrambling, were too soft or too far away to be heard.

Thoughts of firing a second shot skittered in her mind, but the adrenalin-fuelled courage that had screamed through her veins just minutes ago had drowned and taken her bravado with it.

Still, she couldn't stay where she was.

Cinching her wings tight together under her jacket, she stood and stepped tentatively towards the van. Tingling under her unease was the irrational desire to discard the jacket and fan her wings out around her. The lightweight mass of membranes, scales, and hair would shatter into dust at the first touch of a bullet. And yet, there was something about them that made her feel a little more invincible.

She moved slowly towards the van, keeping to a line that would protect her from a direct shot. With each step, she strained to see or hear anything from the van, the uncertainty kicking her heart rate higher and pushing her chest to breaking.

Reaching the van, she pressed herself against its metal body slick with rain. Her wings shuddered at the contact and her mind pushed against the primal resistance of inching closer to an unknown terror.

Only when the side mirror afforded a view of the van's interior did she stop. The driver, a younger female—eighteen year's old? Nineteen?—lay slumped over the steering wheel, a dark river of blood moving sluggishly down her neck.

The drumming of Solari's heart climaxed with a high-pitched screaming in her ears. The rain against her skin burned like acid and her stomach clenched, fighting against the turmoil and endless heaviness that threatened to pull her down.

She retched, bile burning along her throat as she spewed a meagre stream of vomit against the van's side panel. She stayed hunched over, unwilling to look upon the dead body again, letting time stretch and wrap around her.

But, the longer she stayed there, the sharper her anxiety grew. Staying would not make the driver any less dead, only increase the chance of Solari joining her in the afterlife.

Clenching and unclenching her fists in rapid succession, Solari opened the door and braced against the weight of the dead driver as the body slid towards her. She bit down her guilt and revulsion and pushed the body back, winced as it slumped into the passenger seat and then pushed it as far against the passenger side door as she could.

She had wasted too much time. And energy. If another vehicle was to turn up…

With the engine still running and no tyre to replace, Solari shut the driver's side door and angled the car back on to the road. The short-wave radio crackled, sending Solari's heart to her throat and a string of curses to her tongue.

"Transport E16." The static-filled voice echoed in the cabin. "Change of schedule. Proceed to Powranna Compound. We have a grade two ab for immediate transfer north. Confirm. Over."

Solari's heart stuttered with relief. They had Alcaeus.

"Change of schedule received." The voice that replied was younger and brighter than Solari expected. A junior courier? Or trainee? The former would be easier to overpower; the latter, with an accompanying senior supervisor, would deliver a more complicated scenario. "Do we still drop the abnormal at Evandale or has the destination changed? Over."

"No change to destination," the radio crackled. "Proceed to Evandale for change of driver after pick-up at Powranna. Over."

The radio fell silent, leaving Solari alone in the van with her dark thoughts and a dead body. She didn't need to go the compound to get Alcaeus, they would deliver him to her.

TWENTY-TWO

The van shuddered as Solari drove it into a roadside ditch some ten kilometres north of Powranna. Beside her, the dead girl rocked violently against the shattered passenger window.

Just a roadside accident on dark night and wet road.

Cutting the engine and exiting the van, she worked quickly to move the body back to the driver's seat, her heart beating with the rush of anxiety and anticipation. Clambering into the passenger seat, Solari slid down low and readied her pistol.

The radio chatter had announced the arrival of the courier van at the compound ten minutes ago. *Fifteen minutes turnaround, another ten to pass here.*

It was a short wait—less time than it took to cook a batch of tetrahydron, less time than it took to escape to the Gypsy Quarter after Anders had hacked off her fingers—and yet it felt interminable.

Cramps had started itching their way along her nerves three minutes in. Her wings had started to shake after five. And now her body felt plagued by jolts of electricity that branched out along her limbs and grew in intensity and frequency like labour pains. The urge to stand up and stretch put pins in her brain.

Instead, she clenched her teeth and stayed where she was, training the gun on the empty void where the driver's window used to be.

The pain grew to breaking point, tipped over, and grew again. Finally, the lights of an approaching vehicle gave way to the crunch of tyres on bitumen. The sound of the engine shut off abruptly, replaced by the softer rumbling of boots on gravel.

"Rachel? Can you hear me?" The male voice was low and soft. He knew the driver's name, would have already called in the damaged vehicle. It was a complication that could seal Solari's fate no matter how the next few minutes played out.

"Rachel?"

His head came into view—an older man, maybe mid-thirties. Not the grizzled DuPlessis crony she was expecting. Not that it mattered—Solari had come to learn that looks could be deceiving. His eyes registered the dead body before they landed on Solari's gun.

"No sudden movements," she rasped. "Don't look back to your vehicle. Don't make a sound. Put your hands, both hands on the window sill. And don't move."

The man complied. That was the good thing about her battle-scarred face, people didn't doubt her intentions or her nerve.

Gripping the gun in her left hand, she roughly pulled the dead body to the floor of the van and clambered across, never taking her eyes off the man at the end of the barrel. "Now open the door. Slowly. Don't say a word. Don't make a fucking sound."

Her heart was trembling, but neither her hands nor her voice shook. Only her wings, unable to hold back all of their stored anxiety and desperation.

The man's face twisted into an ugly scowl, hinting that he too was capable of following through with threats. And, yet, he opened the door.

"Don't drop your hands," she said, low and clear. "Keep them on the sill."

Solari stepped out of the vehicle, careful to keep the man between her gun and the other vehicle's line of sight. "Turn slowly; no signals, no tip-offs."

He scowled again, but then turned, slowly, just like she had demanded. She pushed the gun into his back, just below the left shoulder blade. "Start walking. No running, no stopping."

Her heart was thundering again, the distance between them and the truck small enough for her to make out the driver: another young female, maybe as young as sixteen, leaning over the passenger seat and peering through the darkness.

The roar of the truck's engine and the sweep of headlights pushed ice through Solari's veins. The light brought everything into hyper definition, before it blinded her. She pressed the gun tighter against her quarry's back. Felt him twitch with intention.

Solari's survival instinct kicked in, but her guilt over the dead girl made her hesitate. Though, only briefly. She clenched her eyes shut, angled the gun lower and pulled the trigger before the guilt could reassert itself.

***

The sound of the pistol firing and the hoarse scream that followed was still echoing in Solari's mind minutes later when she pulled the driver from the truck. The supervisor lay writhing on the ground, liberated from the gun he had been reaching for—and he *had* been reaching for it when she pulled the trigger on her own gun.

The driver, too, had fired a shot, the bullet pummelling into Solari's flak jacket just above her collarbone as she ran to the truck. If Solari hadn't registered the damage on impact, she felt it now as she wrenched the gun from the young girl's grip and wrestled her to the ground.

"Get up!" she screamed, training the pistol on the pretty face free from scars or blemishes. "Get up or I'll shoot you in the face and you can die in the mud."

The girl was shaking as she stood, eyes down and hands out in a futile attempt to protect herself.

"Open the back of the truck."

"I don't—"

"Open it or I'll pull the keys from your dead body."

The girl winced; a tiny movement that damaged Solari more than the bullet that had pummelled her collarbone. She had gone too far; this was all too aggressive, too violent.

Violent.

It was a state of existence she had lived with her entire life, but always as the victim, never the aggressor. Until now.

"Open the back," she repeated, the cold menace still in her voice.

Still shaking, the girl retrieved the keys from the ignition and walked to the back of the truck. Solari strained to hear anything on the other side of the metal, nausea filling her belly as the silence dragged on. There should have been something—cries for help, stamping of feet, clanging of chains.

What have I done? In her wake, a dead body, a damaged man, and a hostage. *For what?* A chance to escape the kind of violence she had just perpetrated? To find her way to the privileged north? To find the mother she'd never known?

The truck doors shuddered as the girl opened them. Inside, rows of bodies—all as young and perfect as the driver at the end of Solari's pistol—sat on narrow benches; blindfolded, gagged, shackled at the wrists, and chained to the floor.

And then she saw Alcaeus. And the relief sent her staggering.

"The one in the back." She was no longer able to keep her voice steady. "Unchain him."

The girl's fingers trembled as she unlocked the chains and shackles around the Metallicari's wrists and ankles. As they fell away, his hands snapped up to rip the gag and blindfold from his face. And, when his gaze fell on Solari, his eyes burned with the dark light of torment and confusion.

"Solari?" He stood, and the driver screamed, her face voicing all the fear and revulsion she couldn't find the words for.

"Take his place," Solari said, ignoring the swell of emotion that threatened to drown her. "Sit down. Now."

Shaking out of her flak jacket, she unleashed her wings and fanned them out behind her. "Sit down now or I'll shake my mutant wing scales all over your pretty face."

"You don't know what you are doing," the girl cried, stumbling as Solari pushed the gun tighter into her back. She fell to the bench, swivelling to face Solari and Alcaeus. How they must have appeared as nightmares to her, the abominations she would have shied from her entire life. "You don't know how bad this will be for you. You don't know who you are pissing off."

The Metallicari moved silently past Solari, his metal plates brushing against her shoulder and making her shiver.

"It's not too late." The girl's voice was high and reedy. "Just let me go and you can live. Let me go and I won't tell him, I promise."

"Won't tell who?" Solari asked, and then to Alcaeus, "Shackle her hands."

The girl shuddered and recoiled as Alcaeus pulled her hands into the cuffs and locked them to the bar behind. "DuPlessis," she stammered. "You don't know what he is like. What he is capable of."

With the girl firmly shackled, Solari handed the gun to Alcaeus and stepped closer. There was a grim satisfaction in watching the girl flinch. Solari reached down, dragging her arm closer to the girl than she needed to, and picked up the blindfold Alcaeus had so desperately discarded.

"He will kill you," the girl shrieked. "He will torture you and carve body parts from you and bring you within an inch of your life just to watch you suffer."

Solari pulled the blindfold tight around the girl's head.

"You don't know him!" the girl screamed. "You don't—"

Her protestations were muted as Solari stuffed the gag into the girl's mouth and tied it in place. Subconsciously she went to drag a finger down the scar on her face, catching herself and hastily wiping her hand instead on her jeans.

"I know," she murmured, just loud enough for the girl to hear over her whimpers. "I know DuPlessis."

TWENTY-THREE

Solari struggled to concentrate. Thoughts of the dead driver abandoned on the side of the road and the two captives chained in the back of the truck still filled her veins with ice, overwhelming her sleep-deprived mind and hungry body. But it was the silence from her passenger that distracted her attention from the road.

Alcaeus' voice had dried up on exiting the back of the truck—the supervisor still writhing in the mud that had turned darker with his blood.

"We'll need to secure him in the back, as well," she had said. The Metallicari had paused, and frowned—with disappointment? Distaste? She didn't have time to ask, and he didn't offer any more conversation, working silently as he bandaged the man's wound and carried him to the back of the truck.

Solari had almost said something to him as he pulled the alijeah pills from her discarded flak jacket and offered it to the man before tying him up. Instead, she had slinked into the driver's seat of the truck and waited for the Metallicari to join her.

"Solari, there's still someone out there," he had said, appearing at the window and pointing to the van she had hijacked less than an hour ago.

"There's no-one. Get in the truck."

"Solari, there's someone in that van."

"It's no-one. Get in."

"Solari!"

"She's dead! She's been dead for over an hour. Get in the truck, we have to go."

Since then, he hadn't looked at her or said a word. Even now, twenty minutes later, he sat rigid in the passenger seat. And it was driving her crazy.

How could he condemn her violence? They lived in a violent world—violence was everywhere. It confronted them at every turn, appearing constantly on the drive north to Evandale: in the dilapidated rest-stops with their shattered windows and billboards punctured with bullet holes, in the burnt-out cars that lay exposed in their roadside graves, in the ugly orange anchors that defaced every abandoned house and storefront.

Her anger and indignation had quickly overshot her guilt and remorse, building in her chest until it bubbled up her throat. She turned to the Metallicari, ready to unleash a diatribe, but the words died on her tongue.

He stared at her, eyes clouded with untold emotion. "Did he give that to you?"

"Did who give me what?" she snapped, her mind still entangled in dark thoughts.

"The scar." His gentle voice a sharp rebuke to her anger. "Did DuPlessis give it to you?"

Solari sighed, releasing some of the tension clouding her mind. So many secrets between her and the Metallicari. Too many. What could one more matter?

*Except…*Maybe if she were to tell him, maybe if she could show him the violence she had lived, he would understand.

"A long time ago, my dad needed something. And DuPlessis offered to give it to him. Except my dad skipped out before he paid his debt, and so DuPlessis transferred it to me."

"He cut you to collect on your father's debt?"

"No." She gripped the steering wheel tighter, eyes flashing to the red icon on the GPS unit. The changeover location was still fifteen minutes away—too far to just dance around the truth. "DuPlessis was going to send me north."

Alcaeus frowned and Solari realised her error. "Before he

knew I was a mutant," she explained quickly, feeling the familiar prick of guilt, even though she was telling the truth, in a way. "He wanted to sell me."

She flushed at the memory, the residual emotion still strong enough to haunt her. Her life under Worcsulakz's protection and rule had faded the memory of her time with DuPlessis. One threat traded for another, one nightmare overshadowing another. It surprised her to feel the strength of its return.

"I tried to escape and he punished me for the insult."

"And then let you go?"

Solari heard the incredulity in his voice and she laughed—a harsh, hacking bark. *Not exactly.*

***

"I'm disappointed." Pierre DuPlessis reclined on a gaudy leather lounge. That was his style—he wasn't happy to just be a gang lord; he wanted the stereotypical lifestyle, the caricature from the movies of his childhood…back when there were movies, and televisions, and mindless entertainment.

A cold sweat exploded against Solari's skin, the salty perspiration agitating the fresh wound cut into her face. DuPlessis' deputy had slashed her when they'd found her hidden away in a half-empty crate of ammunition. The deputy had slashed her, and now DuPlessis would kill her.

But instead he turned his cold stare to one of the guards. The flash of gunfire burned in her vision, but did not end her life.

"You should not have let her escape," DuPlessis said, the guard lying bleeding on the luxe, white carpet.

"As for you," he continued, turning his attention and the gun to Solari. "You shouldn't have tried to escape. Now look at you—your pretty face all messed up. I only trade premium product; you're no good to me damaged. No one pays for broken goods."

"But they'll pay for snowrock!" she cried, her mind twisting to find a way out of her fatal predicament.

DuPlessis paused, lowering his gun ever so slightly.

"Yes," he said, drawing the single syllable out. "And how do you propose to get me enough snowrock to make up for the price I could have

got for you in the North and for the inconvenience of losing a guard and destroying my carpet?"

"I can cook it."

He laughed at the suggestion, but when she told him about her skills, her ability to turn mutant DNA into the purest form of the drug, he tapped his finger against his chin as if entertaining the notion. "Take her to the cells," he demanded of another officer. "Tomorrow you will cook for me. Or you will die."

When the guard came for her in the middle of the night, she cowered and screamed, thinking DuPlessis had changed his mind and reinstated his death sentence.

The stench of stale sweat filled her mouth and nostrils as the gag tightened around her face. She struggled, thrashing about, clawing at her captor until he jammed his fingers against her neck and pulled her into unconsciousness.

And then she woke up. Unlike DuPlessis, the room Worcsulakz's deputy occupied was sleek and minimalist. Instead of a dozen guards, only three stood beside him. And one before—the one who had collected her from her cell.

"So," the deputy murmured, leaning forward. "Avan tells me you can cook snowrock."

***

"He didn't let me go," Solari said, finally answering Alcaeus' question, pushing down the memories before they could possess her. "His enemy smuggled me out. And now I have two debts to pay."

TWENTY-FOUR

The streets of Evandale were no different to the other towns they had passed through; barren and bereft of anything to delight the senses. Nothing. Nothing but the cracked bitumen of the road and the ubiquitous concrete of a failed industrial sector. Rows of empty factories and warehouses streamed past the truck, their grimy facades broken only by the ever-present orange anchor.

Solari glanced at her passenger, the wounded supervisor unconscious in the seat beside her. Alcaeus had traded places with him a few kilometres back; the new driver would be expecting to see both the supervisor in the cabin and the Metallicari in the back. The supervisor's leg had stopped bleeding and, wearing the fresh pants from one of the prisoners in the back, he looked like he was sleeping off a big night in Conara.

The red icon flashed on the GPS screen, the changeover location just a few streets away. The plan she and Alcaeus had hatched earlier was rough at best—Solari would push the drunk supervisor story and lead the new driver to the back of the truck to inspect the 'cargo'. After that...well, after that didn't really matter— as long as it ended with the new driver in chains and the location of their entry point to the Northern Region.

The warehouse at the destination point was as cancer-ridden as the rest of them. There were no visible security cameras, but still she approached slowly—the idling van in the driveway the only indication that the GPS had led her to the right place.

She parked the truck strategically, angling it to allow for a quick getaway if needed. Wriggling in her seat, she pulled at the plaid flannel shirt she had confiscated from one of the prisoners and tied around her waist. Together with the flak jacket, it would keep her wings from view. Adrenalin singing in her veins, she tightened the jacket and tied a double knot in the shirt, gestures as useless as they were comforting.

In the side mirror, she watched the changeover driver approach the truck.

"You're late." His voice was the rough bark of someone whose throat had been stripped from years of barking orders and smoking too many cigarettes. He was smaller than Solari expected, and fatter. *Finally some luck.* It would only make him slower. "What happened to him?"

Solari glanced at her passenger. *I shot him.* "He drank too much at Conara. He's sleeping it off."

"Well, I'm not going to move him," the changeover driver barked.

"That's OK," Solari said, opening her door and stepping out of the cabin. "I'll wake him after you've checked the cargo."

Hitting the ground, Solari's legs felt as though the adrenalin had melted through bone; she clenched her teeth and forced them to move naturally.

"Is it true there's one of those abominations in here?" the driver asked as Solari opened the back of the truck.

Beneath her jacket, Solari's wings threatened to twitch at the insult, and she prayed the wing tips were not visible below the shirt she had tied around her waist. She clenched her fists and stepped into the belly of the truck. "Yes," she said, inclining her head towards the back where Alcaeus sat, chains looped through his shackles but not locked in place.

The driver stepped past her, inching towards the back, growing confident as his advance was greeted with nothing but silence. "I've never seen one so—"

He spun around at the sound of Solari closing the doors, eyes widening in the dim light and fixed on the pistol she aimed at him. Before the driver could reach for his own, Alcaeus sprung from his position and pulled him into submission, wrenching the man's arms behind his back and forcing him to his knees.

"You crazy bitch," the driver roared. "You will die for this. Even if I don't get to you, DuPlessis will have your fucking head."

Solari stepped up to him, grabbing the gag Alcaeus had discarded and ramming it into his mouth. She ran her index finger slowly down her scar—with less self-consciousness and more intent than she thought possible—pressing the finger hard against the raised skin. "He already has."

She watched silently as Alcaeus shackled him to the seat and tied the blindfold over his eyes. Waited for the aggression to leach out of him. When he finally quietened, she nodded to Alcaeus, and the blindfold and gag were removed.

"What's your destination?"

The driver's laugh was rough, coarse, and incredulous. "You did all this to know where I am going? You really are a crazy—"

He spluttered as the gag was reinserted.

"Let's try this again," Solari said, more confident than she felt. "Where's the drop-off?"

She waited again, watching for his eyes to lose the fire of aggression, before removing the manky fabric.

"I'll never tell you. I'll never fucking tell."

Solari nodded and Alcaeus returned the gag. She could use a bullet to persuade him, but they were in short supply and she couldn't afford to waste one. Besides, there were other ways to make the driver talk.

***

They headed west, away from the main road, away from the reach of DuPlessis. Alcaeus sat quietly, face turned away from Solari, gaze set on the damaged world that passed in a blur outside the truck's window. The road deteriorated the further they drove, and the orange anchors of DuPlessis territory became less frequent, until finally they reached the Fringes.

"What are we doing here, Solari?" Alcaeus asked when she pulled the truck over to the side of the road.

"We're getting some answers."

"I won't torture him," he said, staring out the windshield, refusing to meet her gaze.

"I'm not asking you to," she retorted, stepping out of the truck before her anger could get the better of her.

Outside, the air was thick with humidity and carried with it the scent of the Fringes—of life and death and decay, of pungent fertility and damp vibrancy.

The idea had formed in the silence of the drive, growing in clarity as they traded the chaos of the urban word for the chaos of the natural.

"Guard the truck," she called to Alcaeus, her gaze firmly on the verdant Fringes. "If I'm not back in an hour, do what you want."

She strode towards the boundary, not waiting for his response. The drop in temperature pulled the fog from her mind and pushed everything into high definition. Solari scanned the trees for yellow lichen, pulling strands of it from low-hanging branches and stuffing them into her pockets. Mushrooms, leaves, purple bark that broke apart in her hands—it all went into her pockets, her mind ticking off ingredients as she trekked deeper into the dark heart.

Sticks and leaves crunched underfoot as she strode carelessly through thickets of dense scrub, her mind half on the job at hand, half seething with unspent fury.

Alcaeus thought *she* was the monster. Not DuPlessis, who had been happy to carve her from forehead to lip. Not his lackeys, who couriered the young and beautiful beyond the wall like chattel, or Worcsulakz, who would chain her in a steel cage cooking snowrock until her insides bled with the inundation of toxins, or Jerath, who would take the rest of her fingers if he ever found her. But Solari. For what? For doing to them what they would do to her and worse? For doing it to them before they could strike first? For daring to fight her way free of every fucked up situation she kept landing in?

A snarl rumbled close, low and full of menace. Solari turned slowly, her hand creeping to the pistol tucked into her waistband.

The tawny fur of the thylacine was tainted dark in the shadows, throwing into sharp contrast the row of white fangs that girded its mutated body.

It snarled again, stalked closer.

Solari's hand inched closer to the pistol, her skin itching for the cool comfort of its metal. The beast was only a few metres away; close enough for Solari to see the scars on its forelegs and snout, and find dark eyes gleaming with something other than pure violence.

Her fingertips grazed the pistol, hesitating even as the adrenalin pushed her to grab it and kill the tiger before it could kill her.

A breeze, cool and full of the Fringes' stench, washed over their détente. The thylacine paused, lifting its head to catch the scent. Solari's hand tightened on the pistol; she could shoot now, the animal distracted and its throat exposed.

Her wings fluttered in the breeze, shivers running from her shoulder blades to her finger tips. She dropped her hand from the pistol and let it hang at her side.

The thylacine snapped its head to Solari at the sudden movement. She could see the intent in its eyes, knew that it was ready to launch at her. Forcing her breath to slow, she held the beast's gaze and knelt to the sodden earth.

The tiger paused and padded forward. Slowly, Solari unfurled her wings and let them expand behind her. The tiger stopped its advance, rising on its haunches and pricking its ears.

Everything Solari knew about biology told her to act submissive—to lower her gaze, retract her wings, curl her body down. But her instincts told her to maintain her own dominant pose.

With each second that passed, her pulse began to slow. In the light that filtered through the canopy, the beast no longer appeared feral, but regal.

Another low rumble issued from its chest. Solari's wings fluttered, ready to retract. Instead, she fanned them wider and hardened her gaze.

I am not your enemy or your master. I am your equal.

The thylacine went silent, regarding her with its dark and intelligent eyes. And then turned from her, the rows of fangs on its back rippling as it stalked away from Solari and deeper into the Fringes.

TWENTY-FIVE

Solari strode out of the Fringes, the flannel shirt flaring behind her and her heart still racing. The afternoon shadows had stretched to engulf the truck. Alcaeus leant against the passenger door, arms crossed against his chest, metal scales dull in the darkness.

She never slowed, her feet crunching on gravel where moments before they had tangled in organic chaos. In a matter of strides she collided with him. His hands, outstretched to stop the clash, dropped to her waist as she reached up to grab his shoulders, her fingertips pressing hard against the sharp edges of his metal plates.

The kiss was a universe away from their first—hard, where the first was soft; urgent, where the first was tentative.

His hands stilled. His body stilled.

It acted as a circuit breaker. She pulled away, looking down when he didn't meet her gaze. The electricity that had coursed through her veins just seconds ago dissolved into a slushy mess of confusion and embarrassment. She couldn't just stand there, but there was nowhere else to go.

How had it come to this? How had she found herself here? Orphaned. Alone. Scarred, hunted, brutalised. And now, rejected.

Alcaeus tapped his finger under her chin and lifted her face to his. She kept her eyes downcast, unwilling to see the pity or gentle admonishment that would cloud his face.

"Hey." His voice came to her soft and deep.

Please don't look at me with pity. She reluctantly opened her eyes.

She never got to see what was reflected in his. Heat at her lips brought the electricity back with fire. Alcaeus' hands were no longer stiffly by his side; they ran through her hair, over her wings.

She wasn't afraid of him anymore. She didn't know who she was, or who she was becoming, but she knew that whatever it was that she felt for this man who was holding her like a fragile bird, it was as far from fear and revulsion as she was from freedom.

***

"Did they hurt you?" Solari broke away from Alcaeus' embrace and stepped back.

It was unfathomable how much had passed between them in such a short space of time and how much she still didn't know about what had happened while he was in the compound.

"No." He shrugged and looked away. "Nothing but a few scratches."

She smiled at the poor cliché and lifted his white shirt turned dark with dirt and sweat and grease and blood. The raw wounds that ran across his torso and snaked around his back made her baulk. He pulled the shirt down gently and nudged her hands away.

"It's nothing," he repeated.

She frowned, but didn't pursue it. "Did you learn anything for your troubles?"

"They're moving to fortnightly shipments." Alcaeus sighed and leant back against the van.

"Of people or weapons?"

"The weapons are paramount; the people help pay the way and generate some leverage. It sounds like DuPlessis is ramping up his offensive against Worcsulakz."

She remembered the extra brownouts in Hobart; it made sense—DuPlessis had been angling for over a year to steal a larger cut of the Southern Reaches' underground empire. Pulling in weapons from the Northern Region would certainly help, but she wondered where he was really getting the money from; the sex trade was, by all accounts, lucrative, but surely not *that* lucrative.

"Did you hear anything about where they were headed?"

Alcaeus shrugged. "They were going to drop us off in some border town and await further instructions—something '-town'…"

Solari pulled the map from her flak jacket and scanned for border towns. "Youngtown?"

"Maybe. I guess."

"So, we go to Youngtown," Solari said, stashing the map back in the pocket.

"But, we don't know the transfer point. It could be anywhere, could be *anything*—an abandoned building, a brothel, a third-storey apartment in a non-descript building…"

"We need to get the driver to tell us."

"He'll never tell us, Solari. You heard him—he's petrified, like everyone else, of DuPlessis. And I get the sense—subtle as it is—that he doesn't like mutants."

She smiled wryly at his sarcasm and pulled the strange collection of organic artefacts from her pocket. "That's what this is for."

The early years of Solari's biochemistry trade had been sketchy, not that time had really improved things. Back when she had first started out, there had been no decent lab equipment, no gangland sponsor, and very little experience. But, with local suppliers unable to keep up with demand for the basic drugs, Solari knew there was a market gap she could exploit. And, so, before upgrading her talents to producing the more lucrative snowrock precursors, she had scratched out a living cooking crude versions of other drugs—speed, oxycodone, rohypnol.

Most of her batches had been fair imitations, but the rohypnol was always light on the drowsiness and heavy on the talkativeness and loss of inhibition. She had given up producing it after only six months of testing.

"If I remember the right ingredient mix, it will hopefully be the beginnings of a truth serum."

"You know how to make truth serum?"

She could hear the scepticism in his voice. It mirrored the uncertainty in her thoughts.

"I used to know," she replied. "And I'm hoping I can remember."

"That won't help us much if we're using an ineffective serum on the driver—he could tell us anything and we wouldn't know if it is truth or fiction."

"I know," she relented. "Which is why we need to test it."

"Test it on who? We can't test it on any of the…" He looked at her strangely, his frown of frustration shifting to one of foreboding. "Solari…"

"It won't hurt you—I'll make sure whatever batch I make is not lethal."

He quirked an eyebrow. "Not lethal?"

She smiled. "It won't hurt. I promise."

TWENTY-SIX

They travelled north, keeping to the western roads; their destination not Youngtown, but a small outpost town with no direct affiliation to either DuPlessis or Worcsulakz. The town only extended four or so blocks, enough to fit a pub, a motel, a petrol station that doubled as a convenience store, and row upon row of abandoned houses with their windows boarded up. Still, it was all Solari needed.

She parked the truck a block away from the motel—even with the other occupants still gagged, she didn't want to run the risk of alerting anyone's attention. Not that there were many captives, now; along the way, at random towns and road stops, they had released the others—one or two at a time to keep them separated and avoid suspicion—until all that was left were the two drivers and the supervisor.

There was still a risk in having three captives, all who needed to be fed and watered, all who would be plotting to escape, and maybe even kill her. But it was a necessary risk. She needed their answers.

The woman at the motel reception looked up and frowned as Solari walked in, but smiled when she saw Alcaeus. Wearing the leather jacket taken from the changeover driver, he looked like any other person—any other *non-mutant* person. He was smiling at the receptionist; not the seductive smile of Anders or knowing smile of Jerath. A genuine smile; polite, kind, unassuming. The rarest kind of smile.

"What can I do for you?" she asked, still looking at Alcaeus.

"We, uh, need a room," Solari answered, gaze shifting between the two of them.

"How many nights?"

"Just a couple of hours."

The receptionist looked to Solari at that. "Our minimum booking is four hours."

"That will be fine."

"And the rooms are basic amenities, only," the receptionist continued, grabbing a key from behind the desk. "Clean, mind you, but basic."

"That will be fine," Solari repeated, fingers itching to grab the key.

"That will be one hundred dollars."

Solari grimaced, but didn't argue—it wasn't as if she was spending her own money. Reaching down, she pulled the driver's wallet from the pocket of her flak jacket and handed over two yellow notes, snatching the key as soon as the receptionist proffered it.

"Thank you," she said through clenched teeth.

"My pleasure." The receptionist tucked the notes away in a key-locked box. "If there's anything I can do for you, don't hesitate to ask."

Solari didn't bother replying—it was clear the receptionist wasn't directing the invitation to her. Instead, she set off down the hallway, gripping the key and scanning room numbers.

"No need to race, Sol—"

Solari shook her head urgently and put a finger to her lips. Just because the motel's facade lacked an orange anchor or blue trident, didn't meant the receptionist wouldn't pass on valuable information for the right price. Alcaeus nodded and the two of them entered their room silently.

The space inside was exactly what the reception had promised—beige walls that may have once been white, a double bed with a simple frame, a small television tucked in a corner, and a basic ensuite with clean, but chipped tiles.

"It will do," Solari announced, locking the door behind Alcaeus and closing the heavy curtains across the window that looked out onto the street.

"What do you need help with?" Alcaeus asked, flicking the light switch and shrugging out of his jacket.

"See if you can find a kettle and a hairdryer or iron. And grab as many glasses or cups as you can find."

Solari untied the shirt from around her waist and shrugged out of her own jacket. Flaring out her wings and savouring the feeling of freedom, she pulled her collection of items from the jacket's pockets and separated them into things for now and things for later. Lichen, bark, leaves—now. Gun, map, wallet—later.

The headache that had started back in Powranna threatened to break open her skull. She pressed her palms against her temples, trying to hold it together, to squeeze out the pain.

"Hey," Alcaeus said, coming back into view with a kettle and an assortment of cups. "Are you alright?"

"Yeah," she replied, squeezing her temples one last time and letting her hands drop to her side. "Just tired. And hungry."

"Then sleep," he said, putting down the equipment and resting a hand on her shoulder. "Sleep, Solari—we can do this later. Hell, we can both get some sleep, and some food, and then test this concoction of yours."

It was so tempting—she could just let him wrap her up in his strong arms, lay her head on his chest, just fall asleep.

"No," she said, wincing at the pain of shaking her head. "It will work better if you are tired, if you're under stress. Just like the driver."

Gently, he spun her around to face him, his eyes searching hers. After a while, he simply nodded and let his hands drop. "OK, Ms Biochemist Extraordinaire. Let's start our fucked-up game of truth or dare."

***

"So, how does this work?" Alcaeus sat cross-legged on the bed, his back resting against the steel frame.

175

Solari passed him the half-spent pen and the notepad from the side table. "Write down a secret you don't want to tell me. A secret you've kept for a long time that makes you feel guilty or edgy or unsettled just thinking about it. Something you don't want to tell anyone, but something you specifically don't want to tell me."

Alcaeus took the pen and paper reluctantly.

"Drink this," she said, looking down at the mixture she had brewed and transferred to one of the cups. "It will taste like shit—I used to add a heap of sugar and press it into pills, but you get the rough, organic version. It also might make you feel a little lightheaded, which is good, because that means it's working."

"So I drink this and just start babbling the truth?" Alcaeus took the cup and peered down at the brown liquid.

"No, you'll give me a hint of what the secret is about before you drink it—nothing specific, just enough so that I can target my questions; I don't want to be asking you about your ex-girlfriends if your secret is about the body buried in the backyard of your childhood home."

She expected him to smile at that, but he just sat rigid on the bed, his fingers picking at the edges of the notepad.

"So, I'll ask you some questions," she continued hesitantly. "It won't be like an interrogation; the mix works better if it's a seduction. I'll write down your answers. At the end of the session you'll take a cold shower to get rid of the mind-fog and then review what I've written down. If the answers I've written down are consistent with what you've written on your piece of paper, we'll know the serum works."

"And how *does* the serum work?" Alcaeus didn't look at her, just stared at the blank notepad in his lap and tapped the pen against his thigh. "How does it pull this secret out of me?"

"The way I see it, there are three types of secrets. One, the secret you don't really care about keeping, because it's not important, maybe only a little embarrassing, and the consequences of telling it are negligible. Two, the secret you do care about; the one you hide in the dark corners of your memory because you don't want anyone to even know about it, but that eats you up inside to the point where you sometimes dream about offloading it just to be rid of the burden. And three, the secret so big and bad you'll take to your grave; the kind of secret you try to hide from even yourself.

The serum seems to work of the first two—it blurs the edges of the first kind of secret and dulls any concern about telling it, breaking down what little inhibition there is to stop you from divulging; and it sings the siren call to seduce you into telling the second type, wrapping you up in this nice, warm, comforting hug that makes you feel safer about telling it, which is what you really want to do anyway. But it never works on the third type; there's not enough holes in the mental barriers to exploit, I guess."

She paused and waited for Alcaeus to stop the incessant tapping of the pen and look up at her.

"And if it works," he finally said, "you'll know my secret."

"Yes."

"And what about yours?"

She frowned at him. "What about mine?"

He looked up at her. "Well, it's not exactly a fair trade—I drink this mud water that tastes like shit and tell you my deep, dark secret, and you just get to sit there and hold on to yours."

Her mind immediately went to her wings, the secret she was desperate to both hide from him and reveal. *The second type of secret.* "There's not enough ingredients to waste—I'll be stretching it to make enough test batches *and* have enough to use on the driver."

Alcaeus held her gaze, challenging the weak-sounding excuse. Finally, he sighed and leant back against the bed frame. "I'll learn your secrets somehow."

Solari stared at him, heart racing, as he bent his head to write down his secret. *Not if I can help it.*

***

Alcaeus stepped back into the room, wet hair raked back, towel wrapped around his waist, naked torso and metal scales on display. After the third shower, he had given up on getting dressed for subsequent sessions. It would have been an arresting sight if Solari hadn't been so frustrated by the failures of her recent serum batches.

The ingredients that had stuffed her jacket pocket two hours ago looked sparse and overwhelmed on the bedspread.

"Are you sure you've given me the right context?" she asked.

Before Alcaeus had taken the first batch, he had told her the secret was about *'how I ended up in the enclave the first time'*.

"Do you want me to give you more details?" He sat on the bed again, stretching out. They were both tired and frustrated.

"No. It's not about me guessing the secret. It's about you revealing it." She sighed. "Anyway, it's not like the driver will be offering extra hints out of the goodness of his heart."

"So, what do we do?"

Her fingers picked at the ingredients—enough for three more batches at best. She could always drive back to the Fringes to get more, but the extra trip increased the chances of being seen by someone on DuPlessis' payroll, and returning to the motel would attract suspicion. No, she needed to get the next batch right.

"Did the last time feel any different?"

Alcaeus shrugged. "I felt like it was harder to keep track of the story—I could feel my brain really struggling with it. But, that could just be—"

"Lack of sleep, I know. But it's all piling in on the cognitive load of lying—sleeplessness, hunger, stress, and hopefully the rohypnol. And you're in the same condition as the driver. We'll use what we can get and hope that a decent batch will cut the final thread of resistance."

She was slower in making the next batch, her headache making it harder to keep the mix of ingredients and the process straight in her mind. "Do you remember how it felt when you were drinking the last batch?"

"It felt like drinking a rough batch of tequila—like I'd swallowed fire and it was radiating out from my belly."

"Well, that's promising. Any numbness in your fingertips or pins and needles in your feet?"

"No, I don't think so."

She nodded and adjusted the mix, crying out as her fingertips grazed the element she had pulled from the kettle.

"How did you learn to do all this?" he asked, watching everything she did with keen interest.

"Self-taught," she mumbled, trying to measure out precise ratios without precise instruments.

"What motivated you to learn?"

She thought of Denavim. "That's a first type of secret," she murmured, too softly for Alcaeus to hear.

"When I was a kid, my brother was diagnosed with a rare, aggressive form of cancer." She tried to keep her voice even, letting the words flow but concentrating on the rohypnol cook. Denavim's face flashed in her memory, but she quickly pushed it away. It was hard to think about her brother without remembering the way he died. Hard to be reminded of his beautiful, *vibrant*, body that had just…shrivelled. As if all the fire had evaporated from it, leaving him empty even before he took his last breath. It was why she never spoke of him. Why her throat, even now, seized as she spilled her secret.

"It was a few years after my mum died." Her voice faltered at that part. It had been her truth for so long. *Not dead. Sent away.*

"Anyway, everyone was already, I don't know, *messed up*, and then we found out Denavim was dying. And that kind of just tipped us all over the edge. And then things got worse."

The smell of scorched leaves filled the room. Solari glanced up at the smoke detector and then over to the batteries on the bedside table. Alcaeus caught her gaze and she quickly turned back to the concoction. *Keep it together. Just a first type of secret, remember?*

"We all dealt with it differently. Denavim got distant; which was understandable given he was dying from a fucking shit disease."

Easy. Keep the blood pressure down. It was futile to try and stay calm; the same factors boosting Alcaeus' cognitive load were also boosting hers. She couldn't rationalise her emotions anymore.

"My dad got stupid." It hurt to say it, even though it was true. She had loved her dad, *still* loved her dad. But she also kind of hated him. "He sold everything he had, and didn't have, to DuPlessis; all for the promise of a delayed death sentence. Fifteen months. Traded everything—my mum's jewellery, our house, his life, my face—for fifteen months.

"Me, I got resourceful. At first I was looking for a cure, which was as stupid as it sounds. But, I was young and full of misplaced confidence and had nothing to lose. And my mind was thirsty — Hobart offered me nothing, and here was this thing that opened up my mind to a whole other world; a way to escape all the fucked-up shit. And there was *so* much shit: mutant reprisals in full swing, gangland wars at their most brutal, no food, no water, no electricity.

"Biochemistry was my ticket out of the city and into the Fringes, my ticket out of the helplessness and fear. It was so far removed from the senseless violence that suffocated everything else; I wasn't tearing down the world, I was creating it.

"It sounds ridiculous, right? It sounds downright fucking delusional. But that was me."

She slammed her hand against the outlet, shutting off the electricity to the element. The pain exploded through her exhaustion and torment. Biting down on her lip, she clenched her eyes shut and kept the tears at bay.

Stop it, Solari. Stop it now.

Taking a deep breath, she opened her eyes. Alcaeus was still sitting on the bed. It was as if he hadn't heard any of it, or that it didn't happen, or that none of it mattered. And then she saw his eyes, and she knew that it had happened and that he'd heard it and that it mattered.

Reaching into her jeans pocket, she retrieved the photo of Denavim and threw it on the bed next to Alcaeus. He picked it up and unfolded it, damp hair falling over his face as he leaned in to inspect it.

"And when my chemistry experiments didn't work," she said, letting the final words tumble out in a rush, "and Denavim died anyway, and Dad left me alone with his gangland debts, I figured I may as well put my newfound skills to use. So, I started cooking tetrahydron for Yevgeny Worcsulakz to pay off my own debts. And now he wants to put me in a metal basement as his personal cook or kill me. Who knows?"

She offered a weak smile to Alcaeus. He eyes were soft, but he didn't smile back.

"So, that's my secret," she murmured, finishing the cook and pouring the mix into a cup. *One of them, anyway.* She handed the cup to him, returned the photo of Denavim to her pocket, and took up her own position on the bed. "Time to hear yours."

***

"I know you came out of the enclave when you were seventeen," Solari said, her voice low and unbending; it was the key to drawing out the truth—letting the subject know their secrets were already known, that the questioner was not desperate and always in control. She used the insights she had gleaned from the last two hours of testing to push Alcaeus off-centre. "And I know you entered reluctantly."

He smiled, but she saw the truth of it; the smirk of an ugly memory and anxiety masquerading as bravado.

"Who was the first person you saw when you entered?" she asked, still keeping tight control of her voice.

Alcaeus' smile turned to a frown. It was an unexpected question. While every opening question had been different—to keep the element of surprise alive and avoid the build-up of habitual resistance—the sessions had, until now, focussed on life before the enclave.

"Cherise," he said finally, making the fateful decision to offer up what he no doubt thought, under the rohypnol's influence, was unimportant information.

"What did she look like?"

Alcaeus leant back against the bed frame, his eyes softening with the memory. "She was a firecracker from the start. Barking at me to slow down, put my hands in the air, take off my jacket. She grabbed the jacket before I could throw it to the ground, rifling through the pockets. It didn't matter, I hadn't brought it with me."

"Brought what with you?" she murmured, keeping her voice even, despite the racing of her heart at the way the story was unfolding, at the weight of authenticity it carried.

He paused, no doubt seeing the corner he had inadvertently maneuvered himself into. His eyes flitted away from Solari, his fingers tapping out a more hectic pattern on his thighs. Then he sighed. "The gun." His voice was low and gravelly. "I'd dropped it back at the house. I didn't need it anymore."

Solari's chest tightened; the strong, seemingly invincible Metallicari appeared to shrink in on himself, becoming the terrified seventeen-year-old arriving at the enclave gate.

"Why didn't you need it anymore?" Soft, calm.

"Because he was already dead." Alcaeus went still, a man utterly defeated.

"Who was already dead?"

"My dad. I'd shot my dad."

His face crumpled with all of the guilt and fear and regret that would have followed him in the intervening years. And then the truth, finally gifted an open door and gentle invitation, came rushing out.

"He was going to kill me. Said I was an abomination, a punishment sent from God, a monster spawned from the devil. He was drunk. It made him violent, but clumsy. I didn't want to shoot him, I just grabbed the gun before he could shoot me. I was already backing away, heading towards the door. But then he lunged at me, or I tripped; I don't know."

Tears fell freely down his face, weakening Solari's grip on her own emotions.

"I don't know. I just fired.

"At first, there was a lot of silence—as if the sound of the gun firing had sucked up all other sounds into a kind of sonic black hole. And then I heard my mother screaming. She was running; not for me, for my father. She tried to resuscitate him. I tried to pull her away but she just screamed at me. Over and over and over. 'Murderer!' 'Murderer!' 'Monster!'. Screaming all the hateful, spiteful names my father had tormented me with.

"And when she finally stopped screaming at me, she picked up the phone and called the police.

"I ran out of the house, threw the gun into the garden, hotwired my dad's car and headed straight to the enclave."

Solari scrubbed at the silent tears that ran down her cheeks, her throat burning with a rush of emotion that threatened to undo her.

Alcaeus looked up at her, his eyes full of grief and

vulnerability. "And that is the truth," he whispered, handing her the crumpled sheet of his written confession.

Solari fell into him, wrapping her wings and arms around his broad shoulders, a shield that was too late to protect him from his pain. He returned the embrace, trembling arms snaking under hers and folding around her back. Burying her head into the crook of his neck, she hid her tears in the cavern she had made around them. In the dark, hollow space, she could hear the quiet sobbing of the Metallicari.

She clasped him tighter and they stayed like that, bracing each other and themselves against the tide of pain that had rocked them since birth.

TWENTY-SEVEN

Solari woke with a start. The room was dark, no trace of sunlight edging around the curtains. Alcaeus slept beside her, his arm lying heavy over her exposed midsection. She reached out to trail a finger down his metal plates, letting the sharpened edges sing along her skin. How had she ever been repulsed by something so beautiful?

He started to stir and she pulled her hand away, straightening her shirt and sitting up.

"Solari?" he mumbled, voice husky with sleep.

"We need to go."

"Solari..." He grabbed her hand and pulled her back down. She fell reluctantly, bracing herself against his chest with her other hand. He smiled up at her, a quirk of the lips that reminded her of the summer solstice celebration back at the enclave.

His grin grew wider, tempting her to smile back. Daring her to. He tugged again at her hand and this time she fell the remainder of the way willingly.

"Hey," he murmured.

"Hey," she replied.

He kissed her, slow and casual, like they had all the time in the world. Like there was nothing more urgent than being there in that moment; nothing to run from, nothing to get to, nothing else to be but there with each other.

"We have to go," she murmured, pulling away from him.

He sighed and sat up. "OK, OK. Let's go."

***

There was a comfort in walking the darkened streets of a quiet town. For the briefest of moments, Solari allowed herself to let it all wash over her; the shadowed eaves of abandoned houses, the tin letterboxes that creaked with the drop in temperature, the rustle of dead leaves along the street.

All of that shattered when they turned the corner to the street where she had parked the truck. Vague figures hovered around the back, the trailer doors swinging in the night breeze.

Solari ran towards them before her brain could issue the caution. Alcaeus shouted out the warning as one of the figures cried out their own. Closer now, Solari could make out the two drivers—the young girl and the short, fat male—and their liberators. The other two figures were smaller, more petite. Their urgent cries of *'Hurry! Hurry!'* carried easily in the silence. Solari knew those voices; the last of the captives, the ones she had dropped off at the derelict petrol station ten kilometres south.

"What are you doing?" she screamed at them. "They were going to sell you to the North."

"Stay back, you fucking mutant."

Solari turned towards Alcaeus, and then stopped. They weren't screaming at the Metallicari, they were screaming at her.

Shaking off her surprise, she pushed herself to run faster. It was no use; they had the head start, and even if she did catch them, they had the numbers to overpower her.

"Solari!" Alcaeus called to her from the back of the truck, restraining one last figure who thrashed but was in no danger of escaping.

The supervisor.

"Bind him," she said, walking back to the truck.

"Solari." He frowned at her, communicating his reluctance and recrimination.

She rolled her eyes and sighed. "Fine," she said. "Just hold him, then. Tightly."

For a moment, she entertained the notion of using the leftover truth-serum she had cooked up and decanted into an empty plastic bottle the night before. But the fear that widened the supervisor's eyes told her it wouldn't be necessary.

"The second driver," she said, stepping into what little personal space he had left and pulling his face up to meet hers. "The small, fat one that swore too much—he's not your problem. He'll go find his nearest escape route and stay off the grid until DuPlessis calms down. Because you know he's going to be *pissed.*"

The stench of his infected leg wound filled her nostrils, her throat tightening with the urge to gag.

"No," she continued through gritted teeth. "Your problem is the girl. Because a girl that looks like that should be a captive in this little truck of yours, not the driver. Which means she's someone important. Not important enough to have some cushy role somewhere safe and opulent, but enough that she's learning the ropes of the business. And you know a girl like that is going to run straight to DuPlessis and spin whatever story she can think up that will shift the blame away from her and on to someone else.

"And that blame is going to land squarely on you. Because you were the one left behind, the one with the manky leg who can't run away. You'll be shouldered with the blame, and when they find you—because let's face it, there's no real escape route for you, is there?—you'll shoulder the punishment."

She paused, breathing shallowly through her mouth. Slowly, she reached up and dragged a fingertip down her own scar. "And we *all* know, DuPlessis' punishments are no slap on the wrist."

"What do you want?" the supervisor asked, his breathing ragged and hollow.

"We'll let you go," Solari said evenly, biting down the iota of guilt at seeing him deteriorate so rapidly. "You'll have a chance to get away—at least away from this truck and this town; I'll even give you a hundred dollars to help you on your way. And all you need to do is tell me where this truck was headed and how the product gets moved across the border."

He groaned, spluttering on a choking laugh that bubbled up his throat. "I don't know. That's the whole point; why we switch drivers at Evandale, you stupid bitch."

Clenching her fists at her side, Solari fought the urge to kick him in the shin and watch his superiority shatter in an explosion of pain. She glanced at Alcaeus, who maintained his grasp and gave her the slightest shake of his head.

"Well, then, what *do* you know?" she asked instead, keeping her voice calm. "Or should we take our chances in Youngtown finding someone who is more cooperative?"

His eyes widened at that, taking on the feral light of someone that had lost all leverage. "There's a place just outside the town where the drivers drop off the product and buyers come to inspect."

"Where?"

"I. Don't. Know. Why don't you just check the data logger?"

She looked up at Alcaeus. He shrugged. "Hold him," she said, scowling at the driver before making her way around to the truck's cabin.

Running her hands under the dash, she swore as her palms found nothing but smooth plastic. Her fingertip burned as she jammed the nail into the grooves of the fuse box panel to loosen it. And swore again when she found nothing.

"Where are you?" she muttered, glancing around the small space, hands reaching into the glove box and centre console, pulling down the sun visors.

"Fuck, fuck, fuck." She slammed her hand down on the seat. "Ask him where the logger is," she called to Alcaeus.

"He doesn't know," he called back after a minute. But she already knew that. Drivers knowing where the data logger was located defeated the purpose of having one.

She rested her head on the dashboard and stifled the scream that was building in her chest.

Fuck my life. Fuck my life. Why had she thought this situation would be any different? Why had she dared to dream that this time, *this time*, she would be dealt some average cards instead of the usual fucked up royal routine of pain and suffering and torture?

She slammed her hand down on the dash, and again, beating down on it, embracing the pain. Again and again. Hammering. And when the hammering no longer satisfied, she turned to short punches at the steering wheel, the radio, any spare space open for attack.

Skin tore, splitting at the knuckles as plastic shattered beneath the force. She pressed her eyes shut, holding back the hot tears by sheer force and stubborn will. Slowly, she unclenched her fist, only opening her eyes when her breath returned to normal.

And then, she saw it. Behind the broken plastic of the air conditioner vent. The data logger.

TWENTY-EIGHT

Youngtown. In Solari's imagination it had been more militarised, less chaotic.

It was close to fifteen years since she had last visited a border town. When she had been thirteen years' old, just after Denavim had been diagnosed and her father had run out of options, they'd all bundled into the car and driven to Westbury, the largest town in the shadow of the wall.

Every Saturday, before her father's shift at the rail terminal, they had made the journey north. Solari had waited in the car with Denavim, playing simple games of eye-spy and dragon-names, even though they were too old for them, while their dad, with his wearied posture and deepening frown-lines, had bribed guards to smuggle medicine from the North.

Not that they ever did. They'd take his money, but when he would return the next week there were never any life-saving pills waiting for him.

That was back when you could still approach the wall. Back when it had been more a fence than the impenetrable concrete barrier it was now.

"That one?" Alcaeus' voice broke into her thoughts. He pointed to a mediocre-looking hotel on the next corner. It, like every other building they had seen in Youngtown, was plastered with DuPlessis' orange anchors, but there wasn't much activity around its entry and no cars were parked out the front.

She shrugged. "We've got no better option. And it's only for a week."

The data logger had given them the general vicinity of the drop-off point; they had passed it on the way into town—two blocks of squat, single-storey buildings on the southern outskirts. It was a good start, but they would need to wait until the next delivery if they were to pinpoint the exact location. In the meantime, they'd just have to wait.

"What do you want to do with the car?" Alcaeus asked, frowning at the orange Torana they had stolen from outside the motel. For all his aversion to violence, the Metallicari had been surprisingly quick to help her lift the car.

Pulling her flak jacket around her shoulders and tightening the flannel shirt at her waist, she folded her wings in hard and suppressed the shivers that had plagued her since leaving behind the injured driver and the truck. Leaving the car so close might create problems; but if they needed a quick getaway, they would do better in a car than on foot.

"Leave it," she said, glancing around. "And grab what you can. I think I saw a go-bag in the back."

Armed with the bag, a blanket, the left-over rohypnol, and an assortment of protein bars and chip packets, they left the car behind and strode across the street to the hotel. Solari ducked her head to avoid eye contact with the few people loitering around. As her hand reached for the door, someone came stumbling out, crashed into her and sent her falling back into Alcaeus.

The culprit, a twenty-something male reeking of alcohol, leered at her, his gaze tracking slowly over body. And then his gaze found Alcaeus and the leer turned to a scowl. "What are you looking at?" he slurred, brushing clumsily past Solari to push at Alcaeus' chest.

Solari looked around quickly, scanning the street for those seduced by the promise of a fight. In a town like this, there were three types of people: those with their heads down and noses out of trouble; those with their fingers in the forbidden pie, but at arm's length and with eyes averted; and those with their faces so firmly planted in the pie that their lips bled red with the cherries and their tongues screamed for the taste of another before they had finished the first.

Finding no-one looking to intervene, she barrelled into the drunken male, pushing past him and into the hotel, pulling Alcaeus with her. Her shoulder ached as it slammed into the door, her face flushing with the unexpected change in temperature as she stumbled into the room beyond.

It took a while for Solari to overcome her disorientation. The space was larger than had appeared likely from the outside, stretching around a central bar lit by low-hanging bulbs. Bottles of vintage spirits smuggled in from the North sat among the uglier bottles of moonshine liquor, all of them sparkling in the golden light.

And yet, despite the arresting interior, the attention of the bar's patrons was not directed to the bar or its libations, but to the entertainment on offer. Gilded cages, ornate and glittering, dotted the landscape. Rising floor to ceiling, they acted like suns; pulling the bar's patrons into a hyperactive orbit. And inside every one of them languished a mutant.

Except, they were not really languishing. While their dead eyes screamed their despair and desperation, they writhed with a contrived passion that drew the glazed stares and frequent catcalls of their audience.

Beside her, Solari felt Alcaeus baulk and go rigid. Instinctively, she grabbed his hand and pulled him closer, forced him to look at her, to contribute to the illusion of a distracted couple. Because looking at each other was better than getting caught staring at the insanity around them.

"Solari—" he whispered, low and harsh.

She shook her head, reaching up to press a finger against his lips. *Not here, not now.* Her wings felt like a fire was racing along their membranes; the urge to unfurl them and shake off the tremors were tempered only by the pathetic forms before her, once exotic, now a caricature.

Schooling her features into nonchalance, Solari strode to the bar. "We need a room," she shouted above the noise.

The bartender, an older woman with platinum-blonde hair and heavy makeup, nodded and reached for a key. "One-thirty," she yelled back. "Do you want anything sent up?" Her eyes flicked over to the mutants in their cages.

Solari fought the urge to grit her teeth, sliding the notes from the driver's wallet over the counter. "Maybe another time."

The woman winked and threw the keys in the air. Solari reached for them, but Alcaeus plucked them mid-arc.

"I got this beautiful," he murmured. Solari heard the strain in it. She turned to him; he was smiling at the bartender, but every other muscle in his body was tense.

Holy hell, this will not end well.

"Let's not waste any time, then, lover," she replied, grabbing at his shirt and pulling him away from the bar.

***

Solari stared at the wall of their hotel room, with its peeling, patterned paper depicting an idyllic, romanticised concept of nature: flowers crowned with full petals, tightly shaped pastel buds, and tendrils of green vines in symmetrical rows—everything the Fringes was not. She sat cross-legged on the bed, her flak jacket underneath her like a barrier between her and whatever nasties had been left behind on the sheets, and wondered if nature had ever been so submissive and ordered.

The room was quiet without Alcaeus, the music from the bar downstairs reduced to a muffled hum and low rumble of beats, giving time all the opportunity it needed to torment her with its dour plodding. Earlier, they had reached the quick and easy conclusion that it would be better for Alcaeus to run some brief reconnaissance on his own; the two of them together would attract too much attention and Solari, with her distinctive scar, was too recognisable. Besides, with just the one gun between them, a second person would provide no additional benefit and only add distraction.

Still, handing over the pistol had not been easy. She had hesitated, forcing Alcaeus to meet her gaze before she let him take it from her grasp. *"It's OK, Solari—I'll bring it back."* As his hand slipped from hers, she knew her hesitation wasn't concern about him not returning with the gun, but about him not returning at all.

In the first hour, she kept herself distracted by rifling through the go-bag, unloading the makeshift rohypnol and collection of items from her flak jacket, and trying to figure out a way to pull them all together into a coherent plan. That had lasted twenty minutes before she gave up and took up watch beside the window instead.

Two hours of staring at the quiet streetscape had sent her straight to the mini-bar. Another two hours had left her with an empty mini-bar, and back to staring at the wallpaper.

She fidgeted, digging fingernails in under the skin of other fingernails, pressing and pinching, letting the pain shred the boredom. And the anxiety.

Her gaze slid from the wall to the door. She scrambled off the bed, folded her wings into the small of her back, tied the flannel shirt around her waist, and slung on her jacket. Shaking her head at the recklessness of it, but needing to kill her boredom, she locked the door behind her and headed downstairs to the bar.

The music that had been a muffled groan upstairs exploded around her. There were more people now, drunken and stupefied and totally enraptured by the mutants in cages. Reptilia dominated the display, their iridescent scales finer and more fragile than Alcaeus' metal plates, but Osteoclasta and Arachnidia also featured. Some were of a similar age as Solari, but most were older. And all were damaged. Scarred, burned, hobbled, misshapen; these were the rejects, the ones that had never made it beyond the wall. Too flawed to satisfy the tastes of the North, just freaky enough to satisfy the depravities of the South.

Solari took a seat at the bar, sweating in her heavy jacket and the flannel around her waist, but tightening them around her nonetheless.

"What can I get you, love?" the bartender asked, the same one who had handed over the room key.

"Tequila," she said, feeling the rasp in her voice as she strained to be heard over the music.

The platinum blonde nodded and pulled a glass from underneath the countertop. Determined not to look over her shoulder, Solari focussed instead on the wall behind the bar.

Bottles glittered in the warm light, stacked on glass shelves that seemed to disappear. Photographs plastered the glass splashback like a retro form of graffiti; bartenders smiling and pulling lewd poses, patrons crowding around each other in a moment of spontaneity, and mutants. Arachnidia serving drinks with chelicerae gleaming, Osteoclasta dancing in cages, Reptilia with strained smiles perching on patron's laps.

It was almost as bad as watching the spectacle behind her. Solari ducked her head, staring instead at the uneven fists in her lap, looking up only when the bartender slid a shot glass of tequila over the bar to her.

And then she saw it. A photograph at the far edge of the collection, faded with time and torn at the corners. A group of five twenty-somethings grinning in the foreground, drinks raised and grins plastered. And behind them, in one of the gilded cages, a Reptilia grabbing at the bars, resignation clearly etched on her face.

Christianne's face. Her mother.

TWENTY-NINE

Her drink forgotten, Solari spun around to confront the full spectacle of the room, her gaze searching through the crowd to the gilded cages. Searching for her mother.

"Looking for one in particular?" the bartender called, drawing Solari's attention back. "You and your man—did he send you down with a specific request, or do you get to choose the pleasure?"

"My choice," Solari said, her heart fluttering in a vice-grip.

"What takes your fancy? We have—"

"I want her," Solari interrupted, pointing past the bartender to the photo of her mother. "The one at the far edge; the Reptilia with the sad eyes."

There was a slight hesitation from the bartender before she plucked the photograph from the wall. "There's something about her, isn't there? Something that draws the eye…"

"How much for her?" Solari's voice tightened with urgency.

The bartender laughed and replaced the photo, filling the empty space it left behind. "That one is not for sale."

"I have money to pay," Solari said, snapping her gaze to the bartender. "I can pay double what you ask."

"I'm not asking for anything. That one is not for sale." The conversation was over, the bartender moving away to serve another group of patrons clamouring for her attention.

"Where is she?" Solari shouted above the noise, risking the

puzzled glances of the patrons and the irritation of the bartender.

Easy, the contrary voice in her mind whispered. *Don't show too much interest, don't encourage suspicion.* She struggled to heed the words with her desperate hope shouting over them.

"She's not here," the bartender called back. "Choose another."

"Where is she?"

"She's gone. If you want a mutant, you'll need to choose another."

Around her, the music and shouting and whistling and jeering drowned out her thundering heart. She tuned back to the chaos and forced her gaze to rise above the crowd to the elevated cages; not searching for her mother—that would have to come later. "Give me her, then," she shouted again, pointing to an Osteoclasta in the farthest cage.

The soft lighting cast into sharp focus the even sharper bones that jutted from the mutant's forehead and temples; a grotesque tiara to match the bone spikes that erupted from her collarbone. She was older than the rest, maybe ten years older than Solari—not as old as her mother, but maybe old enough to have met her.

The bartender glanced over and grinned. "You have a thing for vintage females, don't you? Do you want her now or should I send her up to your room?"

"To the room," Solari replied, dropping a one-hundred-dollar bill on the bar and standing up.

"I'll send her up in twenty minutes," the bartender said, snatching up the bill and turning it over in the light. "She'll tell you the rules."

Solari nodded and slammed a fifty-dollar bill down. "Tell her to bring the photo."

The bartender nodded and turned away, pushing the one-hundred-dollar bill into the till and the fifty into her bra.

***

The Osteoclasta entered the room with unexpected grace, the bone tiara less grotesque and more commanding now that she was stripped away from the drunken debauchery of the bar. The door

196

closed behind her with a subtle click and her eyes swept the room with an unexpected confidence.

"I was told there would be a gentleman?" Her voice was low and syrupy.

"No gentleman," Solari replied, her gaze drawn to the cuffs linking the Osteoclasta's wrists together. "And you won't need those."

"They're for your protection," the mutant demurred, bowing her head.

Solari took a deep breath and removed the flannel shirt and jacket, still unsure whether this was the right move. Her hand gripped the shard of mirror she had secreted into her waistband and she unfolded her wings.

"I don't need protection."

The Osteoclasta's eyes widened, accentuating the lines on her face that were hidden in the dim light of the bar. And then they narrowed. She was not intimidated, or impressed, or scared. She was suspicious. "What is this?"

"Did you bring the photograph?"

The Osteoclasta frowned and reached with her cuffed hands into the pockets of her leather pants to retrieve it. Solari snatched at the square of paper before the mutant could pull it back.

"Who is he? Your dad? Husband?"

"Huh?" Solari was too distracted by seeing the photograph up close. There in the fluorescent light of the room, she could see her mother's face more clearly. The photo wasn't as old as she had thought, maybe taken within the last five years.

"The photograph," the Osteoclasta replied. "Which man is yours?"

Solari looked up. The Osteoclasta's voice had turned hard.

"Did he leave you when you turned mutant? People can be callous like that..."

"I'm not interested in the men," Solari said, sitting down on the edge of the bed. "I'm interested in the Reptilia. In Christianne. Did you know her?"

"How do you know that name?"

"It doesn't matter how *I* know it, it matters that *you* know it.

Do you know where she is?"

The Osteoclasta stared at her, gaze twitching from Solari's eyes to her wings, lips pursed and frown deepening. "You're too late."

"Too late for what? What happened to her?" Solari persisted, unable to keep the urgency from her voice or her wings from fluttering. It was all she could do to not glance at the wardrobe where the last of the truth serum was stashed. It was an option, for later perhaps—though her gut still twisted at the thought of more violence.

"She's gone." There was a finality in the Osteoclasta's tone that landed like a sucker punch. Solari felt the urgency drain from her body and her wings finally fell silent. She'd been foolish; stupid to let herself hope.

"Christianne didn't belong here," the Osteoclasta continued. "This place is hard. Not difficult hard—although it is that, too—but like an egg falling on concrete hard. Or a glacier grinding down a continent hard. It is brutal, and unforgiving, and violent. It is *hard*. And Christianne wasn't hard. Even after all her years here, she never became hard."

"What happened to her?"

The Osteoclasta walked over to the desk and perched on its edge. "I came to Youngtown when I was thirteen; whatever softness I had when I arrived was beaten out of me early. Christianne arrived three or four years later. She was trying to get to the North, like most of the mutants you see downstairs. And she had a chance, too—the North like their mutants soft, pliable, *genteel*. They make for better ornaments.

"So she went looking for the transfer point, where the Northern buyers collect their pretty ones for the sex trade. There's always been rumours that they occasionally purchase mutants as well, but Christianne was rejected like the rest of them—maybe she had some deformity she kept hidden between her legs, maybe they just weren't interested in Reptilia anymore, and who could blame them? There's always been hundreds of them.

"And so, she ended up here. Not that she didn't try to escape—to the North, back to the Enclave, back to Hobart.

Youngtown didn't beat the softness out of her, but, in the end, it beat out any hope of future escape."

Solari's heart skipped a beat. "She's still here?" Maybe she had misunderstood when the Osteoclasta had said that she was too late, that Christianne was 'gone'. Maybe her mother was in detention, or in recovery from whatever damage her latest patron had inflicted. Both options made her stomach churn, but beneath the rage and revulsion flickered hope.

"No," the Osteoclasta replied.

"Is she dead?" Solair's chest clenched with the effort of asking. She had suffered injuries before—at the hand of Anders; out in the Fringes; generally running from whatever shit Hobart threw at her—and she knew that the worst kind of injuries were the ones that ripped open old scars, then healed, then ripped them open anew.

"Maybe," the Osteoclasta replied. "Probably. I don't know."

"What do you mean, you don't know?" Solari said, acid in her voice. "She was here, you knew her. You said she didn't escape. What else is there?"

The Osteoclasta shrugged. "She was bought."

THIRTY

"Solari? Solari!"

Alcaeus' voice floated to her in the darkness, just like it had back in the enclave.

"Solari, hey, hey, hey. Come on beautiful, open your eyes for me."

Slowly, her eyelids prised apart, blinking in the bright light of the room. And there he was, crouched down on the floor, leaning over her, eyes searching hers.

"Hey, it's OK. I got you." His arms reached under and gently lifted her to sitting. "Want to tell me what happened?"

The pain ricocheting in her skull was dampened only by the fire in her hands. Disorientated, time seemed to skip out of sequence, and thoughts of Anders flashed bright and fresh in her memory. She looked down at her hands. *Old wounds ripped open.*

Everything fell back into place and she remembered—the Osteoclasta, the bottle of tequila she ordered to the room, punching the walls til she bled and passed out.

"I think my mum is still alive," she mumbled, the words slurring with the alcohol still lacing her brain.

"OK, we can get to that later. Who did this to you?"

She shook her head, moaned as the pain exploded behind her eyes. "No-one. I just needed… I just couldn't…"

Alcaeus frowned at her, his gaze flicking to the blood-stained holes in the wall. "OK," he said gently, "up you get."

In one smooth motion he slid his arms around her waist and lifted her up. The room spun and she closed her eyes as nausea swelled in her belly. Blood thrummed in her ears, the sound of Alcaeus' footfalls suddenly lost against the sound of rain.

Warm water hit her hair and trickled across her wings. She shivered as her boots and jeans were removed, her skin hitting the still-cool tiles of the shower. Against the rush of water, she heard cotton tearing, felt it being pulled from her slick skin.

She rested against the shower wall at her back and imagined the water washing away all the shit that had clung to her life since…*since forever.*

"My mum died when I was a baby. That was what everyone told me." The words tumbled out, drunken and raw. They shredded her insides, but she didn't stop. "My dad, my aunty. They told me she was dead. But they lied; they drugged her and shipped her off to the enclave."

"The Reptilia you were looking for," Alcaeus said.

"I thought she was dead. And then I thought she was in the enclave. And then in the North. And now I know she came here. She came here and she was beaten and sold."

"Sold to who?"

"I don't know. I don't know." She repeated the words over and over, burying her head in her hands to hide from Alcaeus' concern, and letting the water drown out the voice of her growing despair.

***

"So what do we do now?" Alcaeus asked around a mouthful of greasy pad thai.

They sat together on the bed, knees touching, boxes of noodles on their laps. Solari, dressed only in a towel and an oversized trench coat salvaged from the go-bag, tapped her chopstick against her lips. The noodles, bought from a street vendor in the heart of Youngtown, were cold—forgotten while Solari sobered up in the shower—but still the best thing she had eaten since the midday feast she and Alcaeus had shared in the enclave.

"The Osteoclasta said that most of the mutants downstairs were rejects from Northern buyers. Maybe we could get one of them to talk?"

"Could work," Alcaeus replied. "They wouldn't know the exact location—if they did, every mutant in the Southern Reaches would be flocking there. But, they would have seen the key players, and maybe that's the more important information."

Solari took a bite of her noodles, her tongue savouring the taste while her stomach roared its protest. Her fragile mind tried to work through the options, grinding against the throes of a wicked hangover. "We'd have to play it smart. These mutants are already beaten down, they're not going to risk pissing off someone who can beat them down further."

Alcaeus nodded and stared at the door. "Or worse," he said, frowning. "They find some leverage in telling that someone that someone else is looking for them."

The thought pulled them both into silence. If they were found out before they discovered how to reach the North, they would lose any hope of breaching the wall. They would likely lose their lives.

"We'll need to find someone green," Solari said. "Someone who's still bitter about being rejected and who doesn't know how dangerous it is to share what they know."

"It won't be enough. We'll need to give them an incentive."

Solari glanced to the wardrobe where the wallet full of dwindling cash was nestled in amongst their other, less profitable, items.

"We'll have to take them with us, won't we?" she said. "We'll have to smuggle them across the wall."

Alcaeus nodded and chewed his lip. "We'd better find someone we can trust, then."

Solari laughed, but it lacked any joy and sent lightning bolts to her skull. She pressed her hands to her temples. "I guess tomorrow we go on a bar crawl and start looking."

The sound of the bar downstairs rumbled softly into the silence that followed. In the quiet, it was harder to keep at bay the questions circled in her mind. Her broken, incoherent, fragile mind.

How did I get here? In this room? With this man, and these wings, and the blood of a dead girl and a dying man on my clothes? With a photo of my dead brother in my pocket and another of my dead mother who is very much alive…

Tears sprang to her eyes, unbidden and unwelcomed. She scrubbed at them, but the effort of stopping more tears from forming put fire in her chest and sandpaper in her throat.

The bed creaked as Alcaeus moved the noodle boxes to the bedside table. She waited for him to reach out, to touch her, to say something. But he just sat there, still and quiet, and gave her the space and time to cry.

"It's all just so *fucked up*," she rasped. "There are no good options, no right decisions, no way out of this fucking, fucked-up life."

She stared at him, daring him to disagree, desperate for him to agree. He remained silent.

"Why aren't you saying anything?" she shouted. "Why are you just sitting there? Damn it, Alcaeus. Say something. *Do* something."

He didn't flinch, just stared back with equal intensity. "What do you want me to say, Solari? What do you want me to do?"

"I don't want you to do anything." It came out spiteful, the violence still leaching from her insides. "I don't want you to do anything," she said again; less angry, but still intense. And, she meant it—she didn't want him to do anything; *she* wanted to do something. She was tired of waiting, of only ever reacting, of constantly running and clawing her way through life and only ever feeling fear.

Solari wiped away the last residues of tears and reached for Alcaeus.

"What are we doing, Solari?" he murmured as she pulled him to her and lifted his shirt.

"We're finishing what we started at the motel."

***

The streets of Youngtown took on a carnival atmosphere at night.

The beacons on the border wall ramparts were obliterated by the strings of lanterns that hung between buildings and the light that streamed from unshuttered windows. Music escaped from doorways as patrons passed each other in a strange trade of those wanting in and those wanting out, the melodies interrupted by rough voices that shouted obscenities and promises of violence.

Solari gripped Alcaeus' hand, their public display of intimacy offering very real comfort. He squeezed back, a quick pulse. Together they strode along the uneven footpath, weaving around the damaged, deranged, and drunk, past the smell of stale urine and fresh vomit seeping from dark corners and alleyways.

Biting down on her cheek provided Solari a temporary distraction; the pain drawing her focus inwards, the flash of blood along her tongue bright and bitter.

It was all DuPlessis' influence. Whereas Worcsulakz was all sharp edges and business, DuPlessis thought himself Dionysus reincarnate; just as likely to drown you in wine as to splatter your brains on a wall.

"We're running out of options," Alcaeus whispered to her.

Solari grit her teeth and kept her head down. They had spent the last three nights on these 'pub crawls', making their way to the town's hotels, pubs, bars, and brothels—sometimes together, sometimes separately, but always spread out over a few hours and multiple blocks to avoid suspicion. Alcaeus had made small talk with the other patrons, while Solari had chatted with the bartenders. All for nothing—the most recent mutant in Youngtown still had two years' worth of beatings behind him.

"Solari. Any more places and we'll start attracting attention."

She hated that he was right. Looking up, she scanned the nearby buildings—a bar on the far corner, a brothel four doors down on the other side.

"OK, OK. One last go. You take the bar, I take the brothel. Keep to yourself as much as you can. I'll meet you back at the hotel."

He grimaced but nodded. "Fine. But stay safe."

Before he could walk away, she reached out and grabbed his hand. Just briefly, just to give it a squeeze. He raised an eyebrow, but squeezed back, the hint of a smile appearing right before the worry returned. She flashed her own reassuring smile and let go of his hand, watching as he took his first tentative steps towards the hotel.

It was easy to forget that this was his first real foray into the world of non-mutants in over a decade. To forget that there was nothing tethering their fates together, not really, not anymore. Nothing to stop him from taking their stolen car and driving it to the Second Enclave further south, where he could find a new home and friends and safety.

Across the street, someone was shouting. Solari risked a glance, turning in time to see the first punch being thrown. The victim, a younger male with a pinched face, stumbled backwards. Pulling his beanie further down his forehead, he roared and launched at his attacker. The older male laughed, set his feet wide and shifted his body just slightly at an angle.

Solari's breath caught. The muscular frame and closely-shorn head, complete with tattoos running from skull to elbow, were all too familiar. *Scotty.*

She turned away quickly, hiding her face and her scar in the shadows. Heading back to the hotel would take her away from the fight and from Scotty, but risked him seeing and following. Reluctantly, she stepped towards the brothel, keeping her body and face angled away from the commotion.

Heart hammering away in her chest, she walked as fast as she could without shifting the crowd's attention. She broke into a jog for the last few metres, her hands slamming against the door as she pushed through, still waiting for the sound of Scotty's voice to ring out behind her.

The door crashed back into place, the sound echoing in the unnaturally quiet room and forcing Solari to stop thinking about the tattooed skull from her past and pay attention to where she was and what she needed to do.

Unlike the other brothels she had checked in the last few days, this one was empty—simply a small room painted in muted colours and furnished with soft lighting and sparse adornments: a few armchairs, a side table with an expensive-looking lamp, a dark-grey chaise.

"I think you may be in the wrong place," a deep voice murmured, drawing Solari's gaze to a leather sofa in the recess behind her and the impeccably-dressed man who reclined on it. He was a few years older than her, but showed no signs of life's torment; everything about him was beautiful. Perfect features in tailored threads—it all screamed money. And the North.

"What place would that be?" she asked, pulling at the dirty flak jacket before she could help herself.

"I'm sorry, but I must ask you to leave. If you are looking to indulge in mutant delights, there are more affordable establishments a few blocks away."

"I have money." She reached into her pocket to retrieve the wallet.

"Not enough," he replied, the slightest hint of exasperation tinging his words.

Solari pulled the notes from the inside fold of the wallet.

"Two hours with our greenest recruit costs three-thousand dollars."

"How green are we talking?" she asked, stashing the notes and the wallet back into her pocket.

"Three weeks."

That will work.

"And what's the tenure of your most experienced recruit?"

"She's not an option."

"I can get the money, if—"

"You can't get the money. Even if under that dirty flak jacket you were dripping with diamonds, it wouldn't matter. She is made available exclusively to our VIP guests. Which you are not. And, now, I must really ask you to leave."

Solari nodded and held her hands up in mock submission. "Alright. I can tell when I've overstayed my welcome. I'll come back when my money and my clothes are more to your liking."

He smiled—all business, no joy—and stepped past her to open the door. "I look forward to that."

***

After leaving the brothel, Solari had taken the long way back to the hotel, circling around the block in case Scotty and his victim were still putting on a show. Even with the detour, she knew Alcaeus would still be an hour or two away, and she didn't have the patience to wait before hatching her next plan.

"You want a repeat performance by Erena?" the bartender shouted above the noise. "She said you weren't that enthusiastic about her."

Solari ignored the Osteoclasta dancing in the corner and turned her attention to the bartender.

"I thought I'd change it up a little," she shouted back. "My husband prefers them younger, more petite. One that looks more like me."

The woman behind the bar laughed. "Men are so boring! With all that freakishness on offer and all he want is a mutant version of you."

Solari smiled back, her lips tense at the edges. *He already has that.* "What about her?" she said, pointing over to a Reptilia who approximated her height and build.

"She's too fair, no?" the bartender asked.

"If I slip you an extra fifty, can you dye her hair?"

The bartender grinned, the seduction of more money no doubt setting the sparkle to her eyes. "That is definitely possible."

"And she needs to lose the outfit. I want her to wear something classy."

"That will be extra, of course."

"Of course. How soon can you arrange it?"

"I'll get my delivery courier to pick something up from Hobart. He should be here tomorrow evening."

Solari nodded and slid over five-hundred dollars, leaving just over a hundred dollars' worth of notes in the wallet—enough to last until she could set in motion the next step of the plan. "Tell him he needs to get a dress, backless, with a coat and some nice shoes. Something sophisticated, that even a Northerner would find appealing. Something distracting, something that screams money and style."

"So, you want a mutant that looks like you, but on the other hand looks nothing like you."

Standing up, Solari drained the last of her tequila and set the glass back down. "Every husband's dream, right?"

"Not mine," the bartender called after her as Solari took her leave. "Mine wants some A-grade hooch from the North."

Solari shook her head and kept walking. "Everyone wants something from the North."

THIRTY-ONE

"I hope your visit was more successful than mine," Alcaeus said, stepping into the room and locking the door behind him.

"A little," Solari replied, glancing over from her position at the window. "We need to sell the car."

"Well, that's going to be a little difficult." He perched on the end of the bed and kicked off his shoes. "Considering it's not ours to sell."

"How much do you think someone would be willing to pay for a stolen car?"

She joined him on the bed, flopping back so that her feet hovered just above the ground and her back sank into the mattress. Overhead, the ceiling was spidered with hairline cracks—a hundred different pathways diverging from each other and colliding back together; lives she could have had, options she could have taken, endings she could have explored.

"Nine hundred, maybe a thousand?" Alcaeus looked over at her. "But why are we selling it? Won't we need it in case the whole plan goes to hell, which, given our track record, seems likely? We can still go the Second Enclave, Solari."

She closed her eyes and shook her head. "The enclaves won't protect us against DuPlessis now that he knows he's looking for two mutants, we need to go north."

"Then maybe we stock up and try to survive Liawanee."

She sat up. "No. Leaving is too risky—being on the road, needing to stop for fuel and food, chancing the car to make the journey—too much can go wrong. Staying is our best option."

"Fine, but why do we need to sell the car?"

"The brothel I went to—it's different to the others. Exclusive. There's a mutant there—someone who's only been there for three weeks. I need to see them."

"You want to sell the car and pay three thousand dollars to see a mutant that may say no to your proposition, or worse, turn you over to DuPlessis?"

Solari nodded.

"Just how exclusive is this place?"

"They have a waiting room full of furniture that costs more than the car, an escort who I'm pretty sure is actually from the North, and mutants that are for the sole privilege of VIPs."

"Why would they have an escort from the North?" Alcaeus stood up and walked to the window.

"Why would they have VIPs?" Solari asked, flopping back down on the bed.

"Because they can charge more."

"Yeah, but who has that kind of cash? Not the locals. Or the small-time delivery couriers." She thought of Scotty, who no doubt had arrived in Youngtown as a courier, and wondered how his fight ended. *Hopefully with a concussion. Or better yet, a dead body.* She had enough problems, she didn't need to add him to the list. Again.

"DuPlessis and his deputies?" Alcaeus asked.

"Maybe. But why would they come here? Why bother? They send their couriers for a reason—this place is a bigger shit-hole than Hobart."

"I don't get it, then."

"You don't need to get it." The words came out too harsh. "Sorry. It's been a bit..."

"Insane," Alcaeus finished for her.

"Yes." She shot him a grateful smile. "What I meant to say, is that we don't need to know *who* goes there, we just need to find a way to get the money for *us* to go there."

Alcaeus shook his head. "Disagree. You could be walking into anything. Anyone. We need to run surveillance, see who turns up."

"Fine. You *run surveillance* while I figure out how to sell a stolen car for three thousand dollars."

They stared at each other in a silent stand-off.

"You're impossibly stubborn, you know that?" he finally said, breaking the deadlock.

"Maybe not *impossibly*."

"You know," he murmured, scratching his nails along his metal plates. "You might not have to *sell* the car to get the money."

"You want me to courier tourists around for a few extra bucks?" she said with light sarcasm. "We'd be here for decades."

"No," he said, smiling over at her. "I was just thinking, if you can't trade for it, and you can't beg for it, maybe you could gamble for it…"

THIRTY-TWO

In the end, Solari convinced Alcaeus that both of them should go to the gambling den six blocks from the hotel. There were other dens that were in the less shady parts of town, but they were more crowded—and being identified was a bigger risk than being stabbed. Alcaeus had wanted to go alone, but she was having none of it, and neither of them wanted to waste more time arguing about it.

"First sign of trouble, we run." Alcaeus looked intimidating, but Solari had come to recognise his tells, and it was clear to her that he was just anxious.

She walked beside him, her hand in his, the act more familiar than a pretence now. The streets were still relatively quiet, but sometimes the quiet was more dangerous. "Just don't go all trigger-happy on me," she murmured. "We run at the first sign of *real* trouble, not just someone looking at us sideways or mangling the English language with their naughty words."

Alcaeus rolled his eyes and barked a short laugh. "Had you even played poker before the enclave?"

"No," she admitted, her wings rustling under the flak jacket. "But I used to watch old games on TV back in Hobart." *When the power was on and the tetrahydron was curing.*

Alcaeus barked another laugh.

"Anyway," Solari said, ignoring him, "from what I've seen of poker, it's all about reading people — and I'm really good at that."

"Oh, yeah?" Alcaeus murmured.

"Yeah," she said, glancing sideways at him. "Like how I can tell that, right now, you are thinking 'I should just snatch those keys from her flak jacket and drive us both south'."

"Alright, smart-arse," Alcaeus said, coming to a stop outside a group of four-storey, red-bricked buildings that reminded Solari of her childhood home in Richmond. The lack of any orange anchors was reassuring. "Let's go see you hustle."

A gaudy neon sign directed them away from the street and down a flight of concrete stairs accessed via a dark and narrow alley. At the bottom, their progress was halted by a long counter protected by thick plexi-glass. Two bouncers stood either side of the narrow gap between the counter and the side wall, and a large sign spelt out the gambling den's rules in thick, black lettering: NO GUNS. NO FIGHTS. NO REFUNDS.

Even from her restricted viewpoint, Solari could see the sprawl of the gambling den beyond. Despite the dingy accommodation, the tables were set up to be evenly spaced and every table had a minimum of four players. The gambling would be serious.

Solari returned her gaze to the barrier that separated her from the action. An older woman wearing fancy clothing that frayed at the edges threw a fistful of jewellery into the deposit tray. Behind the glass, the attendant sorted through it before pushing a stack of multi-coloured chips back through the return. The woman made a show of grumbling about the exchange rate, but picked up the chips and barged past the bouncers.

"Next," the attendant called, beckoning Solari and Alcaeus closer. "Cash or product?"

"Product," Solari said, holding up the keys.

"Make and model?"

"Um, it's an orange Torana. Maybe 1970s."

"Do you have the papers?"

Solari paused, just briefly. "No."

The attendant didn't blink. "Rego number?"

"XHZ-175."

"Current location?"

"We parked it a block away. On the corner of Raglan Street."

The attendant picked up a walkie-talkie and patched through a call with the information, her green-lacquered fingernails tapping against the plastic while she waited for the response. "Take a seat," she said to Solari, inclining her head to the wall behind them where a row of plastic seats was bolted to the floor.

Her wings fluttered against their constraints as she waited, her nerves made worse by Alcaeus's constant fidgeting. The Metallicari struggled to stay still, his hands flitting over and about each other as his knees bounced up and down. Solari tuned him out, focusing instead on the scene beyond the plexi-glass. She counted six bouncers, not including the two that barred the entry to the gambling den.

With her nerves settling into a tolerable hum of static, she shifted her scrutiny from the security detail to the tables, making a mental note of the players and their movements—who frowned, who smiled, who slouched; who was louder than they needed to be; who was drinking too much; and who frequented the counter to exchange more money and jewellery for chips.

By the time the spotter patched a call back to the attendant, Solari had already picked her target. With no hesitation, she collected the fifteen-hundred dollars' worth of chips, gave half to Alcaeus, and moved past the bouncers with only one table in her sights.

She smiled a little as she took an empty seat, bringing the table's population up to five players. In her peripheral vision, she watched Alcaeus sit down at a neighbouring table; close enough to keep an eye on things and to raise the signal if they needed to leave. *Don't get trigger happy,* she whispered to him in her mind, and then blocked him out of her focus.

"New player at the table," the dealer said, smiling as he shuffled the cards. He was easily in his late-sixties, grey hair and deep wrinkles betraying a hard life in the Southern Reaches. "Blinds are twenty dollars, house takes a ten per cent rake each hand."

Solari nodded and looked around at the four other players, each with a sizable stack of chips in front of them, all of them playing a little too loose with too much alcohol and enough time between drinks to have become chummy.

She flexed her wings under the flak jacket to release some of the tension. "Shuffle up and deal."

***

"Flush," the dealer called, pushing the eight, jack, and nine of hearts up out of the line, leaving the king of spades and ten of hearts sitting outcast. Solari's opponent, a red-headed woman adorned with fake gold jewellery, beamed and reached out over her ace and king of hearts to scoop the chips into her stack.

Solari clenched her jaw, staring in disbelief at her useless ace of spades and queen of diamonds, which just seconds ago had spiked her heart rate with the realisation she had hit an almost-unbeatable ace-high straight. *Almost.*

The dealer dragged the cards away. With the felt cleared, the mindless chit-chat around the table continued. Two hours since her arrival and Solari's chip stack, once a tower of lucrative yellows, oranges, and reds, was now a smaller, and bluer, pile of rubble.

She glanced over at Alcaeus, his knee still bouncing. They should have left earlier.

The real sting was that they could have. Forty minutes earlier, her stack had been a veritable rainbow of success, topping out at just under three-thousand dollars. With Alcaeus' chips and the money still left in the wallet, it would have been enough. But, she had been riding high, and thoughts of buying back the car and driving it to the drop-off point had made her reckless.

Then it all crumbled; good money chased after bad bets in a desperate attempt to win it all back. And now here she was, further from the three-thousand dollars than when she had first arrived. Around her, other chip stacks were starting to loom higher. In a few hands, her measly collection would be easy pickings for someone with the cards to push her out. She needed to jag a good hand, and then she needed some luck to convert it into a win.

Luck. The thought of it threatened to unhinge her and push her into fits of laughter.

The dealer passed the deck her way and wordlessly she cut the cards. With the knot tightening in her stomach, she clenched her fists and focussed on controlling her breathing. Around the room, a dozen or so games of poker were in various stages of evolution; each table, each player, riding the peaks and troughs of chance, waiting for the next win, the next victim.

The dealer flicked two cards across the green felt towards Solari. She paused, flexing her hidden wings against the constraints of the jacket and the hard, plastic chair, and then picked up the cards. The ace of clubs and ace of spades stared back at her.

She blinked, and then casually laid her cards back down to the table, squeezing her wings tight against the tremors threatening to reveal them. Around her, the other players lowered their cards and started fiddling with their chips. Solari didn't bother looking down at hers, she knew there was only four-hundred dollars' worth.

Betting started; the first player raised one hundred dollars, the second called. Solari curled her toes—she had done the impossible—jagged a good hand and an insane amount of luck.

"New blood," someone murmured at the table, but Solari kept her focus on the betting. Another raise—three-hundred dollars. A call. Her move.

"All in," she said, loud enough for Alcaeus to hear, and pushed her ragged collection of blue chips to the middle. "Four hundred."

She sat back quietly, still curling her toes; she needed all of the remaining players to call her bet for it to work.

"Call," murmured the man to her left. And like a line of dominoes, the others fell into place—quickly calling to see the flop. Only then did Solari look up. It didn't matter if she showed emotion; her hand was fated now.

She shifted in her seat to look over at Alcaeus, but her gaze was tripped up along the way by the 'new blood' that had arrived at a nearby table. Scotty.

There were only a few spare seats left around the den, and thankfully none on Solari's table, but the small proximity to him was like a knife between her shoulder blades. Quickly she turned away, pulling up the hood of her flak jacket, slouching down in her seat, and silently pleaded with the dealer to move faster.

The flop cards were dealt. Ace of hearts, nine of clubs, queen of diamonds.

Her heart somersaulted in her chest. Trip aces. She couldn't possibly lose. Surely. Around the table, a chorus of 'check' ran in quick staccato.

That's it; a quick game's a good game.

The dealer turned the fourth card; a ten of diamonds. The red-headed woman bet four hundred dollars and was met with a string of folds, a call by a younger man with a crooked nose and greasy hair, and another string of folds.

Solari appraised the two players still in the game. The woman most likely had a straight, the king and jack no doubt colluding under her cupped hands. The man, well, he could have two pair—maybe a suited queen and nine—or he could have nothing; could just be betting on his machismo and loathing to let two ladies take his pre-flop money when a fifth card could still gift him a win.

Not likely. If Solari had any money spare, she would have bet the red-head would walk away smiling with the rest of the pot that was quarantined away from Solari's take.

Behind her, the chatter on a nearby table was ramping up, Scotty's nasally voice like nails against her wings. She bit down harder on her cheek, the taste of blood in full bloom.

The fifth and final card, the river, fell like a feather to the felt. And Solari's heart seized. The ace of diamonds.

Her fingers itched to throw her cards over, grab her pile of chips, and run. But there was still a round of betting to go. Useless, irrelevant betting, except for the two players still vying for the rest of the chips.

"Two thousand," the redhead said. To protect her hand? She shouldn't have bothered. Solari had the other two aces.

"Five thousand," the male quickly countered.

That surprised her. It was high enough to be a push, to bluff the redhead into walking away, but not so high as to rule out an aggressive move to collect more money with a solid hand. *Maybe he has the flush?* Not that it mattered to Solari; four aces still trumped a flush.

"Call," the redhead said reluctantly, decimating her stack of chips to match the bet.

Solari's fingers were like snakes, snapping out to turn over her cards. "Four of a kind," she said almost breathlessly.

The redhead's face fell as she revealed her prophesied king and jack, but then quickly recovered and turned to the man. The larger side pot was still there for the taking.

"Thanks for playing, ladies," he said, his voice fuzzy through his crumpled nose.

At first, Solari only saw the flush. The five diamonds. In that moment, her elation was still attached to her chest. But then the dealer pushed the diamonds up, leaving the ace of hearts discarded. *Four of a kind beats a flush.* The words flew to her lips but died on her tongue.

While four of a kind did beat a flush, it did not beat a *royal* flush.

The man was laughing and the other players around the table were joining in, except the redhead, who sat quietly counting her remaining chips with long fingernails tapping against the plastic, and Solari, whose mind was full of static and unable to form a coherent thought.

Slowly, she stood on shaky legs, her wings trembling underneath her jacket. She could still hear Scotty nearby, but the buzz of static in her ears made it all seem distant. She kept her head turned as she walked past, catching Alcaeus' eyes as he also stood. The Metallicari looked blankly at her, his face stricken and dumbfounded.

"Hey!" Scotty's voice shouted above the general hum of the gambling den. Solari picked up her pace. "Hey, you in the flak jacket!"

Heart in her throat and thoughts of *fuck, fuck, fuck,* transcending the static, Solari pushed past the final two bouncers and raced for the stairs, her feet stomping up the concrete until the chill of Youngtown's night air shocked her panic into something more manageable.

Her head swivelled around to look for Alcaeus. Why wasn't he behind her?

For a moment, she considered running back down to find him, her feet pausing at the top of the stairs. She thought of the pistol that sat hidden away in the wardrobe back at the hotel. The rules of the den meant she wasn't armed, but—gratefully—it also meant Scotty wasn't either.

The sound of footfalls drifted up to her. She took a step back and positioned herself to launch.

THIRTY-THREE

"What are you doing?" Alcaeus shouted as he crested into view, taking the stairs two at a time. "Run!"

Solari blinked in surprise and then darted after him, away from the gambling den and down the street. Three blocks away, he pulled her into a crevice between two tall buildings, jamming them both in tight. Over his shoulder, she could see the sliver of life on the street beyond.

His heart raced against her chest. Or was that hers?

She took a shaky breath. "What ha—"

"Shh." He shook his head and held a finger against her lips. "Just wait," he whispered.

They stayed like that for ten minutes, maybe more, until their pulses were no longer tidal waves.

"Who was that?" Alcaeus asked. "The man with the skull tattoo?"

"He was wearing a cap."

"It fell off after he fell."

"He fell?"

"After I tripped him. He knew your name, Solari."

He knows a little more than that.

Alcaeus frowned. "Is he going to be a problem?"

"I don't know. Maybe." *Probably.* "He stole my jacket. So, I stole it back. And his van."

"Our van?"

"He's a courier." It was the only explanation for why he was there. The best way to replace an old van was to find a job that offered you a new one.

"That's not good, Solari."

She leant her head into his shoulder and started laughing, soft and maniacal. Her whole body shook with it. And then it ran dry.

"I have no luck," she whispered against his chest.

Alcaeus lifted up her chin and looked down at her. "You have terrible luck, but I wouldn't say you have *no* luck."

She shook her head away from his touch. "What luck do I have?"

"Well, you're with me."

She rolled her eyes. "And, what? That makes me the luckiest girl in the world?"

"Maybe." He grinned down at her. "It certainly makes you eight-thousand dollars richer."

***

"I can't believe you won." Solari sat next to Alcaeus on the bed back at the hotel. Her heart still raced; from the brisk pace they took to return unnoticed, and from the sight of the Metallicari holding so much money.

"I won."

They fell into fits of laughter again. They hadn't been able to stop laughing since Alcaeus pulled the thick wads of cash from his pocket.

"Eight-thousand dollars?"

"Eight-thousand dollars."

Solari's stomach hurt from laughing so much. "How did you do it?"

"While you were losing all of our money, I was building a nice little stack. Turns out I know how to read people better than you." He grunted as Solari elbowed him in the ribs and laughed again. "And then I saw you get all nervous when tattoo boy entered the place and then I heard you say 'all in'."

221

"And?"

"And, I was on a pretty good hand myself, so I followed your lead. Seemed like everyone else thought they were on to a winner, as well. But they didn't have four aces."

"You won on *four aces*?"

Alcaeus nodded and there was nothing that could stop Solari from flopping back on to the bed and laughing at the irony of it all, laughing until tears streamed down her face.

The bed creaked as Alcaeus flopped down beside her.

"Maybe you are lucky," she said when the laughter subsided.

"I'm feeling pretty lucky at the moment," he replied, turning his dark, serious eyes to her. Darker than the pre-dawn, tinged with decades of…*life*. Eyes that held promises of a *better* life.

"Still," he continued, turning away and looking up at the ceiling. "We need a bit more luck, don't we?"

***

The young Reptilia arrived the next afternoon gift-wrapped in a midnight-blue dress and woollen coat that just skimmed the floor. The deep colour was a perfect contrast to her olive skin and emerald scales. Her gaze glanced over Solari but lit up when it fell on Alcaeus standing next to the window.

Solari shut the door behind her. "Take the dress off. And the shoes."

The Reptilia ignored her and strolled up to the Metallicari, shrugging out of the coat and throwing it on the bed. Rows of iridescent scales glittered along her spine. "I thought he was calling the shots," she murmured, faltering only when Alcaeus shook his head.

"He's not for you," Solari said, more smug than she intended. Alcaeus raised an eyebrow at her and smiled. She rolled her eyes. "Now, take off the dress."

Silk rustled to the floor, long limbs bending to unclasp bronze-coloured stilettos. Solari kept her gaze on Alcaeus. He glanced at the naked Reptilia but his gaze slid easily back to her. Catching her scrutiny, he cocked his head and smiled wider, calling out her unannounced test. *Did I pass?* he mouthed to her. She shrugged nonchalantly and turned back to the Reptilia.

"What do you want me to do, now?" the Reptilia asked, still addressing Alcaeus.

"You can get dressed," Solari said, grabbing a large t-shirt from the go-bag and tossing it to her. "And you can leave."

"Is there a problem?" The Reptilia looked from Solari to Alcaeus. She looked worried and Solari understood her panic—going back downstairs ten minutes after arriving would have repercussions; she would be accused of failing to meet expectations, would risk punishment for her failings.

"No problem," Solari said. "We just need you to leave."

"It doesn't seem like *he* wants me to leave." The Reptilia remained naked, the t-shirt dangling from her hand.

Alcaeus remained still, arms loosely folded across his chest, face unreadable.

"I already told you," Solari said, picking up the silk dress and laying it on the bed. "He's not for you."

"That's a nasty scar you have," the Reptilia said, voice dripping with syrup.

"That's a nasty mouth you have," Solari replied, stepping into the space between the Reptilia and Alcaeus.

"I can show you how nasty it can be," she said over Solari's shoulder to Alcaeus.

"Not today, you can't," Alcaeus murmured.

The Reptilia looked back to Solari, her face pinched in a scowl. "Fine." She shrugged into the t-shirt and threw a dirty look to Alcaeus as he opened the door for her.

"Sorry for the inconvenience," he said, no hint of irony in his voice. "You can keep the t-shirt."

The Reptilia's scornful laugh was shut off as Alcaeus closed the door behind her.

Solari stripped out of her clothes and into the dress. It fit her better than expected, her wings folding over and around the spaghetti straps and causing the silk to flutter.

"Solari..."

"I know, I know," she replied, bending down to slip on the

shoes. "I'll make it up to her. Maybe we can tip her with the leftover change from today's transaction."

He didn't answer. She stood up and turned to face him, expecting the usual look of wry disapproval on his face. Instead, she found him standing very still, his gaze transfixed on her, and an intensity in his eyes that melted her core and made her want to rip the dress off again.

"How do I look?"

"You look beautiful." God, his voice was so raw. "You look—"

She crashed her lips into his before he could say anything else. Before he could say something that would make her cry.

***

Alcaeus kept a protective arm around Solari as they walked through Youngtown towards the brothel. Dark silk peaked from under the long trench coat and brushed against her normal boots. In the shadows, it was unlikely that any of the town's vagrants would notice the glimpses of expensive material. Even so, she huddled into Alcaeus' side and quickened her pace.

The Metallicari wore her flak jacket, the pockets heavy with the pistol, cash, and stilettos. His stride was easy and confident and his features nonchalant, but she felt the tightness in his grip and knew that the other hand would be constantly brushing against the steel of the pistol.

While the street bustled with a steady stream of people, the space outside the brothel was quiet. Most people passed by with barely a glance, never slowing, never lingering. Even so, Solari's heart rate spiked as she stopped and leant against a nearby wall.

The cool bricks pressed deeper into her wings as Alcaeus covered her. Hidden from view, she reached into his pockets, retrieved the stilettos and slipped them on. Her hands betrayed none of her doubts as she shrugged out of the trench coat and wrapped the wool coat tighter around herself.

Exhaling slowly to steady her resolve, she looked up at him. Alcaeus kissed her, urgent and fierce, stealing her breath and suffocating the butterflies in her stomach. She stayed in the moment for as long as she could, and then, reluctantly, pulled away.

He reached up to trail a finger down her scar. "You've got this, Solari," he whispered in her ear. "Go find us our co-conspirator."

She plunged her hand into the pocket of the wool coat, fingers riffling across the notes stashed tightly away. Three-thousand dollars; it made her heart jump just thinking about it.

"I'll be just across the road," Alcaeus said, flicking his head towards the bar. Solari nodded, unable to say anything in response. Everything hinged on what would happen next, on what she would find beyond the lobby of the strange brothel.

"OK?" He tipped up her face and held it there until she met his gaze.

"OK," she whispered.

Alcaeus stepped back, picked up her boots and wrapped them up in the trench coat. "See you in a couple of hours."

Before she could lose her nerve, Solari nodded and pushed away from the wall.

"Stay safe," Alcaeus murmured after her.

She looked back, the butterflies returning. "You too," she said, and then stepped inside the brothel.

THIRTY-FOUR

The escort stood as the door clicked shut behind Solari and silenced the outside noise. "Can I help you?"

Solari released her clenched fists and pivoted to face him. "Hello, again."

He blinked, surprise briefly washing over his features until he composed himself. "Hello."

"I'd like two hours with your greenest recruit," she said, holding out the cash.

"Of course," the escort said smoothly, plucking the money from her grasp and showing no signs of his former disdain as he led her towards the door on the other side of the lobby.

"Enjoy your stay." He opened the door and stepped aside to allow her through. "Helena will show you to your room."

Crossing the threshold was like stepping through a mirror, the same lobby replicated on the other side with the exception of a staircase that led from a basement level and up to the higher floors. A girl, many years younger than Solari, with flawless skin and perfect teeth, glided over in a long, white dress. "Follow me," she demurred and led the way up the stairs.

Solari gripped the railing, her stilettos sinking into the heavy carpet. Everything around her was white—the carpet, the walls, the tiny statuettes in downlit niches. At the second floor, they turned down a long corridor. Sounds of sex and pain and pleasure murmured through heavy doors; an exclusive, whispered concerto for the three security guards positioned along the way.

"There are rules," Helena said, coming to a stop at a door halfway down. "No biting, cutting, or hitting the face. No penetration with foreign objects. No strangulation.

"There are no second chances—if your mutant raises the alarm, you will be ejected from the property. Any damage will be compensated, voluntarily or by force." She unlocked the door with a silver key. "I will return fifteen minutes before your session is due to expire. Please finish up and be prepared to leave when I return again for you."

The door swung open. "Enjoy," Helena said, ushering Solari inside. "Your mutant will be with you presently."

Solari barely heard the door click shut, entirely absorbed in the view before her. The room was as luxe as the lobby; but where the lobby was minimally-appointed, this room was indulgent. A king-sized, four-poster bed dripped with soft quilts and textured pillows, artwork in gilded frames adorned the walls, and lamps and sconces threw warm light on everything.

Unclasping her stilettos, Solari buried her feet into the carpet, toes curling at the sensation of a softness she had never imagined possible.

"Your desire is my pleasure."

She turned at the soft, rumbly voice and her surprise at seeing the familiar face was mirrored in his.

"You're the—" he started.

"You're the boy from Elysia's."

They stared at each other—the Reptilia boy, no longer cowering in a closet or the back of a truck, and Solari, his courier-turned-mutant herself.

Her wings quivered violently at the recognition and the flood of memories it brought back. The boy stared incredulously at her. Even her desperate efforts to still them had no effect, the wings shaking so insistently that the coat was no longer enough to keep them hidden.

"You're a mutant?" he said as the coat dropped to the floor, his submissiveness forgotten. "I thought you hated mutants."

"God has a funny sense of humour," she replied, even though she had given up on God a long time ago.

****

"What is this place?" Solari sat on the floor, midnight-blue silk trailing over her legs and onto the cream-coloured carpet. Her coat lay discarded on the bed, her wings fanned out and fluttering with residual adrenalin. The boy's eyes still widened at the sight of them.

"It's where you go when you come in second place," the boy replied, lounging in a crimson armchair by the window. "When they don't want you in the North, but when you're worth too much to be common trash in Youngtown."

"You went to the drop-off point?" Solari asked, leaning forward.

"You mean the auction house? Yeah, I arrived there a few weeks ago; hitched a ride in the back of a courier's van."

"It wasn't the Fixer?"

"The Fixer?"

Solari shook her head, waving away the confusion. *Just a First Enclave thing, then.* "What happened when you arrived there?"

"At the auction house?"

Solari was about to nod, thinking the answer already obvious; *Where else?* And then she remembered dropping the boy off at the enclave, and memories of her own enclave arrival came rushing back. The disorientation, the fear, the anxiety, the feeling of being utterly alone and discarded. She shook her head. "After I left you. What happened at the enclave that made you want to leave?"

"I realised I was just swapping out one cage for another," he said, hanging his head. "Mutants are no different from anyone else; we hate and love and fuck and die as easily as the next. And a fist slamming against your cheek or someone holding you down and raping you is the same kind of indignity regardless of who is perpetrating it."

The bruises on his shoulders still shone blue, a clear indication that fists were still beating him, if not against his face. *Because that would violate the rules.*

"How did you end up here?" she asked.

"I wasn't good enough to get beyond the wall. It seems the North has too many Reptilias already. Just like here, and outside. But, they'd be lining up for you—a Lepidopterae, the stuff of legend. If your wings were real."

Too many Reptilias…

Solari ignored his unasked question and pulled her coat from the bed, its soft wool draping around her arm and pooling in her lap. Reaching into the silk-lined pocket, she retrieved the photo of her mother and held it out to the boy. "Is she here?"

He took the picture and stared at it closely before shaking his head and handing it back. "I don't know. I've only been here a few weeks. I don't think I've seen her, but she could be up on the higher levels, for the VIPs…"

Solari tucked the photo back into the coat pocket and settled the soft material over her legs like a blanket. "What kind of VIPs?"

"Mostly buyers from the North. And DuPlessis' deputies, when they come up to inspect the transport lines or make new deals. Sometimes DuPlessis, himself—although, that could be just a rumour."

Thoughts of DuPlessis and his deputies in close proximity caused Solari's belly to flutter, her wings following in a strange kind of echo. "How often do the buyers come?"

"Every week."

"They come that often?"

The boy nodded. "I've had four sessions in just the last week."

It didn't make sense; there weren't enough mutants in the Southern Reaches to warrant weekly visits, let alone mutants of the quality the buyers were apparently demanding. The pogroms in the early years after the wall was built had decimated the initial mutant populations and offspring from mutant copulations rarely survived. Since then, mutant humans had become sterile and while the residual radiation occasionally created new mutations, they weren't emerging at the original rate and definitely not at the level to supply a steady stream beyond the wall, especially if they were rejecting the Reptilia and the flawed.

"What happened at the auction house? How many of you

were there?"

He leant back in the chair and rested his head against the cushion. "It's hard to remember the details—they blindfolded us in the van and drugged us before they let us out."

"What *do* you remember?"

"There was a room, sort of like this but bigger, and there was a kind of stage up the front." He sat forward and shook his head. "I'm sorry, I just don't remember."

"It's OK," Solari said, leaning back and closing her eyes. But it wasn't. Their only chance to get inside information, to gain a partner in their escape, and it was buried under a haze of drugs and trauma.

Maybe Alcaeus had been right all along. Maybe this had always been a lost cause, and their only option was to risk travelling south to the First Enclave.

"They kind of just draped us on chairs, or against tables," the boy said quietly. "I remember trying to say something but the drugs had made my tongue all thick and…weird. And then the people came up the stairs—these tall, beautiful, *perfect* people. Like some crazy, psychedelic dream. I don't know how long it lasted—ten minutes, two hours—it was only when I woke up here that I realised I hadn't been bought."

"Did you really want to be bought?" Solari asked, opening her eyes.

The boy picked at a loose thread on the arm of the chair. Even with his scales and designer clothes, he still looked like a scared teenager. "It's all a set-up isn't it? The false dream they keep selling us. The enclaves are better than the outside, the North is better than the South, and this is better than some dive bar or random brothel down the road."

They fell into an uneasy silence.

"It's funny," he said eventually and nodded at her wings. "I only ever wanted to be a normal again. I don't think I could ever think of a reason why someone would want to be a mutant."

"The North is salvation," Solari said. "Slaves go to the North as chattel, mutants as curiosities."

The boy laughed and looked down at his hands. "Chattel, curiosities—it doesn't matter. Once you're there, you're at the disposal of your host. *Your desire is my pleasure.*"

"But, if you could go—if you could make it to the North—would you?"

He didn't hesitate. "I would crawl naked over the razor wire of the wall if it would get me there."

***

The knock at the door came sooner than either Solari or the mutant boy, *Nico*, expected. An empty bottle of expensive champagne lay discarded on the floor, two crystal glasses resting beside it.

"Fifteen minutes," Helena called through the door.

Solari rubbed her eyes and turned over, the soft mattress of the bed a siren call seducing her to go back to sleep. Beside her, Nico sat up, his face transformed by a wide smile. "That was the best sleep I have ever had," he whispered.

She smiled and shimmied out of the bed. "Me too."

It had been a reprieve to just curl up in the bed side-by-side and sleep, with no fear of discovery or violence. Wrapped up in fresh, cotton sheets and snuggling under soft, woollen blankets, Solari had dreamed of the North—of wide, tree-lined boulevards, of dappled sunshine falling on delicate blue orchids, of Alcaeus' arms wrapped around her and Christianne's face smiling down on her.

Sleeping had been a benediction, and waking a cruelty.

"You'll come back for me?" the boy asked.

Before drifting off to sleep, they had discussed the plan—a desperate, vague cobbling together of ideas and opportunities.

"I'll figure something out," she said, putting on her stilettos and wrapping the coat around her wings. "Find a way to come to this room every morning before dawn. When you see me, that's your cue."

Nico nodded and threw back the blanket to exit the bed; a shower of dusty scales fluttered around them. Solari's heart seized, her panic mirrored in Nico's eyes.

"Quick," she said, racing for the bed. "Help me strip the sheets."

They pulled carefully at the cream-coloured sheets, now

marred with a fine film of wing scales. They were running out of time; Helena would return at any minute.

"Take them to the ensuite," she whispered fiercely. "Drench them. If anyone asks, tell them I spilled the champagne on them."

Nico shook his head. "It won't work." He bent down to pick up the empty champagne bottle and slammed it against the bed frame, glass shattering over the discarded blankets and luxe carpet. Picking up a larger shard, he dragged it across his shoulder, staunching the blood with the sheet and letting the red sink deep into the fibres.

"I have to go," Solari said. "I have to intercept her before she comes back."

Nico pulled the sheet away from his arm and grimaced at the sight. "Go," he said, heading towards the ensuite. "Just come back for me."

Heart still hammering, Solari slipped from the room, closing the door firmly behind her and shutting out the sound of running water. The nearest security guard glanced up at her presence, but otherwise didn't shift from his position. Forcing herself to breathe normally, Solari smoothed her coat and dress over her hips and started towards the staircase.

Helena crested into view a few seconds later, her eyes widening a little at seeing Solari walking towards her. Pausing where she was, the escort waited for Solari to reach her. "Everything was to your satisfaction, madame?"

"Yes," Solari murmured, keeping her strides small and unhurried. "Thank you."

"Allow me to escort you back to the lobby for a digestif," Helena said, turning and leading Solari to the staircase.

"No digestif is necessary," Solari replied, focusing on keeping from stumbling in her stilettos.

"As you desire," Helena said, beginning the descent.

Above them, another escort led a charge down to their level. Solari glanced up, eyes drawn to the contrast between the white dress of the escort and the deep red dress of the woman she led. She expected to see another perfect face of a Northerner, but instead found flawless pale skin adorned with iridescent aquamarine scales.

Her heel caught in the thick carpet and she stumbled, lurching forward before she could grab the railing and steady herself.

"Are you alright, madame?" Helena said, turning around wide-eyed.

"Yes," Solari said, her voice strained; not because she had stumbled, and not because she had drawn the attention of her escort.

Helena nodded and continued down the stairs. Solari turned to look back at the escort and her mutant, but they had already exited the staircase and disappeared from view. Pausing, she kept her gaze on the spot where she had last saw them, silently begging for them to return. Her heart beat counted out seconds she didn't have.

With her chest strained to bursting, she dragged her gaze away and followed Helena downstairs, her legs shaking all the way to the bottom and her hand firmly in her coat pocket and clutching the photo of her mother.

The same woman she had just passed on the stairs.

THIRTY-FIVE

"Are you sure it was her?" Alcaeus asked.

"I am *certain*." Solari paced the room, unable to sit still, itching to race all the way back to the brothel with her pistol and drag her mother back with her. "We need to get her out. We need to get them both out."

"What did you learn about the smuggling operation?" Alcaeus' stillness was as infuriating as it was reassuring.

"Not much. Nico was drugged and blindfolded, so the details are limited. He mentioned a fancy room with a staircase, so we're looking for a multi-storey building." She thought back to the squat buildings on the outskirts of town, trying to recall one that stood taller than the others.

Alcaeus frowned and shook his head. "There were no multi-storey buildings near the drop-off location."

"There must have been. Of all the details Nico remembered, this was the clearest. The buyers from the North came up the stairs for the auction. It has to be a multi-storeyed building."

"No. I remember. They were all single-storey."

"All of them?"

"Anything else would have stuck out. I would remember it."

All of her frantic energy collapsed in on itself and turned her belly to ash. "So, we have nothing." Her throat choked on the words.

"Always the fatalist, Solari," Alcaeus murmured. "You give up your hope like a feather on a breeze."

"What hope is there?" she shouted, rounding on him. "What hope has there *ever* been? Our only chance—our *only* chance—to find a way to the North was with that boy, and the only piece of information his traumatised brain can remember is wrong."

"Not wrong," Alcaeus replied. "Just misinterpreted."

"What does that even mean?" she yelled again, aggression firing in her belly.

"The buyers came up a staircase, just not from ground level."

It was like a key turning in a lock. She could see it—a staircase leading up from the basement, just like the one at the brothel.

"They don't come through the wall," she whispered, slumping down on the bed next to him. "The come under it."

Alcaeus nodded. "They come by tunnel."

The two of them fell into silence, wrestling with the truth they had stumbled upon. In the early years of the wall, Southerners had lost their lives trying to dig tunnels to the North. But they had failed, like all the other crazy attempts, and their efforts concreted in; a permanent reminder—*you will never make it to the North.*

"Do you really think it's possible?" she asked.

"It makes sense," he replied. "It's secure, discrete, elegant in its simplicity."

"So, how do we access it? Where's the map?"

She pulled the map from the bedside table drawer and smoothed it out between her and Alcaeus. "Here is the general location of the auction house," she said, tapping against the small cluster of roads on the southern outskirts.

Alcaeus grabbed a nearby pen and drew an x on the map.

"And this is the brothel," she said, finding the intersection and tapping the spot for Alcaeus to mark.

"And this is the closest town beyond the wall," he said, drawing a third cross through a small, red dot labelled *King's Meadow.*

With a steady hand, he connected them all—a dark, straight line running from the auction house, through the brothel, to the North.

"Our tunnel," Solari murmured.

***

Dawn was just a crack of light on the horizon when Solari and Alcaeus left the hotel and started their walk. It was a strange time to be out on the streets—too late for even the most committed drunk to have not passed out and too early for anyone else to be awake.

Solari gripped the map in her pocket, the line etched well enough in her mind to not need the confirmation of seeing it again on paper.

They started a few blocks from the brothel, navigating the streets and alleys to find a likely candidate for another basement stop along the tunnel.

"How old do you think it is?" she whispered, eyes scanning the buildings for something accessible but discrete.

"The basements would have been there all along, but the tunnel? Who knows? Maybe when they started planning the wall? Maybe afterwards?"

The streetscape opened up, a block or two of buildings collapsed and malformed—victims to more intense periods of fighting between DuPlessis and Worcsulakz.

"I saw a bomb rip apart a block of high-rises in Hobart last year," she said. "I was five blocks away when I heard the explosion, but I felt that sound in my chest. And then the entire street shuddered. DuPlessis had been blowing things up for months, but this was a *statement*—taking down an entire block in Worcsulakz's territory…"

It had been typical DuPlessis—everything had to be a statement, every act had to have a style to it, some flair. The thought made her pause.

"What?" Alcaeus asked, quickly scanning the nearby shadows.

"A bomb didn't do that," she said, staring at the haphazard lines of broken buildings. "Worcsulakz doesn't make statements; he works clean."

She moved closer to the rubble, looking for the tell-tale signs.

And then she saw one—a dip in the road, a slight concave fissure like a massive footprint left in soft bitumen. "The buildings didn't collapse," she said. "The road did. The tunnel is underneath us."

"Or, was," Alcaeus said, looking around and scanning the nearby streets. "If the road collapsed, the tunnel has as well."

"So, they re-routed?" Solari glanced at the nearby buildings. A convenience store sat isolated on the next corner, its neon lights still bright in the pale light of morning.

The two of them hurried towards it—there were no other people in the street, no faces lingering in windows or bodies leaning in doorways. A brass bell rang as Solari pushed the door open and entered.

The store was in good order, its rows of shelves stocked with staple items and treats. To the left, a row of fridges terminated at the far wall by a stairwell. Opposite them, a young man with pock-marked skin stood at the counter leafing through a tattered porn magazine.

"Excuse me," Solari said, grabbing an assortment of things from the shelves—a can of something, a chocolate bar, some gaffer tape—and plonking them down on the counter. "Do you have a bathroom I can use?"

The man put down his magazine, glanced at the wares on the counter and then up at Solari. "Payment first."

Alcaeus pulled a twenty dollar note from his pocket. The attendant grabbed at it and cocked his head towards the stairwell. "Downstairs and to the left."

"I'll be right back," she said to Alcaeus, her voice light even though nervous anticipation spiked in her chest.

"I'll be right here eating this chocolate bar," he said grimly, gaze flitting from the attendant who had already returned to his magazine, to the exit and the street beyond.

Solari walked casually to the stairs, only hurrying when she was safely out of view. Downstairs, a storage room presented a more crowded version of the store upstairs; boxes upon boxes of unopened merchandise filling shelves to capacity. A door near the front ejected the stench of an unclean toilet. She ignored it and moved down the aisles until she found herself at the back wall, where a tower of shelves sat in front of a padlocked coolroom.

Moving aside the nearest boxes, she noted the layers of dust. It had been a while since anyone had touched them, which could mean nothing in a struggling convenience store wasting away in a carnival town, or could mean everything. She tugged at the padlock, but it held. Despite being old and rusty, there was no way of breaking it without attracting the attendant's attention. She tapped lightly on the door, pressing her ear up against the cold metal to hear the long and hollow echo inside. She tapped again, the echo drifting like a pebble skipping down a well.

Solari smiled, pressing a hand to her stomach to control the flutters. She had found her tunnel. Now, she just needed a way to access it.

***

"We break into the store and then the coolroom." Solari's words came out in a rush as she pushed the midnight-blue silk dress into the go-bag. She glanced around the hotel room, sizing up the things she should take and the things she could leave behind.

"And how do you propose doing that?" Alcaeus tossed her the stilettos and she nestled them beside the silk.

"I know how to pick a lock."

"Like you know how to play poker?"

She shot him a scowl, but continued packing; the coat, her old clothes, some of the bag's original t-shirts—all rolled tight and crammed into the soft canvas. "I may have limited poker experience, but I've picked my fair share of locks."

Alcaeus raised an eyebrow, mocking her.

"It's not even that hard," she said, ignoring him and throwing a towel in the bag. "Just two spanners and *click*." She brought her fists up and popped them down, as if she were snapping a rod in half. "Job done."

"That easy, huh?"

How many times had she broken into the locked cabinets of her lab after leaving the keys at her apartment… "That easy. I mean, longer spanners are better, and you have to position them just right—just above the halfway point of the shank—but yeah, that easy."

"It's a wonder anyone bothers to use them," Alcaeus said dryly.

"Yes," she said, volleying back the sarcasm. "Who would have thought humans could be so stupid?"

She zipped up the bag and stood. "I'm going down to the bar to get some tequila."

"Bring back some chips," Alcaeus called to her as she left the room.

She smiled as she walked down the stairs. Even though there was still so much that could go wrong—What if they got caught at the convenience store? What if she couldn't pick the lock? What if they were intercepted at the brothel? Or her mother didn't recognise her? (all equally disastrous, but the last one particularly terrifying)—they were close. Closer than they had ever been.

Tonight they would make their way to the North.

Downstairs, the bar was quiet; the mid-morning hour cast a sleazy tone over the scene. A different bartender—a tall, but otherwise nondescript man—leaned against the counter and surveyed the room.

"What can I get you?" he drawled.

"A bottle of tequila and a packet of chips," she said, slapping down a handful of twenty dollar notes.

Less patrons meant less dancers, and it was easy for her to pick out the familiar mutants in and around the cages. The Osteoclasta was noticeably absent, but the Reptilia girl stood a few metres away, gyrating against a man slouched on one of the lounges. She met Solari's gaze, her face turned ugly with a cruel twist of her mouth.

Still salty, are we?

Solari offered a smile back, but it faltered and then shattered when the Reptilia's patron turned around. Slowly, he removed his dark baseball cap to reveal a shaved head and tattooed skull.

Without hesitating, Solari grabbed the bottle of tequila and held it like a weapon, all the while her brain racing to assess her options. Fight or flee. She glanced from Scotty to the Reptilia to the staircase to the exit. Silently, she cursed the ridiculous, oversized t-shirt she wore, and wished desperately for the protection of her flak jacket and the pistol held in its pocket.

Fuck, fuck, fuck,

Scotty stood. She needed to move.

Solari ran for the exit. She would have to come back later for Alcaeus; running to him now would only cause more problems. Neither Scotty nor the Reptilia had any issue with the Metallicari, their vengeance was directed solely at her.

Run now, get Alcaeus later.

Just metres from the exit, she pushed her arm out, ready to collide with the door and spill out into the street. Something heavy barrelled into her side. She crashed to the floor, the bottle of tequila shattering on impact and pushing glass shards into her side. Desperately, she tried to stand up, but her body screamed with pain and refused to cooperate.

Scotty stood over her, his foot slamming into her side. "Hello, stormgirl. Someone's looking for you."

THIRTY-SIX

Waking was like swimming in amber. Solari's stomach roiled as her eyelids fluttered opened, the dull thud of old pain erupting at her side. Details emerged in her vision, fuzzy at the edges and shrouded in grey shadows. Muted light filtered in around heavy curtains, falling on a wooden bureau and four-poster bed.

Vaguely, she registered the soft, luxurious carpet at her back. Her wings flexed at the familiarity, but failed to unfurl. Discomfort and pain pooled in her muscles and she tried to shift her body into a more comfortable position, to sit up, to stretch. But she could do none of these things on account of the nylon rope stretched taut across her chest and looped around her wrists and ankles.

Hints of fear and confusion tickled faintly in her mind, buried under a disorientation that had settled like a wet blanket over her thoughts. Her mind struggled, and failed, to make sense of everything. And still her reaction was muted. As if she was hungover. *Or drugged.*

Squirming and wriggling, she pulled herself up to the bed and then to standing. A rush of vertigo assaulted her and she leant against the nearest post to steady herself and wait for her mind-fog to clear. She walked on unsteady feet to the window and pulled aside the curtains.

The outside light was fading. Neon lights winked on along the street and the growing crowd announced the death of the afternoon and the onset of evening. She recognised the stretch of road, she knew where she was. *The brothel.*

Her bound hands fumbled at the window, straining against the frame in a useless effort to prise it open. Gritting her teeth against the pain in her fingers, she turned from the window and searched the room for something sharp or heavy. The drawers were empty and the bathroom cleaned out; everything sharp removed, everything heavy either bolted down or too unwieldy to lift.

She stumbled back to the window. The glass was thin; she could break it—wrap her hands in the thick linen sheets and smash her fist straight through. What would one more laceration on her mangled hand matter?

But at four storeys high, a fall would shatter the rest of her. Escaping the room would do her no good if she couldn't escape the scene. And why escape, when her goal had been to return anyway? For the boy, for her mother.

Her mind was clearing, making way for a merciless headache. She shuffled to the bathroom and turned the tap to full force, splashing cold water over her face and letting it trickle down her throat. Glancing up, the wall-to-wall mirror reflected a shadowy doppelganger back at her.

Solari groped in the near-darkness for a light switch, her hands brushing over cold tiles until she found it. Warm light flickered on, growing in intensity as she held down the button. Released from the darkness, the image in the mirror stared back at her through hollow and sunken eyes. Brown and purple bruises formed an ugly camouflage across her face, neck, and arms.

She pulled at the white rope around her chest, but it stubbornly resisted her attempts to free herself from its grip. Her breathing was coming too fast, too shallow; it burned in her chest and rasped along her throat. Black spots flashed in her vision and a shrill was building in her ears. She needed to calm down, but the reflection of her bruised and bound body only pushed her heart to beat faster and her breath to fail.

Her bound hands pawed at the light switch, eliminating the reflection and thrusting everything back into the shadows. Leaning against the tiles, she slid down the wall, hugged her knees to her chest, and tried to piece together what had happened to her.

Like a bad recording, patchwork memories came back in

incomplete fragments. Scotty had been waiting for her. The Reptilia's smile should have given it away; it had been careless to be so dismissive. She had tried to escape, without Alcaeus. *Alcaeus.* His face flashed bright in her mind. He would be worried about her. Would he be looking for her? Where would he search? Not here.

She wondered why Scotty had brought her here. He had said something to her, after slamming her to the floor and kicking her. What had he said? *Someone's looking for you.*

Who was looking for her? She grunted. *Who wasn't?* Jerath, Worcsulakz, DuPlessis—each possibility a death sentence.

She shuddered, the nylon rope pulling at her wings and spearing pain along her nerve endings. Memories of being shackled in DuPlessis' warehouse came back to assault her: the dank smell of the basement, the endless cries and shouts, the beatings, the threats, the singing of steel against skin.

She pulled at the rope at her chest, wincing at the pain in her wings even as the shackles at her wrist pulled angrily at the skin. Tears, hot and sharp, began to well and she blinked them away angrily, until they grew so insistent that they coursed down her cheeks.

The fight was draining from her. She could *feel* it. All her life she had held to it, and it had clawed and scratched and cut her at every turn. It had bled her, and she had recovered, and then it had bled her again. And all this time, she had held to it; gripped it so tight, even as its barbs and spikes had found more vulnerability to target.

And, now, as it started to leach away, there was no final grab, no tearing or scraping as it left her. Instead, its claws seemed to retract, the old wounds coated with honey, everything conspiring to just let the fight drain away. It was easier than she had expected.

Once, there had been something to fight for: Denavim, always Denavim, and the delusional hope that things would return to the way they were—for her family, for her father and a way out of his debt, for herself before her father's debt became hers.

And then the fight had become less about finding a way to the light and more about avoiding the descent into darkness—surviving in Hobart, staying under Worcsulakz's radar, hiding from Anders' violence.

What was there to fight for now?

The thought was a whisper, soft and fuzzy and laced with all of the new drugs they had pumped into her system. Just another coat of honey to help the fight slide away. She had lost so much, had been emptied and hollowed out for so many years. And it would be so easy to let go, to just let this fight slip from her fingers…

And then it stuck, a hidden spoke grabbing hold. She had lost so much, but she hadn't lost everything. Her mother was alive, and here in the brothel. Alcaeus, with his quiet voice and dark thoughts, was out there somewhere. And the North was so close, with its promise of a life that didn't claw and scratch and cut. All of them beautiful, impossible things. All of them worth fighting for.

***

Solari awoke in darkness, her wrists burning again, the rope digging deeper into her flesh. Through the haze, she was aware of someone in the room, grabbing at the rope that bound her. *Alcaeus?* He pulled at the rope roughly, the skin screaming at the insult. One hand now free, she tried to lift it to him, but he batted it away.

"Stay still, you fucking bitch," the voice growled. *Not Alcaeus.*

Solari squinted through the darkness, pushing at the drug-induced fuzziness in her mind and trying to separate out the details in the shadowed room. The restraints around her wrists fell free and the stranger hauled her from the bed. Another man waited in the doorway, his hulking frame a menacing silhouette.

Panic bloomed in her chest and helped push some of the fog from her mind. She thrashed wildly, pushing against her captor and away from his colleague who stepped in to grab her. The punch to her side stole her breath. Arms encircled her, her own wrenched back and tied together.

A push at her back sent her stumbling into the hallway. She fell to the floor, slamming into the carpet with no way of bracing herself.

"Get up," the same harsh voice called.

Her wings shivered and convulsed as rough hands grabbed at

them and hauled Solari up.

"Ugh, it's fucking moulted on me."

"It's what?"

"It's *moulted* on me; its fucking disgusting wing dust is all over my hands."

"So, wipe it off. Not on me, you dick. Get it moving—it needs to be in the penthouse now. The big man is waiting."

The two of them pushed and dragged her up the stairs and along the corridors, laughing as she slammed into walls, grunting as they punched her for her attempts at escape. When they finally reached the penthouse, Solari was out of breath and doubled over in pain.

A cluster of security guards parted from the large double doors, allowing Solari and her escorts to push through into the room beyond. And, there, reclining on a beige armchair, his plum-coloured, double-breasted suit as ostentatious as his smirk, was DuPlessis.

"Hello, Solari."

The room was massive, impeccably furnished, and filled with all kinds of carnal delights. DuPlessis sat in the centre, a gaudy sun around which a constellation of beautiful freaks orbited. Osteoclasta draped in silk, Arachnidia dusted with gold, Tripexes dripping with jewels. But, Solari's attention was drawn to the more familiar faces—the deputy at DuPlessis' side, the same one who had carved her face; the girl from the van, the one too pretty to just be a driver; and the Reptilia lounging on the chaise by the wall, her mother.

"Like what you see?" DuPlessis crooned. Solari's gaze stayed fixed on Christianne, waiting for her to look up, to recognise her daughter. But, she didn't move; oblivious to the spectacle before her, she stared up at the ceiling with bright eyes while her arm trailed to the floor.

"I seem to be interrupting your party," Solari murmured, her voice shivering under the pummelling of her heart. She turned back to the ganglord. "Perhaps, I should come back later."

DuPlessis smiled, his lips pulling tight and thin. "Hmm. It seems Worcsulakz has grown careless and let his pet bird fly too far from the nest. I didn't think I'd see you and your pretty scar so soon." His eyes flitted to the girl on the simple armchair beside him. Solari was surprised she could sit so still surrounded by all the blissed-out mutants. "My niece tells me you stole a van of mine. And killed a driver, maybe two. Released some high-value product destined for the Northern Region."

He stood slowly, like a python emerging to stalk its prey. Solari clenched her hands behind her back, her wings rippling against the restraints, her stomach fluttering with a rage she couldn't expel.

"Interestingly, that is not what surprises me," he said, his voice all jovial sarcasm. This was a performance for everyone but her. He sauntered towards her, around her. "What surprises me, are these."

Her wings fell into spasms as his hands pulled roughly at the unprotected membranes.

"Conrath assures me there were no such mutations when he first branded you all those years ago. And the weasly courier who brought you here said he'd seen you just a month ago with no sign of wings, either."

He tugged on them again, the pain knotting between her shoulder blades. She bit down harder, trying to dispel the sensation, trying to regain control.

"Ordinarily, I might have forgiven such transgressions and sold you to the highest bidder in the North; the payment for a Lepidopterae would have more than compensated for the trail of destruction you left behind." Pain exploded again as he yanked on the wings, harder, rougher. "But, who would pay for a damaged human playing dress-up as a mutant?"

He stepped in front of her, his thin smile replaced with a scowl. Slowly he raised his hand, the slaking of her wing scales like technicolour dust in his palm, and dragged it down her cheek. The skin around her scar tingled and itched.

She ignored the torment and looked over to the chaise. Christianne still lay there, listless, like a bored movie star. But, now she looked over at Solari and DuPlessis, her eyes sharper and more focussed.

"Don't kill me," Solari begged. Not because she was suddenly scared of him, or scared of dying—she had always been scared. But because she didn't want her mother to see it.

DuPlessis laughed, a fake, forced tinkling. "Oh, Solari. Killing you here, now, gifts me no benefit. No, this was just a pre-showing. Northerners may not pay to take you over the border, but they will pay to watch those pretty wings be stripped from your bleeding corpse."

***

Time passed with nothing to mark it. Solari floated between waking and sleeping, the haze of chemicals in her mind numbing the pain and panic, but leaving her with the details of what had happened and was yet to come. The shackles at her wrists were gone, replaced by red bracelets of angry skin where she had thrashed against them; it was easier to subdue her with drugs than ropes.

The click of the door and an avalanche of light announced a visitor. She looked up in time to see a silhouetted figure deposit a tray of food in the room before the door shut and the room returned to darkness. Her last meal.

DuPlessis and his sense of spectacle.

Her stomach lurched at the smell of roast meat, rich and pungent, and she half-crawled, half-stumbled to the bathroom where she spewed a thin stream of vomit on to the tiles. It was so long since she had eaten anything, the vomit was nothing but rank stomach bile. Crawling into the shower recess, she reached up and pulled on the tap, ignoring the call of her stomach to eat.

Starving to death would be a mercy.

The rush of warm water acted as a salve, quieting the torment in her belly and leaching the drug haze from her mind. Sitting back against the tiles, she watched the water eddy around her ankles, jealous as it dropped innocently and unimpeded down the drain. She sat there until the sound of the water could no longer hold back the dark thoughts and rising panic.

Slamming her hand on the tap above stopped the water, leaving her with only the sound of the residual water gurgling down the pipes and her sobbing. Eventually, her tears dried up too and there was nothing left but the cold and the silence.

How was it that she had come so far, drawn so close to what she had dreamed of for so long—the North, her mother, a chance at a better life—only to have it ripped away by the same monster who had started her on this path of destruction half a lifetime ago?

Her chest tightened and she slammed a fist against the tiles. She had thought she was beyond being hurt. After Denavim had died, she had started building her defences—repairing her broken heart and walling it up against future damage. After finding her father swinging from that tree, she had built the walls higher. And with each betrayal, and attack, and disappointment that followed, she had reinforced them. The armour she had built around her heart should have been as invincible as a Metallicari's plates.

She thought of Alcaeus and her chest grew tighter. In all that was dark and despicable in her world, he had been her Helios.

A sob broke from her throat and she forced it back down with all the energy she had left. If she started crying again, she would never stop.

"Solari?" The murmur came to her as a soft echo—too close, too hollow to be real. "Solari?" Louder, more insistent. "Are you there?"

She looked up at the vent, scrambled against the wet tiles to stand.

"Solari—it's me, Nico. Are you OK? Can you hear me?"

"Yes," she stammered. "Yes, I can hear you." She could imagine him in the adjoining bathroom, standing on the vanity, his mouth close to the lattice of the twin vent.

"Have they hurt you?"

Yes. "No, I'm fine." A different kind of sadness pulled at her chest when she thought of the boy. He had pinned all his hopes on her and her promise to rescue him; hopes that would die as readily at the hands of DuPlessis as she would.

"Can I do anything? Is there a way I can help?"

Not unless you can rain down hell on DuPlessis. She barked a sad laugh. Easier to wish for Worcsulakz to appear…

"There is something you can do," she said quickly, her heart and mind tripping over themselves as the beginnings of a plan started to form. "Get a pen. Quick, get a pen."

Seconds—minutes?—later, Nico was back.

"Write this down," she said. "Six, two, seven, seven, nine, nine, zero, zero. Repeat it back to me."

Nico repeated it back, his voice clear and sure.

"Good. You need to find a phone—steal it from one of your clients, but do it soon. You need to call or message that number. And when you do, you need to quote this ID number: one, six, one, one, five, five. Repeat the number."

Her heart was pounding, her mind struggling to stay focused as Nico repeated her manufacturing ID. "And you need to tell whoever answers that DuPlessis and his senior deputy are here in the penthouse and give them the address."

***

Even with the adrenalin and Nico's promise to patch the call, the exhaustion and chemical manipulation won out over Solari's resistance. Wrapped in a towel, she crawled under the expensive bed sheets and fell asleep, plagued by dreams and nightmares—of Worcsulakz and his cronies coming for DuPlessis, only to turn and bury their hooks into her flesh; of Alcaeus rescuing her, only for his embrace to transform into violent tearing at her wings; of her mother racing across the room to kiss her, only for razor sharp teeth to bite into her face.

She woke in a cold sweat and threw the sheets off. Briefly, there flashed a swathe of light, before the room plunged again into darkness. She sat up, rigid with anticipation, and peered through the darkness.

A shadowy figure moved silently towards her. Solari's chest seized—it was too soon, they had come for her too soon.

"Solari?" the voice whispered. A fresh panic gripped her. Why had the boy come to the room? Why would he risk himself and her by coming?

Her eyes were adjusting to the dark, the figure appearing taller.

"My Solari?" the voice whispered again. Solari didn't move.

The stranger was close—just out of reach, but near enough for Solari to make out the fall of silk over slightly-rounded hips, the ribbons of hair tied loosely back from the face, the strong chin and aquiline nose. But, not the scales—the shadows hid those. "Is it really you?"

Christianne stepped closer and Solari finally found her voice. "Mum?"

The sob that broke from Christianne's chest unravelled any last shred of stoicism within Solari. She stumbled from the bed and raced to embrace to her mother. Under all the carefully-maintained bravado, she was still just the child mourning the loss of her family.

"Oh, Solari," Christianne murmured into her hair. "My poor Solari."

Solari buried herself tighter into her mother's chest, afraid that if she didn't hold tight, the illusion would shatter and leave her alone again.

It was surreal to be holding her, as if all the imaginings of her mother had suddenly become tangible—something solid, with warm skin, a beating heart, and soft breath.

As a child, Solari had imagined her mother as someone kind and gentle, someone who smelled of lavender, who let her eat ice-cream for breakfast and had the same sweet smile as her brother. As an adolescent, the image of her mother had shifted away from the stuff of nursery rhymes, but still carried with it the same romanticism—someone who would brush Solari's hair, or intervene when her dad was cruel and distant, or show her how to cook a half-decent meal to stave off the ever-present hunger pains.

Solari scrubbed the tears from her face, and peered at the woman before her. She had spent so long dreaming about a dead mother, and then chasing the hope of a rescued mother; piecing together and constructing an idyllic and romanticised picture of the maternal figure. But Christianne was not that woman.

Even in the shadows, Solari could see the scars. Her mother was a stranger, tormented and abused in her own way, hollowed out and empty and struggling to put herself back together. Just like Solari.

"I thought you were dead," she said, her voice cracking. "Dad, Elysia—they told me you were dead."

Christianne looked down at the floor. "They were trying to protect you and Denavim. And me."

And look how well that turned out.

"You left me," Solari said numbly. "And you never came back."

Christianne reached for her hand, but Solari pulled it back. The hurt that flashed across her mother's face sliced papercuts into Solari's heart and gave her pause. But only briefly. This was a small hurt compared to the wounds that had been inflicted in her absence.

"I didn't abandon you, Solari," she murmured. "I left you with people who love you and could care for you. I left you with family."

Solari laughed soft and harsh, and pushed the stump of her ring finger down the scar of her face. "Does this look like I was cared for? I was left with nothing. When you left, our family broke and it never recovered. You could have come back." Her voice was cracking, but she pressed on. "I know Dad and Elysia sent you away, but you could have come back. You could have saved Denavim. You would have saved us all."

And there it was—the strange, dark, distant feeling she had been carrying around with her ever since seeing the photograph of her as a baby in her mother's arms—it hadn't been hope, or longing, or nervous anticipation, but anger. God, she was so *tired* of being angry.

She stepped back, away from her mother, and sat down on the bed. Christianne stayed where she was, her body still except for her hands that fisted in the silk folds of her dress. "What do you mean, 'saved Denavim'?"

And the anger burning in Solari's chest faltered. It was hard to rage against a mother who still didn't know her child had died.

***

The words came haltingly to begin with, but then, as it had with Alcaeus, they found their own rhythm. Her mother wept openly as the story unfolded, and Solari had given in to the part of her that still wanted to connect with her mother and held her hand as she recounted it: how Denavim had passed away in her arms in the early hours of a spring morning, how she had searched the streets of Hobart for her dad, only to find him strung up in an abandoned part of the industrial centre, the overturned plastic crate less than a metre from where he hung. Her mother's tears stained the silk folds of her dress and fell to their clasped hands, but Solari didn't cry. She had no more tears left.

*****

"I fought them for weeks," Christianne murmured. "I was adamant there was another way."

Solari and her mother sat on the bed, sharing their stories and finding their way back to each other. There was not much time. They already risked too much by Christianne staying as long as she had.

"When I woke up in that van," Christianne said, "I screamed for you and your brother until my voice gave out. The first few weeks at the enclave were… they were *misery*. And I tried everything to get out, but your dad and Elysia were right—"

Solari shook her head, opened her mouth to protest.

"No, Solari." Christianne said. "They were. Even with everything that happened afterwards, they were right. I saw mutants with stumps where limbs had been torn from joint. Literally torn. Can you imagine? The savagery? The complete and utter *hatred* that would cause someone to tear another person limb from limb? And there were others—so many scars, and cuts, and *burns*.

"There was an Arachnidia, who shuffled around the enclave with only five legs, whose body was ravaged by fire. And do you know what would wake her screaming every night? Not the phantom limbs or the melted skin that looked like corrupted bubble wrap. The memory of her children. Her children that had burned alive in the home she had waited too long to leave. They had promised to punish her and she had left too late."

Solari was silent.

"And I was grateful," Christianne finished. "After months of raging against your dad and my sister—hating them. After months of trying to escape back to you and Deni, I was *grateful*, because they were right. They were *right*, Solari." She trailed a finger across the tip of Solari's wing and gave her a sad smile. "This world is not a world for mutants."

"But, none of it mattered," Solari whispered. "Everyone you tried to protect was destroyed anyway. You left to save us, and maybe you gave us a few more years, but in the end it didn't matter. Denavim still died, Dad still died, and I'll be dead within twenty-four hours."

Christianne drew closer and kissed Solari's forehead, her tear-stained cheeks tingling against Solari's scar. "It did matter." She stood up, glancing over her shoulder to the door and then to Solari. She had stayed too long, and yet, Solari's throat constricted and her chest tightened at the thought of her walking out that door. "It *does* matter. I got to see you again. I got to meet my baby girl. And I got another chance to save her."

THIRTY-SEVEN

DuPlessis didn't wait too long before summoning Solari back to the penthouse. The afternoon sun had just started to dip below the border wall when three security guards barged into the room and pulled her to her feet.

The corridors were quiet; no escorts wandered the floors with moneyed patrons, no mutants hurried towards their next session. Deep in Solari's mind, a panic was growing in anticipation of the torture that awaited, but the chemical cocktail that flooded her bloodstream stopped her short of reacting.

They didn't pull or drag her as roughly as they had last time; DuPlessis wanted her to arrive pristine. All the better to showcase the breaking that would follow.

Her mind retreated inwards, away from the thoughts of what would come. Distantly, she could feel the drag of heavy makeup on her face, the itch of bronzing powder against her skin, and the caress of silk at her thigh. They had dressed her like one of the mutants that had been in the penthouse the day before—an exotic freak straddling the line between beauty and horror.

The doors to the penthouse were pinned open, guarded by two large men in dark suits. Somewhere in Solari's hazy mind, she registered surprise at the empty room beyond. Not that it was completely empty—a large four-poster bed dominated the space, the focal point around which armchairs, lounges, and chaises had been oriented.

Solari's guards escorted her through the room, weaving

around the furniture towards the bed. It all looked so innocuous; a room full of furniture but bereft of people, soft lighting dancing on softer furnishings, crystal glasses and champagne bottles sparkling on low tables scattered around. And then she saw the shackles and chains attached to the posts, the black sheet draped over the bed, and the bedside table glittering with instruments that had no place in a bedroom.

Her stomach churned, from the drugs or the rising panic, and the haze of distant observation started to fade. "No," she rasped. She tried to pull away, but her body was still soft and pliable and weak.

They grabbed at her wrists, pulling them into restraints bolted halfway up the posts. Her arms pulled taut, her chest bearing the brunt of the tension. The pain acted as a trigger—her wings unfurling as the pain reached her shoulder blades, their tips brushing against the posts and the restraints.

The guards faltered at that, stopping to stare at her.

"Get her feet, you morons," one of them cried, and hands hastily scrabbled to spread her legs and secure her ankles in the final restraints.

Her weak thrashing achieved nothing. In a matter of minutes, they had strung her up like a sacrificial offering, her body stretched to breaking point in the shape of a crude 'x' against the bedframe.

"Welcome to the freak show," one of the guards said. And then they strung the black sheet over the posts of the bed and let it fall in front of her, cutting her off from the room beyond.

***

The noise increased steadily around her, and still she could see nothing but the black shroud in front of her. Murmured conversations, laughter, indistinct chatter; the room beyond was no longer just a space filled with expensive furniture, it was filled with excited spectators. Half a dozen? Twenty? More? Who had come to watch DuPlessis' sadistic performance?

"Ladies and gentleman," DuPlessis' voice cut through the low buzz, "welcome to this evening's entertainment. I trust you are all comfortable? Your desire is our pleasure." Low, deep laughter rumbled in response. "As connoisseurs of the weird and exotic, you have seen nature's vengeance wreaked on humans, have viewed up close the abomination, deformities, and unnatural mutations. As normals, these monstrosities have repulsed and excited us, but always at a distance—always from the privilege of *being* normal."

There came a rustling close to her and Solari turned her neck, the muscles stiff and resistant. Conrath, DuPlessis' deputy, stepped into view. Ignoring Solari he strolled to the bedside table and the assortment of instruments.

When he turned, she expected to see him clutching a knife or saw. Instead, his hand cradled a syringe. Solari groaned, whimpered. Tears fell unimpeded down her cheeks in a steady stream, reducing her to a weak, pathetic mess.

Conrath ignored her, plunging the needle into her thigh. Ice filled her veins, rushing like a tidal wave and sweeping aside the chemical residues of previous medication, taking with it all the rounded edges and fuzzy vagueness. Pain, once dull and indistinct, roared to life and Solari, her chest close to bursting, released a shattering scream.

The sound triggered the fall of the black curtain, finally presenting Solari with a view of the room beyond. Everything rushed at her in high definition—the beautiful, impossibly-perfect faces of what could only be Northerners; the eclectic assortment of elegant mutants gliding around the space and proffering flutes brimming with champagne; DuPlessis standing at the front like a circus ringman; and her mother, draped in red silk, sitting pale and stricken in the front row.

"So, who would have thought," DuPlessis continued, waving his hand towards Solari with a flourish, "that a normal would wish to be a mutant?"

She screamed again, long and loud and hoarse, her wings rippling with the untethered energy coursing through her body. The Northerners gasped and eagerly sat forward; a few of them stood and fluttered brightly-coloured notes to the floor. Paying for the pleasure, paying for more.

"Shall we remind her of what it is to be normal?"

The crowd clapped, more money rained down, Conrath stepped closer. Solari twisted her head, caught the glimpse of the metal blade in his hand.

Panic, raw and hot, flooded every nerve ending. Solari thrashed against the restraints and screamed again, her wings beating furiously to avoid the machete.

Du Plessis laughed and took his seat in the front, leisurely reclining next to Christianne. Solari wanted to hurl, to pass out, to wrench free of her restraints and torch the entire brothel in hellfire.

Conrath gripped one of her wings in his fist, crushing the membranes and holding tight despite her desperate thrashing. The pain of the rough handling almost hid the sting of the machete's first slice. And then the throbbing began, and it built. The next scream died in her throat as the machete hacked wildly at her wings. She gasped for air, tried desperately to fill her lungs, but the pain denied any comfort and everything swam out of focus.

Pressure, pressure, pressure, pain.

She was dying.

Details flashed into focus—the room seemed to shimmer as the Northerners stood and rained down money with every slash of Conrath's blade. DuPlessis sat smug and satisfied, his grin growing wider as the carpet of colourful notes grew. And her mother, her beautiful, tragic mother, with her skin so pale it seemed to be rejecting its aquamarine scales, and her tears flowing freely.

The blade hacked again, tearing at the tougher membranes of her wings, and Solari screamed—a hoarse, violent rasp. She wept, she retched, and she screamed again.

Pressure, pain, pain, pressure, pressure, pain.

She blacked out, only for the pain to pull her back into consciousness.

The blade was at her cheek. DuPlessis was dragging out the spectacle, seducing every last dollar from the Northerners who looked on in rapture.

Her mother scrambled towards DuPlessis, terror and wild abandon in her face.

No.

Darkness. Pain. Darkness.

Consciousness became slippery, as if it too was slick with the blood that spilled from Solari's back.

The door to the room shattered, an explosion of sound and wood followed by three figures clad in black, their pistols flashing with light and cracking with thunder.

DuPlessis fell to the floor, scrambled in front of the chairs, lay prostrate before Solari's tortured body. A bullet sang past Solari's ear and the scrape of metal against her cheek followed in quick succession. Conrath grunted and fell from behind her, crashing into her back before falling to the bed.

Blood filled Solari's vision, pain building to breaking point.

DuPlessis pushed himself up, his own pistol gripped tightly.

Darkness.

Her mother stumbled towards her, tripping on her red dress.

Darkness.

Her mother was close, her tear-stained cheeks and eyes filled with terror just centimetres away. Her hands fumbled at Solari's restraints, pulling uselessly on them. Her mouth working to say something that Solari couldn't hear through the chaos, and adrenalin, and pain.

Darkness.

A flash of light, her mother's eyes widened, her lips parted.

No. No. No.

Darkness.

***

Fire flared along Solari's veins, her throat burning with the gasp that brought her back to consciousness. Adrenalin coursed through her veins, thick and fast, and everything appeared too bright, too sharp.

"Hello, Solari." Jerath stood over her and, belatedly, she realised she was no longer tethered to the bed but lying on the floor. "Long time no see."

He reached down for her and she reeled with the déjà vu of it. Ignorant or uncaring, Jerath hauled Solari to her feet. The room spun, a brief kaleidoscope of colour, and then the clarity returned.

The space around her was a warzone. Conrath lay dead on the

bed, covered in blood and what looked like black, sticky tar. Solari's wings, devoid of colour and reduced to a crumpled, mangled mess, lay crushed beneath him. Seeing them set off a dull thudding in her back, pulsing at her shoulder blades. A shadowy, vague pain when her body should have been screaming with fire.

"We hit you with some high-grade ampho," Jerath said. "The pain will return, but not for another half an hour or so."

She pushed away from him and steadied herself. The room was empty again, save the other black-clad assassins, DuPlessis' body drilled with a cluster of bullet-holes, and…

Solari blinked, stepping towards DuPlessis' lifeless form even as her brain shouted in protest. Red silk draped over the gang lord's suit like a shroud. Her mother's broken body tangled up in it.

Breaking from Jerath's grip, heart in her throat, Solari staggered towards her mother and pulled her away from DuPlessis. The red of Christianne's dress coated her hands, staining them crimson. Not the dress, *blood*. So much of it; emerging slow and viscous from the wounds in her belly and chest, pooling in the hollow of her throat, but not touching her face. There, her skin was still perfectly pale, interrupted only with the fine lines of age, the aquamarine scales that still shimmered in the soft light, and her dead, brown eyes.

"Time to go, Solari." Jerath grabbed for her.

She shook him away, falling to her knees next to Christianne, her heart fracturing into a million pieces like cheap glass. In that moment, all she wanted was to wrap her wings around her mother and cradle her until they both turned to dust. But Jerath pulled her up.

"Time to go, Solari," the courier's voice was lower, now. Harder. "Worcsulakz is waiting for you."

Shaking him off was no longer an option; his grip tight and uncompromising.

"Let go of me," she yelled, swivelling around to kick him in the shin. The kick connected and Jerath backhanded her in reply.

"Cut the attitude, Solari, or you'll arrive at Worcsulakz's missing more than those ridiculous wings."

"I'm not going back to Worcsulakz," she cried desperately.

"I've paid my debt. I gave you DuPlessis. This makes us even."

Jerath laughed. "If anything, your debt has increased. This is the second time we've come to your rescue, and you still have a month of snowrock production to make up for."

"I'm not go—"

The thud of Jerath's fist into her midsection stole her words and her breath, doubling her over.

"We're going now," he said and dragged her towards the door, the other assassins scanning the space before exiting before them.

Jerath pulled her roughly, dragging her by the wrist behind him, never slowing even though she stumbled and fell most of the way to the stairs. Feet tripping in the long, silk folds of her dress, she grabbed for the railing. At each landing, she scanned the hallways and found dead security guards littering the carpet.

At the lower levels, escorts, mutant and patrons were slowly emerging from the rooms, eyes wide with a mix of surprise and fear. Even with all the bloodshed, the brothel continued to ply its trade.

Jerath grunted as a couple made their way up the stairs from the lower floor. Solari's heart stuttered as she caught sight of Nico. The Reptilia boy ascended the stairs with his eyes downcast, his steps shaky. Nico's escort didn't look at Solari either; his dark jacket did little to hide broad shoulders, but much to hide the metal plates underneath.

"Misbehaved, did she?" Alcaeus asked in the joking way only men of privilege could pull off.

"Something like that," Jerath said, slowing only fractionally.

"Looks like you punished her nice and good. A lesson for you, scale-boy." Alcaeus pushed Nico, the boy stumbling but regaining his footing. And then, as he passed, the Metallicari pressed the cold, smooth metal of the pistol into Solari's palm.

She didn't hesitate. The first shot blew clean through Jerath's skull and, as he fell, he took the other two down with him. She turned the pistol on them and shot without blinking. The sound reverberated in the cramped space and sent a burst of adrenalin shooting along her nerves, gifting her a brief moment of clarity. Details rushed at her: Alcaeus dragging the bodies to the side, Nico

bending to retrieve the guns. At the next landing, an escort—
Helena?—stood pressed against the wall, her hands shaking as she
raised a gun she had no doubt lifted from a dead security guard.
Gone was her unflappable poise, her eyes wild as they took in the
three mutants before her. She aimed her gun at the largest.

"Stop," Alcaeus shouted.

Another crack of the pistol. Except this time it wasn't Solari
firing, but Nico.

"Stop," his high, reedy voice called. "Or the next bullet will
puncture your chest."

Helena stopped, the gun shaking in her trembling hands. She
was terrified, Solari could see the fear plainly in her eyes.

"Nico…" Alcaeus warned in his low, deep voice. But, Nico
wasn't listening. The boy stepped forward, his pistol steady in his
hand. Alcaeus went to reach for him, but he was too far away.

"We can't leave her," Nico murmured. "She'll raise the alarm.
We will never get to the North."

The boy is right. Even in the unlikely event they made it
through the tunnel by the time the woman raised the alarm, they
would soon be hunted down and killed. Everything they had
sacrificed, bled, and killed for unravelled before they could taste
freedom.

And yet, thoughts of her bullet-ridden mother still swirled in
Solari's memory, merging with the dead driver on the road outside
Powranna, and all the other bodies that had accumulated along the
way.

Before she really knew what she was doing, Solari stepped in
front of the boy.

Distantly, she heard the sound of the pistol firing, the heat just
below her shoulder obliterating all other senses.

"Solari!" Alcaeus roared and ran to her.

Another crack of gunfire. Alcaeus stumbled and looked up
wild-eyed at the escort, before crouching down to Solari. Another
crack and Helena fell, the gun clattering from her grip, her perfectly
white dress tainted with blood.

"Are you OK?" Solari's voice sounded wobbly in her ears.

Alcaeus smiled grimly and flared open the flak jacket. While there would definitely be some bruising and maybe a cracked rib, the jacket had done its job in helping him avoid a more fatal injury. "We need to get you out of here."

THIRTY-EIGHT

The basement was empty, as minimalist as the ground-floor lobby and devoid of bodies. The fire at Solari's arm and between her shoulder blades was building in intensity, and her hands trembled with the urge to reach over and touch what she knew would only be stumps. It didn't matter; even if she could get past the fear of such a visceral confirmation, lifting her arms even slightly sent white-hot electricity arcing through her body.

She stumbled, leant too heavily on Alcaeus, and the fire flared hotter. Alcaeus sat her in one of the ornate chairs and crouched beside her, raising a plastic bottle to her lips.

"What is it?" she croaked around the dirty liquid.

"The rohypnol," he said. "I was going to use it on your admirer with the skull tattoo, but all he needed was a hundred dollars and the threat of a bullet."

She took a large gulp, gagging on the rank taste, forcing herself to keep it down. It wouldn't be as effective as the ampho Jerath had given her, but the boiling along the skin of her back settled to a simmer.

Handing the bottle back to Alcaeus and taking his outstretched hand, she let herself be hauled to her feet. Nico was already at the tunnel's entry, his face glowing in the soft light thrown by the sconces along the wall. He looked exhilarated. Solari envied his happy ending.

"We need to move quickly," Alcaeus said, his voice taking on that distant, surreal quality typical of the rohypnol's effects. "We don't want to encounter any more Northerners in the tunnel."

***

Time became a fuzzy concept. In Solari's shattered mind, it felt as though they had been walking for days. She stumbled alongside Alcaeus, the lights swimming in her vision, the floor undulating beneath her feet. Occasionally, she shook her head, trying to cast off the fog. But, with each step, the rohypnol pulled her further into her own mind, her scrambled thoughts circling around the image of her mother dead on the brothel's penthouse floor, merging it with images of her dying brother and suicidal father.

The wail that broke free from her chest sounded warped and tremulous as it bounced against the walls of the tunnel. Alcaeus's face loomed before her, pulled into a tight mask of fear and concern. "Shh, Solari."

His grip around her arm was too tight. She tried to break free and stumbled, the floor of the tunnel coming up to her in slow motion. The impact sent shockwaves through her body and not even the rohypnol was enough to stop the pain between her shoulder blades from exploding into white-hot fire. And this time, her scream pierced loud and clear.

Alcaeus reached for her, strong arms lifting her from the ground and settling her back on her feet. "Shh. Let me take the pain away." Time looped around and back on itself. Alcaeus pressed his fingers into the tender spot where her neck met her shoulder, and she succumbed to the darkness.

***

"Careful," the voice murmured to Solari through the fading darkness. "You'll damage your wing stumps."

With a fire racing along her skin, and knives scratching at her nerves, she opened her eyes. Nico sat next to her, the only break in what seemed an endless white room. "Where are we?" she asked, her throat sore and voice scratchy.

A shadow appeared over her, metal plates glinting in the

fluorescence. Alcaeus. "The convenience store coolroom."

"What happened?" she asked, her brain still fuzzy.

"Things were getting a bit noisy," he said softly. "We couldn't risk anyone knowing we were down here and figuring out where we were going, so we took a bit of a detour. How's the pain?" He crouched down beside her and offered the bottle of rohypnol.

Fucking brutal. But she left that thought unsaid, grabbing at the bottle and washing away the taste of blood on her tongue with two large gulps. She waited for the chemicals to kick in, but even as the pain started to dull, the tightness stayed in her chest. Belatedly, she realised it was wrapped in the flannel shirt she had been using to hide her wings.

My wings. The image of them hacked and useless, lying wasting on a penthouse floor, brought new pain to the fire between her shoulder blades, sucking the breath from her lungs.

They were only ever supposed to be a temporary adornment, a key to enter the enclave to hide from Worcsulakz. It had been the plan all along to rip them off and discard them as soon as she was safe; they were never anything more than an unnatural disguise, a necessary means to an end…

And, yet, somewhere between entering the enclave and finding herself hidden away in an empty coolroom, they had become something else. A connection between her and Alcaeus. A connection between her and her mother.

Her mother. In an instant, the memory of her wings lying on blood-stained carpet expanded to pull in the image of her mother lying only metres away, her body riddled with bullets. And if the loss of her wings had sucked the breath from her lungs, the loss of her mother stole the blood from her heart.

"They killed my mother," she murmured, the words faltering as the emotion caught up with them. "I was supposed to save her, and they killed her."

Supposed to save her. How many times had she been entrusted to save the people she loved and failed? The only one she had ever succeeded in saving was Alcaeus…

"I'm sorry, Solari," he said, and from the gentleness in his voice and softening of his face, she knew he meant it. And his authenticity shamed her.

"I lied to you," she said, hanging her head to avoid his gaze. "I've lied to you all this time."

"Solari…"

"They were never my wings; not really. I was just someone trying to escape a punishment I thought was worse than death." The rohypnol pulled the confession from her lips before her mind could catch up, the words releasing her from a burden she had suffered too long under. *A second-type of secret…*

"I cut them from a dying moth. And used them to get into the enclave. They weren't meant to be forever. I just needed a place to escape to, somewhere I could be safe, if only for a little while, until I could figure it all out. I was never a mutant—never a Lepidopterae—just someone who needed to hide."

She glanced at Alcaeus beside her, but he kept his steely gaze ahead. And in that moment, she knew—her terrible secret, her carefully-maintained deception, had been the hidden death blow all along. The final thread holding in place the barrier between her mind and the pain disintegrated and she gripped her head in her hands, trying to hold back the hurt and failing. She had lost everything—her family, her home, her wings, her mother, and now Alcaeus.

"I'm sorry," she rasped, the weight in her belly pulling at her words. "I never meant—" The words died on her tongue as Alcaeus stood and strode through the door at the far wall.

"You should sleep." Nico's voice was a gentle salve to the harsh wound. "It will be better tomorrow. You'll feel better tomorrow."

But she kept her gaze trained on the doorway until the rush of exhaustion and lull of rohypnol overcame her, and only then did she heed his suggestion and close her eyes.

***

"Is he back yet?"

It was hard to keep track of time in the coolroom. The rohypnol was playing with Solari's mind and it was difficult to tell moments of lucidity from the nightmares that had drifted in between. There had been moments when she had thought Alcaeus was holding ice to her burning skin, others where her mum had been rocking her back to sleep, and others still where Nico, Denavim, and her father had taken turns watching over her. But in every instance of true clarity, the Metallicari had been absent.

"He's out scouting the tunnel," Nico whispered.

In the hours—days?—since they had sought sanctuary in the coolroom, she had learned that it was one of many 'offshoots' of the main tunnel, a viable alternative in case part of the tunnel collapsed. Tucked away from the main thoroughfare, it was a safe option for hiding, if not for the threat of discovery from above.

"Is the store clear?"

Nico looked towards the larger door. "He closed up shop about an hour ago."

"I'm going to look for supplies."

That was the other advantage of the coolroom safe house: the endless supplies just beyond its door. Alcaeus and Nico had quickly appropriated the water and food, but Solari wanted to find more useful products—like painkillers and antiseptics.

"I'm not...I don't know if—"

"It's OK, Nico. I won't tell him if you don't."

The boy ducked his head and smiled. It was heartening to see that he still held to his humanity, that paradoxical mix of strength and vulnerability, despite all that he had witnessed. All that he had lived.

On wobbly legs, she stood up and pushed through into the storeroom basement beyond. Just as it had been the last time she had seen it, the basement was a maze of shelves and boxes. The coolroom door lock hung broken and askew. She could almost imagine Alcaeus with two spanners snapping it open, but more likely he had shot it in the midnight hour when the store was closed and loud noises not uncommon.

The first boxes she opened were full of cat food, and inwardly she cringed—how decadent had previous generations been to lavish money and food on animals they kept as pets? That aside, it was a good sign—boxes of things from a bygone era bode well for finding old school ingredients, like beeswax and tea tree oil, which she found a few boxes later. Together with a bottle of olive oil, rolls of plastic wrap, three bowls of instant noodles, and a bunch of cotton t-shirts with "Tsamania" printed boldly in black, she hauled her loot back to the soundproofed confines of the coolroom.

"What is that stuff?" Nico asked, helping her unload the items and arrange them on the floor.

"My medical kit," she said jokingly, even though the fire in her body was starting to build. "I need your help—can you start tearing up the t-shirts into strips, as long as you can make them?"

The boy nodded and got to work as Solari sat down beside him and took another gulp of the rohypnol, stopping herself from a second as she eyed the remaining volume. Enough for one more dose. Not enough to withstand the pain that would inevitably come if she couldn't halt the infection. She looked over at the alijeah pills Alcaeus had left behind. It was too soon after she had taken the last dose and, in any case, she would need to ration them.

Sighing, she reached for the noodle bowls and tore off their paper lids. The ingredients inside were stale and mouldy, decades past their use by date, but she merely tipped them into a pile in the corner and used one of the t-shirts to wipe the bowls clean. The she turned her attention to the real ingredients, mixing the oils and the beeswax in carefully-measured quantities, and testing the consistency and potency on the smaller cuts on her arm where Conrath's machete had sliced in his urgency to hack away her wings.

It felt good to lose herself in biochemistry experiments again, to let the smells and stings fill her senses and the demands of the process push aside extraneous thoughts from her mind. When the antiseptic salve was ready, she turned back to Nico and the two of them finished tearing the cotton shirts together.

"Did you really cut the wings from a moth?" The boy kept his gaze down in his lap as his fingers tore through the degraded fabric.

"I did," Solari answered, marvelling as her own mangled hands made light work of the cotton.

"Why?"

It was easy to fall into the retelling of her story, her mind seduced by the rohypnol and no longer afraid of what she risked in sharing her secrets; there was nothing of value left to lose. So, she told the boy about her brother, and her father. About the debts owed to DuPlessis and Worcsulakz. About the day she had found the moth, had her fingers hacked off by Anders, and discovered that Elysia was her aunt, and her mum a mutant—the same day she had first met him as he cowered in the storage room of Elysia's container.

"I'm sorry for how I treated you," she said, stilling her hands and waiting for him to look at her. He shrugged, but kept his head down and his hands moving.

Solari's heart twinged. She could remember how easily she had spat out her bigotry back at Elysia's, how normal it had been for her to blame the mutants for all that was messed up in her life. It had taken becoming a mutant and falling in love with one to realise that life in the Southern Reaches wasn't broken because of mutants, but because of people like her and their corrupted humanity.

She reached out and touched Nico's hand, holding it there until he finally let the torn cotton drop from his grip and looked up at her. "I'm sorry," she repeated, her throat tightening with shame and contrition. "I was wrong and I was stupid and I was so, so blind. You didn't deserve that. You didn't deserve *any* of it."

Slowly, he pulled his hand from under hers. It was a tiny gesture, and the hesitation in it showed no malice, but it stung more than she thought it could. Not that she could show him; he was right to withdraw from her. Just as Alcaeus was.

"I'm sorry," she whispered.

And then his hand was gently gripping hers. She stared at him, and this time he met her gaze, and smiled. "You drove me to the enclave," he mumbled. "You tried to hide me when the van was ambushed. You rescued me when you found me at the brothel."

She smiled back at him. "I also gave you my last protein bar."

"See?" he said. "You weren't all bad."

"I really am sorry, Nico."

"I know," he said, dropping her hand and picking up the t-shirt again.

Together they fell into an easy rhythm, the sound of tearing cotton filling the space and removing any awkwardness.

"So, what made you…attach them?" Nico said.

Solari smiled. That was an easier story to tell, even without the rohypnol. Memories, thick and bright, washed over her and spun the words without her needing to dredge them up. She told him about escaping Jerath and Zjelko, which brought a smile to her face, and running to the only place she thought she could be safe. About meeting Alcaeus, which brought a sadder kind of smile.

"He really likes you," Nico said when her words began to falter.

She shook her head. "I don't think he does anymore."

The boy fell silent, out of words for her. Not that words would have helped.

With all but a few shirts finally reduced to a small pile of cotton strips, Solari pulled the bowl of antiseptic salve towards her and filled the second bowl with water.

"Can you help me pull this off?" She tugged at the blood-stained flannel shirt around her chest. Nico sprung from his spot to crouch behind her, pressing and pulling to unwrap the makeshift bandage. With a final tug it came free, the shock of pain ripping the anguished cry from her lips before she could contain it. Without hesitation, she reached for and drained the last of the rohypnol.

Her breath came fast and shallow. Grabbing one of the strips, she pushed it into the water and handed it dripping to Nico. "Can you…"

"It's OK, Nico." Alcaeus' voice murmured behind them. "I've got it."

Solari went rigid. She was too emotionally spent after her confessions to Nico; she wasn't ready to see him again, to face his disappointment and disapproval.

"I don't mind," Nico said.

"I know," Alcaeus said. "How about you keep watch on the tunnel for a bit?"

"Is that OK, Solari?"

"Yeah, kiddo," she whispered, not trusting her voice. "I'll be OK."

THIRTY-NINE

For a long time after the door clicked shut there was nothing but silence. With the flannel shirt removed, only the thin cover of silk covered Solari's body and she shivered in the cool air. Gentle hands swept aside her hair and draped it over her shoulder, and her shivering increased, peaking as Alcaeus pressed his lips on her bared nape.

"You were right," he murmured, his voice husky and tickling against her skin. "He didn't deserve any of it. But, neither did you."

The warmth of Alcaeus' kiss lingered for a few seconds longer. She held to the feeling of it, long after it had faded, as a torrent of ice and fire exploded on her wing stumps and through her back, ratcheting higher with every brush of a soaked cotton strip against her mutilated appendages.

Held to it until the pain bore too heavy down on her and darkness swept her up in its clutches.

***

The warmth had returned by the time Solari came to, broken only by the cool touch of Alcaeus's metal plates against her cheek. The Metallicari sat against the padded wall of the coolroom, cradling Solari in his lap. Nico lay sleeping on a pillow made of t-shirts that he must have recovered from the same box Solari had found earlier.

A familiar tightness pulled at Solari's chest, but this time it had nothing to do with the fresh bandages that wound around her back and over her wing stumps, and everything to do with the feeling that she had finally found her family.

***

The alijeah pills made it hard to focus. Faintly, as if through the grimy glass of her old apartment building, Solari was aware they were moving, the soft lights of the tunnel appearing every now and then to hint at her journey. *Their* journey.

Alcaeus was a guardian at her side, his metal plates a familiar assurance as she gripped his forearm and tried to steady her feet. Ahead, Nico turned back to them and motioned to the wall ahead. Solari vaguely realised this was an important moment, but the thought floated just out of reach, nebulous and unformed.

"Stay behind me, Solari," Alcaeus said, pulling her behind his massive bulk. Then, to Nico, "Hang back—make sure she stays conscious."

The boy moved behind to flank her, his face twisted in concern and nervousness. "Hang in there," he whispered to her. "We're almost there. We're almost free."

"There's no way of going unnoticed after this," Alcaeus said, directing his words to the boy. "Be prepared to run. If trouble finds us, take Solari and run. Don't wait for me."

There was something wrong with what he was saying, something terrible and final. Solari's brain tried to process the words and their deeper meaning, but the chemical haze kept everything at a distance.

Thunder crashed into her thoughts as Alcaeus stepped up to a door, wrenching at the handle and pushing his shoulder into the heavy panels. The door flew open. Solari squinted, trying to see further into the shadowy darkness beyond. Had they got it wrong? Had they stopped too early? Were they still south of the wall?

"Let's go," Alcaeus called to them, motioning to Nico as he doubled-backed for Solari.

"Did we make it?" she asked, as he guided her through the door and into the darkness beyond. A cool wind brushed over her sweat-soaked skin and raised gooseflesh along her arms. Shadows began to materialise, shimmering in the haze of the alijeah still lacing her mind and stealing heat from her wounds.

Faint lights twinkled in the distance and Solari's heart dropped. *Youngtown.* The tunnel had not taken them beyond the wall, only further into the South. She let go of Alcaeus' arm and slumped against him, utterly defeated.

The Metallicari gently lifted her, careful not to disturb the stumps at her back, and cradled her against his solid chest. She buried her face beneath the flak jacket at his neck, her skin still craving the touch of his metal plates, and cried.

"We did it, Solari," he murmured as she strode along the empty street.

She looked up at him, his face blurry through the chemicals and the tears. "But the lights," she protested feebly. "The town."

She looked back to where Youngtown sat in the distance, a cancer at the base of the border wall. Alcaeus smiled down at her, twisting his body so that she could see what he was walking towards.

Nico ran ahead, stopping occasionally to turn back to them, before running on. Running towards the deeper shadows that emerged beyond the darkened streets. The Fringes. Except Youngtown was kilometres from the Fringes.

She turned around slowly, her eyes seeking out the border wall's ramparts and finding the spotter lights that seemed to hover above it. The dark wilderness of Tasmania's west coast stretched away to her right.

The wrongness of the direction pulled at the fog in her mind. She glanced again from the wall, to the Fringes, to the lights that flickered in the distance. Orienting and re-orienting herself to confirm the cardinal points of her inner compass.

Alcaeus threaded his hand in hers, but she couldn't tear her gaze away. Whatever town glittered in the distance, it was not Youngtown. They had made it to the North.

ABOUT THE AUTHOR

MIKHAEYLA KOPIEVSKY is an Australian speculative fiction author. Her short stories have been longlisted for the EJ Brady Prize and published in *Etherea*. Her debut novel, *Resistance,* was a semi-finalist in Hugh Howey's inaugural SPSF Competition.

Born in Sydney, Mikhaeyla now lives in the Hunter Valley with her husband, son, two rescue dogs, four Australorp chooks, a hive of cantankerous bees, and the occasional herd of beautiful Black Angus steers. When she is not writing or reading, Mikhaeyla enjoys cooking with the produce harvested from her kitchen garden, going to the beach, stargazing, and training to be a ninja.

You can discover more about Mikhaeyla and her writing at:
www.mikhaeylakopievsky.com

Sign up for author updates and exclusive give-aways at:
https://mikhaeylakopievsky.com/sign-up-for-exclusive-content-giveaways/

Follow Mikhaeyla on:
Bookbub: https://www.bookbub.com/author/mikhaeyla-kopievsky
Twitter: @MikhaeylaK
Instagram: @MikhaeylaK
Facebook: https://www.facebook.com/MikhaeylaKopievsky/